# DEAD DRAGONS, NEW TRICKS

# DEAD DRAGONS, NEW TRICKS

## DRAGON'S DAUGHTER™ BOOK 2

KEVIN MCLAUGHLIN

MICHAEL ANDERLE

Copyright © 2020 LMBPN Publishing
Cover Art by Jake @ J Caleb Design
http://jcalebdesign.com / jcalebdesign@gmail.com
Cover copyright © LMBPN Publishing
A Michael Anderle Production



LMBPN Publishing
PMB 196, 2540 South Maryland Pkwy
Las Vegas, NV 89109

First US Edition, December 2020
Version 1.01, December 2020
eBook ISBN: 978-1-64971-376-6
Print ISBN: 978-1-64971-377-3

THE DEAD DRAGONS, NEW TRICKS TEAM

**Thanks to our Beta Readers**
Rachel Beckford, Larry Omans

**Thanks to the JIT Readers**

Dave Hicks
Wendy L Bonell
Jeff Goode
Deb Mader
Allen Collins
Dorothy Lloyd
Peter Manis
Diane L. Smith
Paul Westman

*If we've missed anyone, please let us know!*

**Editor**
The Skyhunter Editing Team

The edges of the portal in front of Kylara Diamantine swirled with blue magic that resembled mist but was most certainly something far more unusual. Her friends had already stepped through. The only people left to be transported to the school were Kylara and Amy Williams, the mage who powered the portal.

"Are you ready, kid?" Amy asked.

"Did you see the frozen lake when you came here? Did you see the place where my parents fled to keep me safe from the dragons?" She knew she should step through the portal and that the mage who had lured her there would be back. But what if she never came? What if she had learned she wasn't a dragon at all but a mage, only to have that secret family history taken away from her again?

"There's a lake near here but it's not frozen."

"There was a house at the bottom of it. Aunt Cassandra had rebuilt it."

"It's gone, Kylara. It has to be."

She hung her head.

"It's time, Ky. Your friends went through a harrowing experience and I know for a fact that they won't let anyone take them to the medical wing until you're with them."

Kylara nodded. As much as she wanted to find her Aunt Cassandra and Hester Diamantine, the dragon who had raised her as her daughter, she knew Amy was right.

Reluctant but resigned, she stepped through the gateway. Immediately, the magic coursed through her and joined her inner magic. In the next instant, her body was no longer in the far northern reaches of Canada but the desert of New Mexico and the Lumos School campus.

"Oh, my God, Ky! You took forever. I was worried sick about you. Don't you ever make me worry like that again!" Tanya Fastwing talked at about a mile a minute. She was a vanilla—a somewhat derogatory term for dragons who had no powers beyond the regular slew of dragon abilities—but sometimes, Kylara thought her special ability might be the number of words she could get out of her mouth in a given period of time.

"I was there for maybe thirty seconds longer than you two," she protested.

"Sure, Ky, but now that we know you're a mage and not a dragon, you shouldn't be off by yourself." Samuel smiled, although it didn't reach his sunken eyes. Almost being drowned seemed to have had a notable effect on the golden dragon. His normally perfect hair and haughty expression were both rumpled, but something else bothered him too, however.

"I'm still a dragon with diamond scales," Kylara said, somewhat confused that she had to point this out at all. She had saved them. What did it matter that she was a mage when she could turn into a dragon?"

"I agree with the two hostages," Amy said and pointed at Tanya and Samuel. "You three need to stick together and get your butts to the medical room to be examined before I tell Headmaster Amythist to put you all in detention."

"For being kidnapped?" Tanya sputtered.

"Exactly!" Amy winked at Kylara. "Now come on. The nurse is only a few doors down from the headmaster. I've decided I don't trust any of you." She said it like a joke but she escorted them to the medical bay all the same.

They entered and were immediately accosted by a female mage who was particularly skilled in healing magic.

"Well, well, well, if it isn't our missing students. Now, what exactly seems to be the problem?"

"Nothing's wrong," Samuel said quickly.

"Oh? Because I don't think I've ever seen you without gel in your hair," the nurse snapped before she put a stethoscope to his chest.

"I'm fine. Truly. Okay, yeah, I was saved by one of the people my honor demands I protect and she had to use my powers to do it." Samuel's head lowered even more.

"Sam, I don't need protection. And it's good that I used your light powers to heal you. If you hadn't shown me that was possible, who knows what could have happened? Right, Tanya?"

"Ky's right, Sam. Come on, it's not her fault she can absorb powers. It's not like some of us were sent to this school to learn how to do exactly that and still have nothing to show for it."

Kylara looked from one friend to the other. Samuel stared constantly at her like she was a kitten who had magically turned into a tiger and scratched him. Tanya's expression seemed to indicate that her dragon mage friend was some type of endangered bird that if not watched carefully, might steal her keys.

"You guys are acting like I didn't save both your butts," she protested, but that only made them wilt even more.

While they talked amongst themselves, the nurse fussed around the two of them, listened with her stethoscope here and prodded there before she finally declared them both fit enough to eat something and return to their rooms.

The woman pushed Kylara back into her chair with a blast of hidden magic when she stood to follow her friends. "Not so fast, young lady. I see evidence of recently healed burns, as well as lacerations and bruises. Not to mention that your aura is all over the place. It's almost like…like… Never mind." She shook her head.

She went ahead and finished her sentence for her. "It's almost like I'm a mage masquerading as a dragon?" Deliberately, she ignored the other two students who lingered in the doorway, most probably waiting for her.

"I…well…that would explain some things," the woman said and studied her carefully as she appeared to replay the recent conversation between the students in her head. "There's all types of magic flowing through you. It'll take me a while to make sense of it, all right? You two, go get some food. She'll be along shortly."

Kylara intended to protest and ask her friends to wait, but the healer's glare convinced her otherwise. They left, although they both hesitated and cast long looks at her over their shoulders. As they walked away, they leaned closer so they could whisper to one another. Whisper about what? She felt suddenly isolated and alone.

"This shouldn't hurt, all right, sweetie?" the nurse said as she began to move her hands over her body.

"You won't take any of my magic, will you?" she asked. Although she had only now learned she was a mage and not a dragon, she was already embracing the shift in identity. The last thing she wanted was to be stripped of these fledgling powers.

The healer laughed. "Of course not. That's impossible. It's simply that magic needs to flow. Yours feels all trapped inside."

Kylara sighed. "I have no idea why that could be," she said as she watched her two best friends—the two people she had risked her life and her place in this school to save—walk away from her.

# CHAPTER TWO

Tanya didn't want to feel the way she felt in that moment. Kylara was her friend. The girl had been nice to her since the moment they'd met. They shared a room, ate meals together, and helped each other with homework. She had also saved her from that jerk Karl Midnight when he'd attacked her for not having powers.

And yet, she struggled with the implications of what they had learned.

"Do you think Kylara knew what she was?" she asked Samuel once they emerged onto the U-shaped stretch of green grass between the three main campus buildings.

"You mean a mage?" he asked.

She nodded.

"I don't know. I don't think so. But, honestly, it now seems fairly obvious. We all know mages can learn different powers and that's not something dragons can usually do. Oh, no offense."

The young dragon wished she had one of her parasols to hide her reddening face but the one she had carried had been ripped to shreds when the mage—Kylara's aunt—had whisked her away with an air elemental. "No, it's fine. I know you're right. I am only a vanilla. I don't know why the headmaster expects me to accomplish anything when Kylara Diamantine is here on campus."

"Hey, Tanya, don't beat yourself up about what happened," Samuel said as he opened the door to the cafeteria for her. "It's me who should have done better. You don't have powers yet, but I do. It's inexcusable that I let a mage get the best of me."

"Do you mean Kylara or her aunt?" she asked as they piled their plates with food.

He shook his head and huffed a sad little noise. Some boys were cute when they were sad but in Tanya's opinion, he wasn't one of them. He looked like all the light had been taken out of him. Instead of radiating confidence and strength, he simply looked tired—not that he didn't have a perfectly good reason to be exhausted.

"I mean her aunt but honestly, I guess I feel that way about Kylara too. Dragons aren't supposed to be saved by mages. That's not how it's supposed to work. Part of the social contract is that dragons—as the most powerful and the most privileged—should protect the less fortunate. I should have been able to take care of myself." His plate piled high with smoked pork ribs and more potato salad than Tanya would dare to eat in a week, he moved toward a table.

She garnished her salad, took a whole chicken—she was a dragon after all—and followed to sit opposite him. "I don't think that's fair. Not anymore, anyway."

"What do you mean?" he asked around a mouthful of meat.

"The Steel Dragon changed the way the world works. A huge part of that was because of her mage. That's why I was so excited to attend the Lumos school this year. I would be the first dragon to learn how to do magic. But Kylara went and blew that record out of the water."

"Did she, though? Okay, yes, she has a dragon body and can fight like a dragon, but she's not one of us. She's a mage. I feel so crappy that I wasn't able to stop that air elemental from taking us away and that we needed her to save us."

"But Sam…it was a mage who kidnapped us in the first place." Tanya shuddered at the memory which remained fresh in her mind. It was almost unthinkable that mere hours before, she had been chained to a wall with a bracelet that had denied her access to her dragon strength and speed.

"I know." He lowered his head into his hands and didn't move for a long moment. Tanya could still read his dragon aura easily enough even though she knew he was trying to control it.

"It's ok to feel weak," she said gently. "I was captured by Karl greasy-hair Midnight. There's no shame in being captured by that mage. She was…she was something else. I'm in two magic classes, if you didn't know, and those elemental beings… Well, they're not easy to use, by all accounts, and the fact that she controlled three of them says something."

"There was a fourth," Samuel said. "Something moved in the earth. I could see it now and then when the light changed."

For a moment, neither dragon spoke. They sat in silence and recalled what it was like to be chained to a wall and treated like cattle while the mage Cassandra grandstanded about how Kylara —a mage—would come for them and that if they were good, she might let them live long enough to see her.

"You were brave, though. You talked back to her and tried to get under her skin. All I did…all I did was—"

"Me acting tough would have been worthless if you hadn't cried," Samuel said so quickly that she knew he was lying to make her feel better. She had learned—while being "interrogated" by the mage Cassandra—that lies came to the tongue quite quickly if the brain thought they might stop the pain more effectively than the truth.

"I can't believe she was right," she said after another long moment.

"You mean about Ky?"

Tanya nodded. "I thought it was all nonsense. That maybe she had an ax to grind with your great-great-however-many-greats grandfather Lumos."

"That's what I wondered too," Samuel responded. "But Kylara knew from the beginning that this was about her. She's the special one, not us. We're merely…what did Amy call us?"

"Hostages."

"Yeah." His tone sounded sulky. "Hostages."

They finished their meal in silence. It was hard to talk about anything except the trauma they had both been through. Not only did it remind them of what they had endured for two days, but they also had to confront the truth they would have much preferred to avoid. While they both struggled to survive, they had come slowly to the realization that the only person who would save them was the very person the mage wanted to come.

They had been used like pawns, plain and simple. And what hurt Tanya most was that the person she had tried so hard to help fit in only proved that she never could. She would only ever stand out.

It was a petty, childish thought and she knew it.

And yet, as Sam escorted her to her dorm and she wandered to her and Kylara's shared room, she couldn't stop thinking it. She had worked so hard to get into this school. It wasn't a small achievement. She was the first vanilla dragon to ever be accepted there and one of a tiny handful who attended this year. All her life, she had grown up in the shadow of more powerful and more spectacular dragons, and she had thought that the Lumos School would be her chance to shine on her own.

But it was already clear that Kylara was the most interesting student on campus. It didn't matter that she was a mage. It truly didn't. What mattered was that she was brave and strong and could learn new powers and use them to save people too weak to save themselves.

Compared to her, Tanya was merely a footnote.

Thinking this made her feel petty, guilty, and jealous all at once. She was miserable for judging her friend so harshly, and yet she couldn't pretend that Kylara accomplishing everything she wanted with no difficulty was easy for her to accept either.

So, with nothing left to do and her feelings wreaking havoc on her exhausted body, she curled on her bed and let herself cry.

# CHAPTER THREE

The nurse had been right and fixing the flow of her magic had helped. Kylara had been upset with her friends, but she saw now that they were merely tired and scared from what they'd been through. They'd be fine soon, she assured herself.

With food in her stomach, she already felt better, although she wished she'd caught up with Tanya and Samuel in the cafeteria. She knew that by now, her roommate would most likely be asleep but that was fine. They could talk in the morning and things would hopefully be easier if they were both rested.

She had almost reached her dorm when Amy Williams swooped out of the sky and landed on her skateboard.

"Yo," the mage said by way of greeting.

"Yes?" she asked.

"The headmaster wants to see you."

"Right now?"

"Do you think she would have sent a flying, skateboarding mage if it wasn't urgent?"

Kylara looked quickly at the hallway to her room, hoped Tanya was okay, and followed in silence to Amythist's office.

Once they reached their destination, Amy knocked three times, opened the door, and let her inside.

"Oh, Kylara—please, have a seat. Amy, tea?"

"I'm fine, ma'am, thank you. I prefer beverages with actual flavor."

Amythist clicked her tongue at her. "You never were particularly good with subtlety."

"Why go soft when you can go hard?" the mage asked rhetorically. "If there's nothing else?"

"There's isn't, not for you anyway. Thank you."

"Wait—you're leaving?" Kylara looked pleadingly at Amy. She had never attended a school before coming to the Lumos School, but that didn't mean she was ignorant of what it meant to be left alone in the headmaster's office.

"Oh, Kylara. I told you when we first met that I don't bite," Amythist said kindly as Amy saw herself out.

She turned to the headmaster, squared her shoulders, and tried to prepare herself for what was coming.

"I'm so glad you're safe, Kylara. It's not an exaggeration to say I was more concerned with your hiatus from our campus than I would have been with most students'. We've had some run off before, of course, but they always return to their parents' estates. We checked your old home for you and when we didn't find you…" The old dragon shook her head. "Tea?"

"I appreciate your concern, ma'am. It means a lot to me," she said, released some of the tension knotted within her, and nodded as the headmaster proffered a cup of tea.

"Your situation is a unique one, my child," Amythist continued. "With your mother…missing, myself and all of the professors on campus feel a special responsibility for you. Every minute you were gone, we feared the worst. I've…adopted… many strays in my day. I know you followed the exploits of the Steel Dragon, so you likely know that it was me who decided to teach the dragons the technomages had been harvesting bones and teeth from for all those years."

Kylara nodded and sipped her tea. She'd read leaked reports of what had happened to those dragons. It hadn't been pretty. Truly, even horrific fell short of the injustice that had been done to them.

"You're even more special than them, of course. Especially in light of what we know you to be now."

"Thank you, ma'am, but I don't see how being a mage who can turn into a dragon is fundamentally different than a dragon who can take the body of a human." She tried to keep her voice calm as she spoke.

The headmaster set her cup of tea down. "That is because you have grown up somewhat isolated, child."

"Excuse me?" She almost choked on her tea and ended up coughing and sputtering.

"Do we need to add an inability to listen to your record? Or will it be fine to leave the documentation with 'cannot follow directions' instead?"

"I saved Tanya and Samuel!"

"A lucky turn of events, to be sure." Amythist's words cut like crystal. "The only reason you are not already expelled is because when this happened, you didn't know what you are. That is true, correct? You had no idea that you were a mage?"

"Of course I didn't know that—"

"Then I am going to pretend that your recklessness isn't entirely different from the behavior that other, equally irresponsible dragons have perpetrated in the past. But hear my words, young lady, and hear them well. If you do anything as absurdly insane as leave campus again to go on a deadly adventure that took you deep into dwarf country, you will be punished —severely."

"What was I supposed to do?" Kylara demanded, leaned forward in her chair, and smacked her palm on the desk. The gesture earned a scornful look from the elder dragon until she removed her hand meekly from where it had rested on the surface.

"You could have come for help, Kylara. This campus is filled with dragons and mages whose very profession is to help young, foolish people, like yourself. You could have come to me. You could have gone to Amy. You could have gone to Professor Sharra. You could have gone to anyone. It was profoundly dangerous for you to attempt to rescue other students alone. They could have died, Kylara. You could have died."

"If I had told anyone, Sam and Tanya would be dead already." She was tired, confused, and already mad about being given the cold shoulder by her friends. Now, she was being reprimanded for saving two students? They should have given her a damn medal.

"Do you honestly think that was the first instance of a kidnapper ever saying 'come alone?' She relied on your fear to create a situation in which she stood a chance at fighting back. If you had told us, she would be in custody right now."

"For your information, she had an air elemental spying around campus. If I had told you—if I had told anyone—Sam, Tanya, and my mom would be dead right now. Plus, it's not like Amy's security team was exactly doing a great job with the elementals Aunt Cassandra summoned. While they all fought against one fire spirit, the cafeteria—where we were supposed to be safe—was attacked by two."

Amythist took a deep breath and some of her anger seemed to dissipate. "Amy told me all that happened—all that transpired. Do you believe it, then? What the mage told you? That she is your family?"

"Yes, I believe it! Of course I do. How else can you explain my absorbing all these dragon powers? Why else would my mom—" She ground her teeth at having to continually revise what the dragon she thought was her mother truly was to her. "That is...

why would Diamantine have kept me hidden from the dragon world?"

"There may be another explanation."

"She looked exactly like me, Headmaster, and wore an amulet that was identical to mine. I'm positive she was telling the truth, without any doubt. Plus, she showed me a kind of…of vision."

"A vision?" Amythist didn't sound as angry now so much as curious.

"On the frozen lake where I found her. She made all this mist and in it, I saw my mom and some other members of Dragon SWAT show up and…and…they destroyed the mages who were simply trying to live there. They killed my real mom or—" She shook her head, not ready to kick Diamantine out of her heart. "They killed my biological mom, I guess. I saw myself as a baby. I got my diamond scales when Diamantine touched me. Can…can magic like that be faked?"

Amythist took a breath and held it for a long time before she exhaled slowly. "No, not really. No. Some mages might be able to do it but…tell me, how did you know it was Diamantine?"

"From the way she fought and from the way she flew. I lived with her for my whole life. I know it was her."

"Then what she showed you was likely the truth. It would not have been possible for her to fake her movements well enough for you to believe it." The old dragon did not look pleased to admit such a thing, which only pissed Kylara off.

"But if it's all true, shouldn't I have been told before? You knew something was different about me when I got here. So did Kristen when she talked to me at the Steel Guard station. You've known this all along."

Amythist sighed. "I assure you, we did not. The world of dragons and mages is a complex one, my child. Many powers have been gained and lost over the centuries. I would be lying if I said I suspected nothing unusual when I met you, but I swear it to you, I never suspected that you were a mage. If it means anything to you, we will do our best to verify that what this… Cassandra…told you is true."

"But how? How could you know that something was wrong with me?"

"There is nothing wrong with you, child," the headmaster snapped. "This is exactly the kind of thinking Kristen is working so hard to wash out of the world. There is nothing *right* about being a dragon, just as there is nothing *wrong* with being a mage or even a regular human. It is unfortunate that we were all so blinded by our expectations. Now, it seems so obvious that you were special."

"What does?" Kylara couldn't help but wonder if Tanya and Sam had picked up on this same "specialness," whatever that meant.

"Well, your aura, for instance. It's different than most dragons. I had thought when we first met that you were doing an exceptional job of controlling it, especially for a young dragon. I see now there must be another explanation."

It was her turn to sigh. "I have an answer to that." Her hands went to the pendant around her neck.

Amethyst raised her eyes in an unspoken question.

"Aunt Cassandra told me her father made this." She brandished the silver-and-turquoise amulet. "She said it was designed to help disguise us from dragons."

"Do you mind if I see it for a moment?" the old dragon asked and when she saw her expression, she added quickly, "I promise to give it back immediately. I wouldn't keep a piece of your history from you. I'm simply curious."

Kylara nodded and removed it from her neck. She couldn't recall the last time she had taken it off but it was certainly not since fleeing her home and enrolling in the Lumos School. She felt strangely naked without it.

The old dragon took the pendant and turned it this way and that in her deft fingers. She sniffed it, tapped it with a finger turned into a dragon claw, and touched it with the tip of a forked tongue. "It presents a fake dragon aura."

"It does?"

"Yes. That explains why all of us dragons thought we could read something off you. It was this amulet. It generates enough of an aura to make me and the rest of my staff think you were simply better than most at controlling your emotions. Truly, it's a clever piece of magic. And you say your…aunt, had its equal?"

Kylara nodded.

"That explains how she was able to infiltrate my campus, anyway." Amythist continued to turn the amulet in her hands. "We have different techniques for looking for mage and dragon intruders. This must have split the difference and let her get close enough to release those elementals." The last observation seemed to be said to herself, rather than her student.

"Does it do anything else?"

"I believe so, yes. There's a kind of shield to it—something I can't penetrate with my powers. I wouldn't be surprised to discover that this amulet shields the wearer from being manipulated by aura powers as well."

Kylara nodded. It all made sense. In fact, it all made too much sense. Hester Diamantine had never bothered to train her to control her aura. Was this why? She had spent enough time to make sure the young mage who could take the body of a dragon understood what auras were and knew how to sense the most basic of aural emotions, but this was something all people could do. That's what dragon auras were. If a dragon wished for someone—anyone—to know their anger, their aura made sure of it.

"What about…what about my aura now?" she asked.

"You don't have one at all," the headmaster said, a little too clinically for the words to be of comfort. "Without this amulet, you read like a human. I can tell you're a mage—and a powerful one at that—but I'm not even sure most dragons could discern that. I have practice with magic in a way that most of them do not."

She nodded reluctantly. It wasn't that she tried to agree so much as she tried to understand all of this. Mere hours before, she had *known* she was a dragon. She had *known* she was the daughter of Hester Diamantine and she had *known* the person who had taken her mom was a monster.

Now, all of that was in question.

"I realize this is probably a fair amount to take in," Amythist said haltingly.

"Has anything like this ever happened before?" Kylara asked, her mouth dry.

The old dragon shook her head slowly. "There are records of mages with your ability but nothing like it has been seen for centuries. Even then, I don't know if those mages could absorb powers from multiple dragons. I'm sure it feels overwhelming but Kylara, this makes you truly special. With your powers, you could bridge the gap between the two worlds in a way that not even the Steel Dragon has been able to do."

"I had just started to adjust to life here," she said, not realizing until she said it that it was the truth. "Now, I don't even know if I should go back to my dorm room."

Amythist sipped her tea and rubbed her chin. "I suppose it might make sense for you to move in with the mages. It's likely you would accelerate your acquisition of the more traditional powers, but—"

"But I'm not a traditional mage."

"Precisely. You were raised as a dragon and have dragon abilities. I certainly don't want you to leave Practical Dragon Powers or the Silver Bullet's tutelage."

"Of course not," she said and wondered how exactly she could face a group of dragons once the rumor got around that she could steal their powers.

"Or you could stay where you are. You and young Miss Fastwing seem to be getting along well enough. I will let you decide which feels more appropriate to you. Does that sound fair?"

"Yeah, sure," she said but her mind returned to Tanya and Sam's looks at her once they'd reached the campus.

"Excellent. If anything changes, you know where to find me. Now, go get some rest. You've certainly earned it!"

Amythist chuckled behind her as she left her office, but it did little to lighten her mood. At least she now knew that with the pendant around her neck, no one would know how crappy she felt. It wasn't much of a comfort.

# CHAPTER FOUR

By the time Kylara returned to her room, a cauldron of rage bubbled in her stomach. She had tossed any self-doubt or nervousness she had into it and was left with only the righteous anger of the young.

When she pushed the door open, Tanya sat on her bed, reading a tome about magic. Her roommate didn't look up from her book but that didn't stop her from venting.

"So it seems it was very, *very* stupid of me to come and save you and Sam," she said by way of beginning the conversation.

"Is that right?" Tanya replied without looking up.

The words were like sprinkling hot peppers into the cauldron of rage. "Yeah! She didn't want to hear that an air elemental was following me or that if I hadn't gone, I wouldn't have found out who I was. I can't believe her. You two could have died, and all Amythist can talk about is how weird it is that I'm a mage. It's unbelievable."

"It truly is." The young dragon still didn't look up.

Kylara glared at her. Normally, Tanya Fastwing's words seemed to be proof that her last name was indeed rightly earned.

But now, she had nothing to say? "What's that supposed to mean?" she demanded.

Finally, the young dragon looked up from her book. She didn't deign to lower the tome at all and simply flicked her gaze to her roommate. To Kylara, it felt like a profoundly arrogant gesture. "It means it's truly weird that you're a mage."

"It's not like I knew that when I met you."

Her friend remained silent.

She felt like she had to keep talking since the girl was uncharacteristically quiet. Not only that, but she had to get these feelings out. She had to get her friend back. "And, get this—Amythist thinks it might make sense for me to move to a mage dorm. She said since I wasn't a dragon, I might not even belong here. That my time might be better spent with the mages so I could learn more traditional powers or something."

Kylara realized she was paraphrasing and that the old dragon hadn't been quite so assertive, but she didn't care.

"Well, maybe she's right," Tanya said quietly.

"Wait, seriously?" She couldn't believe what she was hearing.

"I don't know! I mean…yes? What will you learn from me, a crappy vanilla dragon who couldn't defend herself against a few other students, let alone your aunt." The way she said "aunt" stung.

"You're kidding," Kylara said. It felt like the cauldron of rage bubbling inside her had been upended and dumped on the very flames that gave it heat. While before, she had overflowed with anger, she now felt like there was nothing inside. "You think I should move out?"

"I don't know, Ky. I'm only saying that you've learned all these new powers and that I haven't. If you stay here, I'll simply hold you back."

"But I don't care about that, Tanya. We're friends. You're my *best* friend!"

"Oh, please, Ky. We hardly know each other," Tanya snapped.

Kylara felt her heart break a little in that moment. It wasn't burned to a blackened lump like it had been when Diamantine had battled and lost to the fire elemental on her behalf. This was more like having a single dragon talon thrust into her chest. "You don't mean that." It was all she could manage to say and she knew it wouldn't be enough.

"Well...I kind of do," Tanya said and her words gained speed now. "I get that you say you didn't know what you were—"

"I didn't!"

"But it doesn't change the fact that we've only just begun the semester. It's barely October and it's not like we have all that much in common. I let you borrow my dresses and stuff when you needed them, but now that Ruby took you to get your own clothes, all you wear is jeans and sneakers."

"And that means we're not friends?"

"It means I don't know what we have in common," the young dragon said and sounded both angry and hurt at the same time. "We're not from the same worlds and we're not the same kind of dragon. What am I talking about? You're not a dragon at all."

"And that means me saving your life doesn't matter? What? Since I'm a mage I should have let you die?"

"That's what it felt like you were doing, Ky!" Tanya shouted. "You showed up and your...your aunt gave you a freaking tour of her secret hideout. Do you know what she did to me and Sam? Do you have any idea what we went through while you were... were what? Flying up there on wings you stole from a dragon you tricked?"

"That's not fair."

"None of this is fair!" Her roommate was on her feet now, her hands clenched and face red in distinct contrast to the yellow silky pajamas she wore. "I was supposed to be someone special! I was going to learn mage powers. And then you show up and suddenly, I'm worthless. Do you think Professor Sharra will care about me at all if I don't have powers like you? Do you think anyone will care about me now when some ancient freaky form of being a mage has been rediscovered?"

"I…I came for you because we're friends."

"You came for me because you wanted to know about your powers." Tanya scoffed.

"I saved you from Karl Midnight and his goons." It was weak but it was all Kylara had left.

"You stole Karl's powers. Tempest's too. You're nothing but a thief."

That was it. She'd had enough and her rage boiled hotter than before. It surged to like an inferno as if the cauldron hadn't extinguished the fire but sent sparks up that now consumed an entire forest.

"At least I'm something!" she raged. "You're nothing but a vanilla—and you don't even do that well."

"Ex-excuse me?"

"You act like being a dragon isn't enough, Tanya. Don't you realize that one of the buildings of this school is named after a dragon without any special powers? Emerald defeated a powerful diamond-encrusted dragon in hand-to-hand combat because he trained. All you do is complain."

"It's easy for you to say. You don't even have to train. All you need to do is…what? Let some other dragon attack you? I saw you use Karl's dark powers. Is that why you defended me from him in the first place? You wanted his abilities?"

"I didn't even know about my powers then!" Kylara screamed. This, out of everything Tanya had said, was what hurt the most. The insinuation that she was only there to steal powers from other dragons was too much. "You know what? Maybe I should go to the mage dorm. At least they didn't grow up whining that their mansions weren't big enough."

"Oh, shut up, Kylara. You act like you grew up in poverty or something, but your mom owned so much land you couldn't even see anyone else. My parents have jobs. Did yours?"

"She did until she had to go into hiding to protect me from dragons like you," she retorted. "Dragons who act like mages are less than them."

"Mages are different, is all! You're different."

"Yeah, well, maybe I should be in a different dorm."

Tanya furrowed her brow long enough for Kylara to see her pain, then she focused on her yellow pajamas. "Maybe you should."

"Fine! I'll go, then." She marched out and slammed the door behind her and found Ruby Firedrake, the floor supervisor, waiting for her in the hallway. It was immediately apparent from the expression on her face that she had heard if not every word of the conversation, then at least the most hurtful parts.

"Is…everything all right?" Ruby asked with a forced smile.

"Yes! No. I don't know." She wiped her eyes. Thankfully, she hadn't cried in front of Tanya and she wasn't about to start now. "It's been a very long day."

"Yeah…the headmaster said you've been through some…stuff. Do you want to talk about it?"

She snorted, which in itself almost forced more tears from her eyes. "No. I truly don't." Especially not with a dragon, she thought, but she didn't say it. "Can you help me move to the mage dorm? Do I have to fill paperwork out or something?"

"The mage dorm? Kylara, look, I'm not gonna lie. I heard that you're not exactly a dragon, but that doesn't mean you have to move. Mages have only recently started coming to this school. There's no difference between the mage dorms and those for dragons who sleep in their human form. In fact, we had a big debate before the school year about separating everyone at all. You don't need to go."

"It seems my roommate disagrees."

"Tanya's been through trauma. She was missing even longer than you were, right?"

"I guess so, yeah," Kylara admitted.

"Plus, she was held hostage or something, right?"

"It's good to know the headmaster doesn't care too much about privacy."

Ruby chuckled at that. "Two of the students from my dorm were missing for two days. Do you honestly think I would let her fill me in when she felt like it? I've been a part of this school for longer than she has. You'd better believe I busted her chops to tell me what was going on as soon as I saw that portal open."

She smiled and continued. "Look, all I'm saying is that you and Tanya haven't known each other for that long. Y'all seem to be getting along well, but you can't expect a relationship—especially one that has been through what yours has—to always be effortless. Give it a night. You can bunk with me, and in the morning, you'll feel differently."

"In the morning, I'll still be a mage," she responded obstinately.

"Kylara, that shouldn't matter."

"But it does matter," she said. "Thousands of years of history say it matters. The Steel Dragon fought a war last year because mages and dragons are different."

"But it doesn't have to be that way, not anymore. That's why Lady Steel fought that war in the first place. Things are changing."

"You can't all expect me to be the person who makes things change." Kylara felt deflated like the entire world was trying to crush her. "I'm only a kid. I didn't even know I was a mage until today. Maybe I can...can help change people's perspectives or whatever, but I don't know how I'll do that if I don't learn anything else about mages."

Ruby sighed. "If you're very sure, go pack an overnight bag

and give me a few minutes to talk to the supervisor of the mage dorm. I'll find you a place."

"Thank you, Ruby, and yes, I am sure," she said firmly. Unfortunately, the truth was that she didn't feel sure about anything at all.

# CHAPTER FIVE

Ten minutes later, Kylara stood outside the entrance of the mage dorm while Ruby talked to the resident director of the building. At least the building looked the same as her old dorm, she thought in an attempt to boost her confidence. With any luck, she might get a room to herself.

Ruby emerged and waved for her to come inside. "Well, I didn't tell him everything but I assured him that you…uh, would. I hope that's okay."

"Yeah, that's fine. I don't want to keep secrets," she said.

"Great, that's great. Then come this way, Kylara, and I'll introduce you. And remember, if this doesn't work out, you're welcome back in our building. I've already spoken to Mr. Hinesburg about it and he agreed that this can be a temporary situation. All right?"

"Thanks, Ruby. I appreciate everything you've done for me."

"So much so that you want to hang out with me tonight and talk to your roomie in the morning?"

She forced a smile and shook her head.

"Sorry! Sorry." The dragon's eyes looked pained. "I had to try. All right, this is his office," Ruby pushed the door open to reveal the most modern-looking room Kylara had seen on the entire campus.

The walls were adorned with framed diplomas and awards. One of the twitching, fake perpetual motion machine thingies stood on the desk. Behind it stood a man who—to her shock—did not wear a robe but a sweet checkered vest over a bright green shirt with no tie. His glasses looked like something Buddy Holly would have clamored to own.

"Hello. You must be Kylara Diamantine. Ruby told me about your…request. My name is Warren Hinesburg. It's nice to meet you." He bowed slightly to Kylara.

"Oh, you don't need to do that," she said.

Mr. Hinesburg raised an eyebrow.

"I'll leave you to it then," the dragon said and saw herself out.

"Ruby said you wished to be transferred to the mage's dorm and that you had a very good reason for doing so—not that we necessarily need one. I think some integration would do this school good." He seemed both curious and suspicious of her, not that she blamed him. That was how everyone else had treated her since she returned to campus.

"It's nice to meet you, Mr. Hinesburg."

"Oh, such formalities. There's no need for a dragon to address me that way, Miss Diamantine."

"That's the thing, sir. I'm not a dragon."

He didn't look surprised. "I know it may shock you to hear this, but even though it's my first year at this campus, I am familiar with the antics of college kids and dragons in particular. If you intend to create some kind of prank, I assure you that you will be punished."

"No, no, no, this isn't a joke. Uh…look," She ignited her hand with light.

Mr. Hinesburg was not impressed. "We have a few dragons with light capabilities here, Miss Diamantine. I had heard you have diamond scales, but I see I was mistaken."

Kylara put the light out and placed her hand on the table. Black threads emerged from her fingertips and traveled across the desk like slime mold. One of the threads of darkness found Mr. Hinesburg's motion machine and wound around it to arrest its movement.

"How…how did you do that?" His face was the picture of surprise and his mouth hung open. He pulled his soul patch with one hand while his eyebrows raised almost to his hairline. "Those are…those are dragon powers."

"That's the thing, sir. I'm a mage who can absorb dragon powers."

"But…but that ability hasn't been seen for…for centuries! Maybe a thousand years." As he spoke, his tone went from fear to excitement. "Tell me, what powers do you have?"

"I have the ability to turn into a diamond-scaled dragon from my mom. Since then, I've absorbed the light and dark powers. Oh, I can also control the weather."

"This is…this is—quite frankly, this is incredible!" Any trace of hesitation was now gone from his voice. He stood quickly and paced the area behind his desk while one hand tugged his vest and the other stroked his tiny soul patch.

"It won't be a problem that I can take the shape of a dragon?"

"A problem? Why, of course not. Well, don't change into a dragon while in your room, but no, no, no, no. This isn't a problem at all!"

"Well, it's good to see that at least someone is excited about it." Kylara pouted with the resentment that still roiled within.

He stopped pacing and turned to her. "You're one of the students who were gone from campus, aren't you?"

Kylara nodded.

"You only got back today, correct?"

She responded with another nod.

"You must be exhausted and, if you're coming here after a day like you must have had today, I can only imagine that you're experiencing your first taste of how dragons treat us mages."

"I'm so confused," she said. "I was raised to think mages were as strong as dragons. My mom—or my adopted mom, I guess—named me after a mage."

Mr. Hinesburg shook his head and uttered a low whistle. "You know, that might be even more rare than your ability to take dragon form."

Kylara couldn't help but smile at the attempt at humor despite her black mood. "She was fairly weird."

"I bet!" He smiled. "Look, I'm sure you've heard this probably a hundred times today, but this is special, Kylara. We'd be honored to house you for as long as you'd like to stay here. If there's any training you need or questions about theory, please don't hesitate to— You know what?" He slowed when he noticed the bags under her eyes. "I think I'm getting ahead of myself. Let's get you settled in. And please, I ask all the mages to call me Warren. I don't see why I should treat you any different."

"Thank you, sir."

"Warren."

"Thanks, Warren."

"No problem." He had picked up a clipboard and now flipped through the papers on it. "And look, I'm sure all our mages would be happy to have someone like you bunking with them. Let me find a slot...and—oh."

"Is there a problem?"

"No...no problem. We have only one vacancy in the women's mage dorm. I might be able to find something else if you give me a few days to shift some people around."

"I couldn't possibly ask everyone to do that for me," Kylara said. "Wait...I thought you said you had a slot."

"I do. And you know what, it'll be fine. In fact, it might be... enlightening. It's not only dragons who cling to the old ways, you know."

"What does that mean?"

"I make it a policy to not gossip about my students. I have a room for you, but promise me you'll come and see me if Miss Patel gives you any trouble."

"Oh, I'm sure she's not as bad as my last roommate," she said wistfully.

Warren frowned and looked like he wanted to pry but instead, he nodded and led her from his office. He guided her down a hallway that was identical to the dragon dorm, then knocked on a door.

The girl who answered was almost breathtakingly beautiful. She had full curly black hair that made Kylara's straight black hair look like uncooked spaghetti. Her skin was a shade darker than her coppery tone, but it had none of the pockmarks that acne had inflicted on Kylara. Her eyes were like dark chocolate and her lips the color of dark cherries. She wore pajamas that covered her skin but nevertheless showed off a figure few girls, dragon or mage, would ever attain.

"Who is this?" The first words out of the girl's mouth quite effectively shattered the effect of her beauty.

"Good evening, Jasmine. This is Kylara Diamantine. Kylara, this is Jasmine Patel."

"And is there a reason you have brought a dragon to my room without me being properly prepared?" She had begun to curtsy to Kylara the moment Warren had said "Diamantine."

"Actually, Jasmine, Kylara is not a dragon at all."

"But her surname—"

"Yes, I know. It's quite unusual," He beamed despite his earlier discomfort when he'd first mentioned who she could bunk with. "Kylara was raised by a dragon but has recently discovered that she is a mage. In her lives the long-lost ability for a human to take the body—and in Kylara's case—the very powers of the dragons around her."

"How fascinating," Jasmine said in a tone so flat it made the marbled floor of the school's cafeteria look like the Rocky Mountains.

"She has yet to learn the more classical mage skills but will bunk with you while she sorts all that out," Warren explained. When the girl discovered that her new roommate wasn't a competent mage, her expression somehow soured even further.

"It's nice to meet you." Kylara extended a hand.

The girl looked at the outstretched appendage with barely concealed disdain as if touching her might sully her perfect skin. "Charmed—oh wait. You wouldn't be able to do that, would you?"

"Not yet, no," she said and tried not to grit her teeth.

"And how long will she stay with me? I had grown rather accustomed to having a single." Jasmine's accent was mostly American with a slight trace of British and what Kylara would later realize was Indian. It was hard to pin down, although the accent made it clear she was far more cosmopolitan than her new roomie would ever be.

"Given that your family did not pay for you to have a single," Warren stated firmly, "Kylara will stay here as long as the school wishes her to, Miss Patel."

"Of course," Jasmine responded, but her tone was cold.

"If there's nothing else, I'll leave you two to get acquainted. Kylara, I'll have your things delivered in the morning unless there's anything you need right now."

"No, I have sleep clothes and a toothbrush, thanks."

"Very well. I look forward to getting to know you," Warren said, although the way he said it made her feel like he was far more interested in getting to know how she worked instead of who she was. Not that she currently knew the answer to that question.

Warren left and Jasmine closed the door behind him.

"I've seen you around. You're the girl from the desert, right? The orphan."

Kylara ground her teeth to avoid biting her head off. "I grew up on a ranch here in New Mexico, yes."

"A ranch. How quaint. All the dragons my family have served lived on estates."

The insult was obvious, but she'd had a long day. She wouldn't rise to this right now, not without sleep. But Jasmine didn't look like she was ready to let her new roommate go to bed either so she tried to think of something else to say. "So…did your family go to this school too?"

Jasmine rolled her eyes back in her head with such force that Kylara feared she was casting a spell. "I am the first of my family to attend this school. I thought that would be obvious, given that no mages were allowed a year ago."

"Oh, right, sorry. I've been on the dragon side of things so I forgot. How did you get in, then? Was it hard?"

"I could ask you the same thing." The girl all but purred menacingly like a lion deciding whether it wished to eat the mother antelope or its young. "Despite my family's long esteemed history serving dragon kind, the application process was rigorous. Rumor has it that you were admitted by the Steel Dragon herself—that she took pity on your situation."

"My house was burned to the ground by a fire elemental, so yeah, Kristen got me enrolled. Is that a problem?" There was a difference between putting up with her new roommate being rude and letting the girl walk all over her.

"No, not for a dragon. Of course not. My family has always believed that dragons are entitled to the privileges they claim. I merely wonder what your status is now that you're a mage."

"I'm not sure, that's why I asked to be moved to this dorm. I grew up thinking I was a dragon, so don't know much about mage culture."

"Well, in that regard, I suppose you should count yourself lucky to join me in this room."

"And why is that?"

"Because the Patel mages are the absolute pinnacle of mage culture. If you need to learn about how the world of magic operates, there is no one better than a Patel to teach you. I can—at the very least—assure you that with my help, you won't fall into some of the social traps so many mages seem to slip into since the Steel Dragon's…uh, revolution."

"That's weird." Kylara knew she should shut up but she was so tired. It took too much energy to be kind, patient, or politically correct.

"Weird?" Jasmine inquired as if she had not used the word before and had never dreamed it might be applied to her or anyone in her family.

"My mom used to work with a mage. She always talked about how much of her money went to Lara. I would think that if the Patels are the pinnacle of mage culture, the least your patron dragon could do would be to provide their first student at the Lumos School with a room of her own."

Jasmine's cold, haughty demeanor blew away with a vortex of wind that rose out of nowhere and swirled around her. The effect made her look like a goddess—a beautiful, powerful goddess of something like vengeance, retribution, or slapping bitches across the face.

"The Steel Dragon's new world order has thrown our contracts—contracts that lasted centuries—into questionable legal standing. We are currently exploring…our independence. Rest assured, Kylara, our days together in this room are numbered. I suggest you watch your tongue in the meantime."

"I'm exhausted," she replied. "Do you mind if I get the light?" She didn't wait for an answer but sent a tendril of dark magic out to snuff out the source of illumination.

Jasmine squeaked at the display of a dragon power before she threw herself into her bed and turned her back.

Kylara crawled onto her bed. It was identical to the one in Tanya's room, yet this new space seemed much colder.

# CHAPTER SIX

Cassandra almost felt bad for Hester Diamantine. Almost, but not quite. She had hunted her for a very long time. Sixteen years of hiding out, mastering magic her father had always warned her against, then hunting and tracking dragons who deserved nothing better than a quick death and a shallow grave.

She had killed them all. Almost every dragon who took her family from her was dead. They had all died at her hands—or, more accurately, at the hands of the elementals she had learned to control during her quest for vengeance. The only one left was no longer capable of running. She was chained with cuffs that kept her dragon powers from her. Cassandra could kill her if she wished—and she had wished exactly that for so long but now, she hesitated.

"She knows the truth now. You understand that, correct?" she said to Diamantine. "There will be no going back to her thinking of you as her mother."

"Kylara is alive?" The prisoner wheezed and raised her head slowly.

The mage knew it wasn't an act for the dragon. As long as she was cuffed, her healing powers would be unavailable to her. The bruises on her face wouldn't heal any faster than a regular human's. She would have no super-human strength to pull on.

But she had worked a long time to get to this moment. She wouldn't release the dragon from her restraints, even if part of her—the part that cared about her niece—wished she could.

In reality, she felt like she could release Diamantine if she wished to. It wasn't like there was anywhere the dragon could go. They were in an abandoned mine hidden inside a rarely visited stretch of the Rocky Mountains.

She had ordered an earth spirit to expand and strengthen this room long before. Over the years, the being she most often summoned had almost warmed to the task. What was once a rough-hewn space choked with coal dust was now something far more refined. As the earth spirit had widened the room, it had put in pillars of stone to support the ceiling. It had gathered most of the coal and moved it to another part of her lair.

It was no longer economical for people to remove the coal from this mine and hadn't been for decades, but that simply meant there was a good supply for her to feed her fire spirit with. She kept the spirit in a brazier that she stoked with coal every few days. As long as it could keep an ember or a spark in this realm, it would not need to be called again.

The summoning was a demanding process, especially if one wished to harness the abilities of the more powerful spirits. The coal was the perfect solution to keep her fire spirit well-fed and strong while she bided her time. She used her telekinetic powers to dump more coal into the brazier now, though. She wanted to see Diamantine's face.

Cassandra approached the chained dragon trapped in her human form. She was secured to one of the pillars the earth entity had made long before. The anchor links were buried deep inside the rock, something the being could do as easily as a child could dig in sand.

Surrounding the pillar to which Hester was chained was a

shallow pool of water. In that swam a water spirit, the first she had summoned. For years, it had haunted the frozen lake where she had lost all her family—everyone except her niece Kylara—but when that location became compromised, she had put the spirit in a bottle of water and brought it here. It moved through the water and created a wake as if a large fish swam through the pool.

In addition to these three powerful beings, an air spirit was in the cavern as well. Water and fire spirits were simple enough to control. They needed fuel and water to survive in this realm. Earth spirits were trickier still, but there were ways—most of which she had learned the hard way. The air spirit was certainly the most difficult, though. Cassandra often threatened to banish it to where it came from. She hoped she was never forced to do it as it was a powerful ally.

With these four spirits and her formidable magic powers, she didn't feel particularly threatened by Diamantine. Not that she intended to release her from her bonds.

She waded through the water and stepped onto the tiny island that surrounded the pillar to which her prisoner was shackled. As she did so, the air spirit blew the water from her leathers so when she stood in front of the dragon, her hair blew back from her face.

"You dare imply that I could kill my niece?" she said, her voice barely above a whisper.

"Honestly, I don't understand why you haven't killed me yet. You already eliminated everyone else on my team. Why drag it out for me?"

It was all bluster. She knew that, of course, because she had known who Diamantine was long before she had captured her. Still, she was impressed.

"You're only alive because of Kylara."

"So, she is alive!" And in a split-second, the dragon's tough exterior chipped away to reveal the face of a worried mother. She did care for Kylara. Cassandra was sure of it.

She smirked. "Yes, she is. I lured her away from campus to tell her what she was and took her to the place where you found her —the place where you killed her family."

"It wasn't me who killed those mages."

"Yes. I wasn't aware of that until I discovered it with Kylara. I saw what you did. You and your mage tried to talk to my family. It was very uncharacteristic of a dragon, I must say. And look what it got you." Cassandra jabbed a finger into the palm of Diamantine's scarred hand. It was rare for a dragon to scar at all and rarer still for one to keep a burn.

"Her father gave this to me," the captive said. "It's less than I deserve." Her head lowered.

"I find you so curious, Diamantine." The mage began to pace around the pillar, leaving the dragon's sight and returning on the other side of her.

"I'll tell you anything you want to know but please, tell me where Kylara is. You're not...keeping her like this, are you? You wouldn't do this to her."

"No. No, I wouldn't," Cassandra said and stopped a little beyond Hester's peripheral vision. "She tried to fight me to free her friends—an admirable response, I will admit. Rather than risking any permanent damage, I let her go."

"I swear to the gods of dragons and mages alike that if you so much as hurt her, I will—"

"Oh, calm down. Threats no longer become you." Cassandra cut off the former Dragon SWAT member impatiently. "She battled three of my spirits and almost overpowered them. The dragon healing ability she stole from you has no doubt mended her wounds already. She's powerful with magic, exactly like her mother and her grandfather. To think what she would be already if you hadn't stolen her from us."

"I'm...sorry. I truly am." Diamantine choked the words out.

"Those mages—your family—weren't doing anything except trying to live a life of freedom. When I found the baby, I knew that if I told anyone, she would be killed. I didn't know what she was but when she touched me and took my shape, I knew she was special. I kept her safe as long as I could."

"You did well in that regard," Cassandra told her prisoner. "You were almost impossible to find, unlike your partners. Tormentus and Rubonus were almost painfully easy to find. They were even easier to kill."

"Then why not me? Why keep me in these shackles when you could kill me?"

"Because of her. You could have incinerated that baby or abandoned it, or even eaten it like the monster you are, but you didn't. I never suspected that the reason you were so hard to find was because you had gone into hiding to protect my niece."

"Then…release me. I love Kylara like my own daughter. If you mean her no harm, we can be allies."

The mage shook her head, even though she still stood beyond where Diamantine could see her. "It's not as simple as that. It never is. You may have saved the girl, but you and your team killed her mother, father, and grandfather. They had committed no crime except refusing to live under the yoke of dragons and for this, you executed them without trial."

"And I've regretted what I did there every day of my life. I regret not stopping Tormentus and I regret agreeing to the job in the first place. What I did to Kylara—to you—is unforgivable. But please…I understand I have no right to ask this of you, but please tell me. Where is Kylara? Is she all right? Tell me where she is and tell me the truth, and then do with me what you will."

"She is alive and well." Cassandra saw no point in lying to the woman about the girl. She obviously cared for her. That was why she was still alive—because of the bond the two shared. "She reached a Steel Guard station—no doubt at your command, I'm sure—and has been enrolled in the Lumos School since then.

Although who is to say how long that will last now that she knows the truth about what she is?"

Diamantine sagged with relief. "Thank you, Cassandra. From the bottom of my heart, I thank you."

"You thank me? When I hold your life in my hands?"

"If she's at that school and she knows what she is, she'll be safe. I know the Steel Dragon herself has taken an interest in it. Even if dragons begin to understand what she is—and the threat she poses—she'll be safe. You may take my life if you so desire. Now that I know Kylara will be safe, I have no more reason to live."

"Oh, don't be so melodramatic," Cassandra snapped, turned her back to the dragon, and walked across the pool of water again. "I might kill you in the future. You do deserve it, after all, but you endeared yourself to my niece. I won't have your blood on my hands, not when it would cost me the trust of my family."

What she didn't say was that Kylara was more than simply family. She—and especially her powers—were the key to her people finally taking their rightful place in the world. Although she didn't know if she and her niece could become close. She had seen the look of rage on the girl's face and the look of shock and betrayal when she'd seen her friends bound by her aunt's hand. But Cassandra still had to build a bridge to her if she could.

The ability for mages to turn into dragons could not be lost again.

CHAPTER SEVEN

Kylara had secretly harbored the hope that the next day would be a normal one. She had entertained the fantasy that perhaps her nature as a mage was too special to share widely and that the rumor mill would be shut down before knowledge of what she was became widespread.

This was not the case.

Her day began with her roommate waking her with a flurry of magic.

"Pardon me, Kylara, but I am so accustomed to mages being able to absorb the extra magic I throw around."

She removed the other girl's panties from her head and threw them on the floor. Before they could so much as land on the tile, Jasmine whisked them away and into a laundry hamper using nothing but telekinesis. "I must wash those now," she said then as if it needed clarification, "Not that I wore them."

Well, it was a small comfort that at least the underwear on her head had been clean. She considered making another jab about how the girl wasn't as rich as she once was, an obvious sore point, but Jasmine's powers were too awesome to ignore.

In the blink of an eye, her clothes came from her dresser,

unfolded themselves, and slid over her almost perfect body. With a telekinetic burst of energy, her hair did itself into a bun so elaborate Kylara didn't even know what to call it. With another flick of her wrist, her make up applied itself as well.

In the time it had taken her to wake up, the mage was ready for the day.

"Catch you later," Jasmine sneered and left.

The young dragon mage dressed and tried to blame the grumpiness she felt on her hunger as she hurried to the cafeteria. It seemed she had slept in and when she arrived, the beautiful eating space was mostly empty. She considered it a blessing and ate in silence, listening only to the sound of the mages in the kitchen as they cleaned up the breakfast mess. Fortified with a good meal, she hurried to her first class.

Dragon Law class passed as slowly as ever, but at least the professor didn't seem to care that she was no longer a dragon. It was when she reached her Magical Theory class that she understood her world and her place in everyone else's had changed.

Before—a scant few days earlier in fact—she'd had friends in this class. Or if not friends, then acquaintances—classmates she sat with, gossiped with, and talked about how difficult magic theory was for dragons.

Now, though, her former place was taken by a dragon she didn't know. Whoever he was, he was the only one at her old table with the courage to look at her while she tried to find a new seat. Even Tanya avoided eye contact, although she didn't look haughty so as much as hurt. Kylara felt bad about what she'd said to her, but it wasn't like she would beg the young dragon to kick this new kid out so she could have a seat.

She glanced at the empty chair near Jasmine, only for the mage to take a ballpoint pen and balance it on the chair next to her with her mind. An obvious—if childish—threat.

Kylara finally sat next to the only person in the class who might have been less popular than her—Karl Midnight, the dragon who had attacked Tanya and from whom she had gleaned the ability to control dark magic.

"Do you mind if I sit here?"

"It's not my chair. You can sit wherever you like," he replied, which wasn't exactly polite but was better than anyone else had been. She sat in silence and didn't look at him.

"All right, dragons, mages, and students beyond the binary," Professor Sharra said as she hurried into the room with a swirl of her cloak and winked at Kylara, which didn't in any way make her feel like she fit in at all.

"We now all understand the basics of theory—"

"Speak for yourself," Karl Midnight muttered.

"So we'll move along to the next section of our class," the woman continued. "As you know, the world is changing and our understanding of magic as both an intellectual topic and practical discipline is always evolving. To that end, for the foreseeable future, we have a special guest who will assist us. May I present Petalwing to you."

Something knocked at the window and everyone turned to see what it was. A tiny human—no larger than a bird or perhaps a decent-sized squirrel—thrust itself repeatedly against the windowpane.

"Oh, for goodness sake," Professor Sharra opened the window with a gesture and the tiny creature burst through the opening and into the classroom.

"I thought we had discussed my grand entrance through the window," Petalwing complained as the tiny person darted above the students' heads and showered them in gold sparks that dissipated to nothing before they reached the floor.

"Yes, that was why I left the other window open." The professor pointed to the window directly beside the one that had given Petalwing so much trouble, which was wide open.

The class laughed at this and rather than offending the creature, it seemed to amuse her. Kylara could see now that the pixie was female, but it was hard to tell. If her hair was a little shorter and her breasts a fraction smaller, she could have easily passed for a boy. Her eyes were much too large for her face, and two pairs of wings sprouted from her back. They were shaped like dragonfly wings but were the off-white color of lilies.

"Class, Petalwing is a pixie. She will work with us as we prepare for a field trip."

The class burst into chatter at the mention of a field trip. Kylara and Karl didn't talk to each other, of course, which meant she overheard some of what the others were saying. Many were surprised that a field trip would be tolerated at all in light of the recent attacks on campus. Others simply hoped to go somewhere outside the desert. But one dragon's voice cut through them all.

"I don't understand what the heck pixies can teach us about magic."

"Well, Sir Galen, there is a considerable amount that pixies can teach us about magic."

The offending dragon, one Galen Stormwing, didn't seem particularly pleased about being called out, but he didn't look like he was about to apologize either. As usual, he wore a scowl on his face.

Galen was a vanilla dragon, which was odd because he was related to a family of dragons—the Stormwings—who had become infamous in recent years for their powers. Kylara didn't know if he idolized the dragon who had teamed up with a mage to bring a tornado of fire on the city of Detroit, but she knew Galen wasn't embarrassed by being related to him. That alone rubbed her the wrong way.

"I've seen any number of pixies at parties. I honestly don't see why I would want to learn how to make colorful sparks."

"I would think he'd settle for anything," Karl mumbled to Kylara. "Right now, his only power is having a pissed-off aura. All. The. Time."

She laughed loudly enough to take Professor Sharra's attention from Galen to her.

"Not all of us can turn up our noses at certain powers," the woman said, which made her wish she had the ability to melt into a puddle from embarrassment.

The professor faced the class firmly. "As I dearly hope all of you know, pixies were made by mages during the Second Mage Rebellion. They are beings of almost pure magic, and we hope this can help you to improve your magic skills."

"It shan't be easy, but I think if we all agree to not sing out of tune, it should go swimmingly," Petalwing said. She landed on Professor Sharra's desk long enough to pick a feather up, which she now danced with above everyone's heads.

"As we prepare for this trip," the woman continued, "I need you all to understand how important it is to follow directions. When you agree to come with us, you will essentially agree to risk your life, so it is vitally important that you all listen to Petalwing as if she were your professor."

"There will be no gallivanting about, that is for certain," the pixie stated, dropped the feather, and landed on it so she could use it like a surfboard.

"She has graciously agreed to escort us into the pixie world," Professor Sharra explained. "Once we're there, we'll be met by a team of pixies who will lead us in exercises which may help us to learn new aspects about the magic that flows inside us."

"If I have to hear once more about flowing magic, I'm going to pee," Karl mumbled.

Kylara forced herself to not laugh, but she couldn't help but think he was kind of funny. At least he didn't take everything so seriously—although that didn't change the fact that what he had done to Tanya was messed up. The thought of her friend made her turn to steal a peek, only to see the girl staring at her. She, at least, had understood that she had been laughing at Karl. Of course, she was the one person who she did not want to know that.

"The pixie world is extremely dangerous," Petalwing said from somewhere inside a chandelier. "Creatures from this realm are quite squishy over there."

"So why are we going at all?" Galen asked in a tone that made it a little too obvious he was trying to regain face.

"There is a place—a meadow, in fact—that is quite lovely," the pixie said and made a spiraled descent from the chandelier to land on Professor Sharra's desk. "The meadow is safe. As long as you stay in the meadow, all will be well."

"We think," the professor interjected quickly.

"Yes—we think. The only dragons who have come to the pixie realm have, uh… uh…Miss Sharra, what was the phrase you said to tell them?"

"What Petalwing means to say is that all the dragons who have been to the pixie realm have suffered horrible and excruciating pain." The woman's hands did not leave her hips. "Which means that none of you are under any kind of obligation to go. This first trip will be a test run—a type of pilot program, so to speak. We hope that, with Petalwing's help, we can build this into the curriculum, but we won't require any students to make the trip unless they choose to do so."

"Are you saying there are no grades on the field trip?" a bookish mage asked.

"That's correct. To remain here is probably the smarter move, to be honest, so please, if you have doubts, stay behind."

"Then why go at all?" the same mage asked.

"Because, if all goes as we hope it will, there are great mysteries to be unlocked in that meadow," Petalwing said dreamily.

"She's right," Professor Sharra agreed, her hands still on hips like a tough magic sheriff. "Some dragons—like the Steel Dragon herself—have earned incredible powers from a trip like this. Of course, we can't guarantee those kinds of results, but we hope this visit and more like it in the future will give you all some of the gifts this academy wishes you to have."

"So...what is the expression?" Petalwing scrunched her tiny face in thought. "Ah, yes! Raise your flipper if you do not wish to go."

"Hand, but yeah, you get the idea."

Another excited surge of conversation rippled through the class, but no hands went up. Everyone grinned and discussed what powers they wished to have and which weren't that great.

Kylara decided that she wanted to go on this trip, even though she didn't care about unlocking more powers. If this meadow was where dragons learned new powers, perhaps she would be able to discover something about how she had learned the powers of a dragon.

It was possibly wishful thinking, but she felt that if Kristen Hall had been able to release her hidden abilities there, it wasn't too much of a stretch for her to learn who she was—whether that was a mage, a dragon, or something of both.

CHAPTER EIGHT

After the interesting addition of a pixie into Magical Theory, Kylara managed to leave the lesson not feeling like total crap, which was both a surprise and a relief. She still didn't know who she was or where she fit in, but perhaps this trip to the strange realm would give her a clue.

There certainly weren't any clues that might suggest answers to all her questions to be found in the cafeteria. She entered the beautiful dining hall with its marble floor and carved wooden tables to rediscover somewhat uncomfortably that a hundred pairs of eyes suddenly wanted nothing to do with her. She had become accustomed to this kind of response from most of the student body, but it hurt to walk past Sam and Tanya and have the girl pointedly ignore her.

He at least looked like he wanted to say something, but a look from his companion was more than enough to remind him that his allegiances lay with the dragons, not mages, and certainly not with whatever the heck she was.

Kylara loaded her plate with food—even if everyone hated her, at least the meals were good—and located an empty table tucked into a nook of the cafeteria. She had almost reached it when a cord of dark energy whipped out and flicked in front of her face.

"Midnight, now is not the time," she snapped.

"Oh, calm down," Karl replied from the table she had walked past. "Someone of your…stature shouldn't sit alone in a dark corner. Join us."

"She's a mage, Karl," one of his cronies said, a female dragon by the name of Esme who had venomous claws in her dragon body.

"And a weird one," added Tempest, his other crony.

"And I couldn't care less, so no more of that crap. She is far more powerful than either of you two chumps." He sneered at his two tablemates. "Please, Kylara, have a seat. If these two give you any trouble…" Black snakes of dark energy crept out from his fingertips toward his two friends. They both looked at the tendrils and shuddered, a sure sign that he had used his powers on them before.

Kylara, not sure why he had defended her and even less sure why she cared, took a seat.

"Hi. I'm Kylara Diamantine."

"Oh, shut up, Kylara, we know exactly who you are. You're in our Dragon Powers class." Esme hissed her annoyance.

"Right, duh. Sorry."

"You don't have to take that from her. Not with the powers you control," Karl said.

Esme huffed and continued to eat.

"You're Tempest, right?" Kylara said to the other dragon, although she knew exactly who he was. It was his lightning strike against her that had given her the ability to control the weather. "I don't know your first name."

"That's because everyone calls me Tempest," he said obstinately.

"Everyone calls him that because his first name is Hubert."

Karl grinned before he shoveled a spoonful of pudding into his mouth.

"My mom named Galen after grandfather because she thought he would get powers. But it's me who gets the family name," he said.

"Ask us if we care," Midnight snapped.

"I kind of care," Kylara said. It was vaguely interesting. She hadn't known that Galen and this Stormwing were brothers but it made sense.

"You don't have to kind of care about anything anymore," Karl said and polished his dessert off with the help of his dark tendrils of energy. She had only managed to use the power to make string-like threads, but he seemed able to make them move as if they were snakes. It was something she would like to learn to do.

"What do you mean by that?" she asked, watching him absent-mindedly use the magic she had gained from him.

"I respect power and skill," he said as if it were obvious. "You have both. You beat me fair and square more than once, and even once when the odds were against you. I don't think I would have won our last duel if you hadn't been distracted."

"You didn't win that duel," she said.

He didn't contradict her but simply smiled. "I won't argue with you, not with the powers you have, but if you don't believe me, ask the Silver Bullet."

Kylara decided to let it drop and focused on her food. For a moment, they all sat and ate quietly but before long, her curiosity overwhelmed her.

"I have to say I'm surprised you invited me to sit here. I know many dragons think mages are beneath them."

"You can say that again," Esme muttered into her dessert.

"Dragons only think that way because they won the first two mage wars and managed to cuff most of the mages." Karl shrugged as if they were discussing pizza toppings rather than centuries of horrific slavery. "Look at her." He nodded at Amy, who was seated at a table in front of the cafeteria with some of the other professors. Bottles of different condiments floated in the air around her. "She's one of the most powerful mages who ever lived. She's stronger—much stronger—than many dragons."

"She can't heal, though," Esme pointed out. "Not like us."

"I could crush her skull and there's nothing she could do about it," Tempest declared.

Karl shook his head. "Not true. She has powers that—when used properly—could defeat almost any dragon. Sure, she might not win a test of strength, but only a fool would fail to respect that she's smart enough to leverage her powers to win in almost any situation."

"And you're no fool," Esme and Tempest said together.

He beamed. "See? You two are learning! The fact is, power is power. It doesn't matter if a dragon or a mage has it. Amy Williams has power, so I respect her. The same could be said for you, Kylara. You've proven yourself to be powerful, so I'm inclined to treat you with respect."

"Is that why you treat us like your personal mages?" Esme asked quietly.

"Quite right," he replied. "If either of you had ever beaten me in a fight, I might not be as inclined to treat you the way I do and you might not be as inclined to take it." To prove his point, he launched a snake of inky magic that snatched a bowl of ice cream off Esme's tray.

She sighed and stood. "I'm going to class."

"Me too," Tempest said. "All the 'power' at this table is getting to be a little much."

That left only Kylara and Karl.

"Ice cream?" he asked and placed the bowl in front of her. She couldn't be sure but thought she discerned a twinkle in his eyes that hadn't been there before.

"Sure." She slid it closer and took a mouthful. While she let it melt in her mouth, he began to talk about the upcoming field trip.

"I can't believe we'll have a pixie escort. My dad says they can hardly think in straight lines. I don't see how one will keep us safe."

"Do you honestly think it's that dangerous?" she asked.

Karl shrugged. "Probably. But it might simply be that our healing powers don't work there."

"Is that true?" she asked.

"You don't need to be scared."

"I'm not!" she blurted.

"Good. I want to see it for myself," he said. "There are rumors about creatures that live there—things that were there before the pixies. I wonder if they are true."

"That's why you want to go?" she asked. "I would think you'd want to learn a new power like everyone else."

He shrugged again. "I like my powers. You can do so much with them. I'm sure you'll learn that too. I mostly want to see if what everyone was saying after the Steel Dragon gained her light powers is true. I would think you would be more excited, though."

"Why's that?" she asked as she finished her ice cream.

"It might be a good opportunity for you especially. You got my powers from what? Me touching you? Or was it when I used them on you?"

"I'm…I'm not sure yet."

"Well, whichever it was, this seems like the kind of place where you can either touch whatever creatures are there that grant these abilities or, if they don't like that, simply piss them off and trick them into giving you their abilities anyway."

Kylara realized that the bitter taste of this idea—the idea of stealing powers against the wishes of the user—stuck in her mouth far longer than the taste of the ice cream, as delicious as it had been.

# CHAPTER NINE

To Tanya, even the concept of a field trip to the pixie realm changed everything. She hurried to class, eager to see Professor Sharra for once. To say that learning magic was frustrating to her was a profound understatement. She had found it to be all but impossible—as had the other dragons—and sitting through class each day was torturous. It was like being outside in hundred-degree weather while looking through the locked storefront of an ice cream parlor.

She reached the class, took her seat, and looked around for Kylara before she recalled their fight. In her excitement at the prospect of the field trip, she had managed to forget the horrible things she had said to her and the things her friend had said in return. She knew she should apologize. At the time, she had been tired, scared, hurt, and honestly, more than a little jealous.

Plus, Kylara was nice, and even more importantly, she was Tanya's friend. It made the vanilla dragon's stomach churn that part of her mind rebelled against the idea of apologizing to a lowly mage. It was both unfair and bigoted, but there it was and it squatted stubbornly in the middle of her mind.

This field trip had been the only thing that could get her mind off the issue, although it seemed like she wasn't the only one who was excited.

As more and more students filed in, the energy in the room built like storm clouds harboring hidden lightning. Before the class was halfway full, Professor Sharra arrived with six pixies in tow. This only added to the electric atmosphere and increased both the volume and speed of the gossip at least twofold.

Samuel Lumos came in and took a seat next to Tanya. She had known he was in the class before Kylara and she had started fighting, but it had been in an academic way. He had always been more than her in her mind.

Unlike her, he had special powers—and not simply any old abilities but light magic, the very same magic that had been used against Lord Boneclaw in one of his final battles against the Steel Dragon's forces. Until the two girls had fought, he had sat in the back of the class and hadn't paid much attention but now, his gaze watched the Professor as eagerly as anyone else's.

"How are you doing?" he asked by way of greeting.

"I'm crazily excited," Tanya said as she watched Petalwing and the other five pixies dart around the room. "Honestly, I'm terrified too. Like I dread the idea of all of us going and everyone getting a new power except me."

"I don't exactly think we'll all go to this place and come back with fresh powers," he chided her.

"Yeah, I know, I know. It's only…I've been focused on learning a special power ever since being accepted to the Lumos School, and that was months ago. This might be my first real opportunity to learn something. I know that not everyone will get powers, but…well…"

"You want some?"

"Yeah, exactly." She giggled nervously. "And after everything that happened… I don't know. I don't feel safe anymore."

Samuel nodded. "Well, I hope you find something. Better you than…" The golden dragon trailed off, not wanting to finish the statement with the obvious. Kylara, the mage who could absorb dragon abilities at will—her friend and her rival. Tanya didn't know which word fit better but fortunately, she didn't have to think about it today.

"All right class, it looks like everyone's here." Professor Sharra checked her clipboard. "Funny, we get perfect attendance on the day of a field trip that might grant some of you new abilities."

Nervous laughter rippled through the class. Many of the dragons had skipped Magical Theory at least once or twice but she was right. No one had cut class today.

"We're serious about the warnings from yesterday," she said. "No one is to leave the zone where we arrive. Is that clear?"

"How are we supposed to know where this zone ends?" Karl Midnight asked.

Tanya saw—to her horror—that Kylara was seated next to him again. If she had known that her friend would rebound from their fight by spending time with a dragon like Karl, she would possibly have been more tactful in what she had said.

"It is an unmistakable zone," Petalwing exclaimed and swooped around the young dragon's head. "We will enter through a portal into a place with the most lovely grasses and pools of water. You are all free to walk in the grass and get in the water. Nudity does not bother us."

Mumbles about that followed from the students. The boys said they liked the idea of skinny dipping, while the girls seemed more hesitant, although Tanya could tell from the way the boys looked around that they were mostly interested in the girls doing some skinny dipping rather than themselves.

"But you must not enter the dark and spooky forest!"

Tanya had never heard anyone put such force behind the word "spooky" before. Petalwing continued as she landed on top of Karl's head. His aura radiated annoyance she could feel even where she was seated. "There are creatures there—or perhaps beings is a more accurate word. They are not to be trifled with."

"Exactly," Professor Sharra confirmed. "If anyone leaves this meadow area, you will most likely not return. Is that clear?"

The girl wondered if so many dragons had ever said, "Yes, ma'am," as respectfully as they did now to a mage. Probably not, she decided with a small smirk.

"All right, then." Professor Sharra's hands were planted on her hips as if she did not trust any of her students to obey, which was probably wise on her part. "Petalwing, if you and your helpers would be so kind?"

The pixie nodded and flew to the back of the room where there was more space. Her companions followed her and within a minute, the six of them swooped in a circle at different speeds. It was like watching the face of a clock with far too many hands try to tell the time in multiple dimensions.

After they found a rhythm that was only comprehensible to them, they began to sing. This, at least, was something Tanya could understand. It was a beautiful, haunting melody, with harmonies that were both alien and familiar and pulled on her badly bruised heartstrings. She glanced at Kylara, whose eyes were also locked on the creatures, and sighed.

But before any other thoughts could form from the music's influence, the space between the pixies seemed to shimmer. In one second, they circled a random space in the back of the room and in the next, they ushered in some kind of a change. The music they made seemed to yank on reality itself and suddenly, the space they circumnavigated was swallowed in a gush of purple smoke.

Half of the class startled at this and either flinched or cursed aloud, or—for some of the special dragons—flared their powers. Samuel's hands were certainly glowing, as were his eyes, an effect that Tanya had to admit was freaking attractive.

The purple smoke seemed to get sucked into some point

behind the pixie's circle. It looked as if the creatures had generated a type of wind tunnel and the smoke was pulled into it. Nothing was visible through the smoke despite her intense focus. When she had traveled via Amy's magic portal, she had seen the destination but now, it remained veiled.

It seemed her hesitation to enter a magical portal that led somewhere she couldn't see wasn't a universal feeling. Already, other dragons were lining up to step through.

"Are you coming?" Samuel asked eagerly.

"Yeah, of course," she said, looked for Kylara, and noticed that she had already joined the line. She stood with Midnight, who she chatted to like he hadn't bound Tanya simply to teach her place at the bottom of the dragon hierarchy.

She dragged her focus away from her estranged friend and moved into line. The students in front of her vanished one by one into the swirling purple mist.

Almost too quickly, they moved forward until it was finally her turn. She stared at the portal ahead of her, took a deep breath, and wondered briefly if the air in the pixie realm would taste different before she stepped through.

Her mouth gaped when she realized that she was, in fact, in another world. It wasn't simply another planet but an entirely different kind of existence. That much was immediately clear to her. Something about the light confirmed that she no longer stood on Earth. Everything was too saturated, she decided. The sky above was a rich blue—darker and fuller than the skies of her home, especially those above the desert. Her gaze moved to find the tops of trees in the distance, all rich green and lush like they were well-tended tropical plants in a greenhouse rather than a forest edging a meadow. She continued to study her surroundings until she settled her focus on the meadow itself.

Tanya was a city girl. She had grown up in LA and loved it— the rooftop pools, underground clubs, hidden eateries, and everything else the metropolitan landscape had to offer. But seeing this meadow made her understand that truly, she had never seen beauty in the city.

Something almost soulfully tranquil infused the green area before her. The grass was tall, perhaps two or three feet high, and bowed and swayed gracefully in a gentle breeze. It was green with yellow seeds—colors not altogether unusual for grass—but when it moved, the stems shimmered with a thousand colors. The seeds sparkled like gems.

Above the tops of the grass, butterflies in a hundred different colors and insects of every shape and size flitted and buzzed.

Between all this lush grass and intriguing insects were beautiful pools of water. Each of them was lined with rocks and more plants, often heavy with flowers, dangled gracefully over their surfaces. A tiny waterfall trickled into each pond and another coaxed the water out. They were all part of a stream that must have been dammed and diverted into these pools. Before her eyes could track the stream between them, a dragon boy ran past, leapt upward with a surge of dragon strength, did a triple front flip, and splashed into one of them with a triumphant call of, "dragon ball!"

He transformed into his dragon form immediately before he entered the water, and the resulting splash was epic.

"Thomas! We do not do pool jumps into the sacred pool!" Professor Sharra chastised the boy, who was human again and now completely naked.

"Yes, ma'am," he said, took some of the water in his mouth, and squirted it at one of the girl mages, who in turn deflected it at him and splashed his face.

"Melissa, now is the time for meditation, not splashing our peers!" While the professor moved about and reprimanded the students for all the myriad ways they were disrespecting their hosts, the pixies who had made the portal seemed to do exactly the opposite. They swooped and darted about to splash dragons and mages, bump kids into pools, and steal piles of clothes that had prudently been left out of the water.

Tanya watched it all and thought of all the parties she had been to in California where they had behaved in the same way. If only she had known that splashing and dunking each other was how to activate one's latent magical potential, she might have taken those parties more seriously.

But now, like then, she was most comfortable in her flowing gowns. She moved through the pools, careful to avoid those with the most vigorous splashers, and tried to simply soak in the atmosphere while not becoming soaked. She twirled her parasol as she walked, breathed deeply, and enjoyed every minute of this spectacular place. Her gaze was drawn constantly to the forest. It was warm in the meadow, even under her parasol. She didn't want to get wet yet, but the shady forest floor looked enchanting.

Petalwing streaked past and fired sparks at a dragon who had walked past the pools and into the grassy field toward the trees. "You must stay here in the meadow," she said as her sparks made her point more effectively. They streaked with perfect precision to catch the dragon on the seat of his pants until he finally stripped down and dove into a pool for safety.

Tanya smiled at the sheer delight everyone was having before she turned and walked into Kylara.

"Watch where you're going, vanilla," Karl Midnight snapped at her. He stood next to her ex-friend and scowled at all the fun.

"Hey, don't talk to her like that," Kylara said to him, which she appreciated until the young mage added, "Hopefully, she won't be a vanilla for much longer—right, Tanya?"

She felt bad about what she had said to her, but did the diamond dragon feel the same way? It certainly didn't seem like it.

"Do you want to talk for a minute?" she asked.

"What, now? In this realm?" It was so hard to read Kylara. It always had been. Her aura was a locked box. *Oh, that's because she doesn't have one. She's not a dragon.*

"I would think you'd want to use this opportunity to improve yourself." Midnight sneered at her.

"Hey, Karl, not cool," Kylara said.

"Whatever," he retorted and wandered off.

The girl watched him go for a moment before she turned to her. The lingering glance felt way too long to Tanya.

"Can we talk later? I want to—I truly do. My new roommate is…" She shook her head and smiled shakily.

Tanya longed to be able to sense her friend's aura. Did that look mean she liked her roommate? That she found her frustrating? That she had already given her mage powers?

"But right now…well, I think we should try to use our time here wisely," Kylara finished.

She nodded. It hurt that she didn't want to talk to her now, but maybe she was right. "We'll catch up later," she said, knowing that her aura must make her seem phony but also relieved that a mage not being able to read it was a good thing sometimes.

"You promise?" the girl asked.

"Sure, of course," she replied and watched her walk away. It was a small comfort that at least she didn't follow Karl to his pool.

With a sigh, she turned her attention away from her former roommate—but hopefully still her friend?—and decided it was probably time she found a pool for herself. Not all the dragons had settled into the water, but those that hadn't were mostly the dragons with powers who had never taken the class particularly seriously. For those who wanted powers as desperately as she did, the water seemed the right place to be.

But not for all of them.

As Tanya scanned the meadow in search of a pool where she might be able to remove her dress without it getting completely soaked by rowdy classmates, she noticed a dragon slinking away.

She might not have thought he was slinking and only wandering if not for the fact that it was Galen Tempest, a fellow vanilla dragon who was perhaps even more desperate for powers than she was. What was he up to? Professor Sharra had been quite clear about her expectations for the students. What did he hope to accomplish?

Tanya looked for the professor, not sure how to draw the attention of a pixie. She should tell someone about Galen or he would ruin this trip for everyone.

Or maybe not.

He darted through the grass and hunkered down when a pixie moved in his direction. When it flew past, he pushed to all fours and managed to crawl to the darkness of the woods.

She was vaguely impressed. How had Galen managed to slip away completely unseen given that he had no powers to speak of? Did he know something about this realm that the rest of them didn't?

The questions made her think back to the rumors that had coursed through the dragon world after the Steel Dragon had returned from this very place. She had traveled for a long time, Tanya knew that much, and along her journey, she had gone through some kind of tribulation or ritual that had granted her the ability to use light magic. She had heard nothing about Kristen Hall lounging about in a pleasant meadow.

Did Galen know even more? After all, his father had battled the Steel Dragon and her forces. Perhaps he had gleaned some piece of knowledge?

Tanya wasn't sure what to do. She was still wondering whether she should tattle on Galen or follow him when a dragon with the ability to control the flow of water leapt up from a pool and dove back in to make a splash so huge it soaked everyone in a twenty-foot radius.

"No dragon bodies, please!" Professor Sharra said and hurried toward the students as the pixie chaperones all darted toward him as well. "I distinctly said no dragon bodies!"

She didn't remember the professor saying that but she didn't much care. This was her chance.

Throwing caution to the winds, she took it. Instead of reporting Galen, she hurried through the grass to follow him into the darkness of the woods.

# CHAPTER TEN

Kylara left her conversation with Tanya weighed down by the horrible combination of guilt at being a crappy friend and feeling judgmental for believing she was in the right. It had seemed like her ex-roommate was ready to talk, and she had snubbed her. The truth was, though, that Karl had a point. They would only be there for a short time. It wasn't exactly the right moment for a heart-to-heart.

That didn't mean it was time to soak in a pool with Karl Midnight either, however. He stared at her now. His pale skin was a stark contrast to his stringy black hair, but he still had the physique of a dragon. He was handsome—all dragons were handsome—but she wanted a moment to explore on her own. Ignoring him, she wandered toward the pixies who had managed to persuade a dragon to change into his human body and put clothes on.

This truly was a beautiful realm. It was so different from the desert where she had grown up. The sky was bluer and the greens were greener, and the insects didn't seem to be armed with poisonous stingers to defend what precious moisture they had managed to accumulate. Not only that, but the sheer variety of plants was almost mind-boggling to her. She had watched documentaries about jungles and rainforests, of course, but seeing something on television was very different than stepping into an environment that could be best described as a magical tropical paradise.

It wasn't only the look of it that made her feel differently, though. There was magic in the air—far more than she would ever have imagined was possible. She could feel it in every blade of grass and the wingbeats of every insect. The pools of water teemed with it, and she knew the other students weren't wrong for getting into the water. She seemed to remember something about the Steel Dragon being in the water? Or following the water? She wasn't exactly sure and wished she had studied her adventures in this realm last night instead of dealing with more of Jasmine Patel's haughtiness.

Kylara looked for Tanya but couldn't see her. While she searched, her gaze settled on Karl, who dangled his feet in a pool and smiled. She decided the water must be magic if it could get him to show his teeth in anything but a sneer.

She chose not to go to him and instead, she meandered toward Petalwing, who was leading some of the students— mostly mages and vanilla dragons—in an exercise.

"You must feel the magic," the pixie said. "Feel it with your toesie-woesies and feel it with your fingertips and your eyelashes too!"

Some of the mages, desperate for more power, took their shoes off, while others mumbled about not wanting to get any of the pixie realm in their eyes.

Kylara joined them and tried not to laugh at Petalwing as she followed her movements carefully.

"You must remember that you are all special magic creatures," the creature said excitedly. "That is always true. In this realm, there is more magic in the air like there is more popcorn in a bowl of popcorn than there is in a bowl of chips."

"Are you saying our realm has no magic because it's the bowl of chips?" a mage asked.

"Ah…but both bowls have salt, do they not?" Petalwing enquired rhetorically.

She shook her head at the impish little being and wandered away to find Tanya. While she hoped some of the other students could learn from Petalwing, she felt fairly certain that she wouldn't learn from such whimsical methods.

Diamantine had taught her how to fight in her human and dragon forms through physically demanding and at times emotionally exhausting exercises. All the new powers Kylara had acquired and later used had come from moments of stress. She didn't want to say that she relied on stress to learn, but she knew she did better in stressful situations than most people.

Certainly better than poor Tanya.

Where was she? She thought the pixie method might be good for the girl. She could probably at least understand whatever Petalwing was babbling on about.

Although she scanned the area carefully, didn't see her anywhere. Instead, her gaze once again found Karl, who had managed to choke an entire pool of water with his dark energy.

"What are you doing?" she asked him. "Fishing?"

"The water is wonderful, Ky," Karl said. He had no doubt heard Tanya and Samuel use the nickname, but it was the first time he had said it. She didn't exactly know what to think about that. She felt like a few days ago, she would have bitten his head off, but it didn't seem important now.

"Is that why you won't let anyone else in the pool? You want it all to yourself?" she asked.

"Nah, nothing like that. I'm simply flexing my powers." As he spoke, some of the black tendrils spreading through the pool retracted and a patch of clear water appeared across from him.

Kylara—who still couldn't locate Tanya—approached and sat.

She put one foot in the pool and immediately understood what he was talking about. The water coursed with magic. Feeling it like this made her wonder if it was water at all. It seemed more likely that it was pure magic disguised as water. "It's…exhilarating." She gasped.

"Yeah, and it makes it super-easy to use my special power. I hardly even have to think about it."

"That's because your inner magic channels the magic here," she said.

"How do you know that?"

"Have you completely ignored Petalwing since we arrived?" Kylara asked. "She's leading a group mediation session in how to use the magic the way you are."

Karl snorted, which was as good as a guffaw of laughter for him. "If this is all the pixies are teaching, then no, I won't go over there. They're annoying. Plus, Professor Sharra won't shut up about safety protocol. I'm good here, thanks."

"So you have zero interest in learning new powers?" she asked, somewhat incredulous.

"Well…yeah, I don't. It's not a big deal to me. I'd way rather learn to control my dark powers like this." He gestured to the pool. When he did, all the tendrils pulsed like snakes or some type of coral reef. "If I could do this in the real world, that would be amazing." He smirked. "Do you want to try diving under with me?"

"Are you hoping to drown her or something, Midnight?"

Kylara turned to where Samuel stood nearby. He was shirtless and had the chiseled body that most mortals could only accomplish with nonstop exercise and a diet devoid of all fat, sugar, and flavor. The difference was that while Karl's hair was long, black, and stringy, his was cropped short and slicked back with water. While Midnight was pale, Sam was tan.

None of this was lost on Karl. "Get out of here, pretty boy. You're sucking up all the tan."

"Is that what you're doing to Kylara? Sucking up so she doesn't kick your ass again?"

"Sam—"

"Don't worry about it, Kylara. You don't need to stand up for me like you do for your other, weaker friends," Karl said.

"Do you want to do this right now?" Samuel clenched his fists.

"No, I don't. But I'd appreciate it if you did," Midnight retorted.

The young golden dragon ground his teeth for a moment and his eyes flared with light before he turned to her. "Do you mind if I borrow you from the asshole for a minute or two if that's not too much trouble?"

She was tempted to simply say no. While she didn't exactly want to swim with Karl, she did want to test what the water would do to her with all her powers. Still, it seemed like the universe was telling her this was the time to have difficult conversations with people she cared about, so she acquiesced to his admittedly less than perfect invitation, stood, and followed him away from the pool.

CHAPTER ELEVEN

They walked perhaps thirty feet away before Sam stopped, turned to Kylara, looked her in the eyes, and put his hands on her shoulders like he was about to confront her about a drug habit. "What were you doing hanging out with that jerk anyway?"

"Wait, so let me get this straight. You don't want anything to do with me, so therefore I'm not allowed to talk to anyone else either?" she snapped.

"Wait, what?" Samuel asked.

"I saw the way you snubbed me in the cafeteria. You wouldn't even look at me," she said.

"Yeah, but I shared my guilt with you when you walked past and showed you that I was trying to console Tanya—which, of course, you didn't understand because you're not a dragon."

It was her turn to be surprised. "You did what?"

Sam shook his head and rubbed his face with obvious embarrassment. "Oh, my God, Kylara, I'm so sorry. I only...it's been a crazy couple of days. I guess knowing you're not a dragon and remembering what that means are two different things."

"Yeah, well, I guess it's all right," she said, impressed with an actual apology from a dragon. "And Karl's not that bad. He merely has a thing for power."

"And that means he's allowed to abuse the powerless?" he asked, and some of that fierce tone returned.

"I'm sorry?"

"You and Tanya told me what he did to her. That was disgusting—unforgivable, I'd say. He doesn't get off the hook because he tried to befriend you when he sensed an opportunity."

"If you mean he talked to me, then yeah, I guess he did sense an opportunity," Kylara responded.

Sam held his hands up in a gesture of surrender. "You're right, you're right. I haven't been fair. I simply feel like our relationship has already changed so much."

"Our relationship?" she demanded, not sure if she was comfortable with the term.

"Yeah. I mean, we do have a relationship. Not a romantic one or anything but...uh, not that you were thinking that. Or me!"

"Anyway, you were saying?" she said and saved the dragon from his dragon-puberty brain.

"I'm saying that we met in that canyon and you saved my life. Then we got to know each other at school, and you learned my light power after I healed you. I don't want to stop being friends, Ky. We already have a past together. I still want to be in your future."

"Okay..." she said, not sure what else she could say.

"And then I was captured by...by your aunt! I should have been able to protect you instead of becoming a helpless prisoner in need of a rescue. I messed up badly and I'm sorry."

"Oh, shut up, Sam." Kylara shook her head and the words spilled without thought. "You being captured by a mage who spent her life hunting dragons is not something you need to apologize for. You were taken and I helped. End of story. If the roles had been reversed, would you have tried to save me?"

"Of course! But it's different. You're a mage."

"Can you give that a rest? If I had been taken by Cassandra instead, you wouldn't have even known I was a mage. What would you have done then? Expected me to save my own dragon hide?"

"Well, no. Of course not. She was dangerous."

"And she was a mage! You know, that's one thing Karl gets that you don't. It doesn't matter if someone's a dragon or a mage or whatever. Power is power. Even though I'm technically a mage, I still have the power of a dragon. And if we continue to have a relationship or whatever, you'll need to respect that."

Sam stopped and appraised her for a moment before speaking. "Wow, Midnight said all that?"

"There was more ruthless sarcasm, but yeah, basically," Kylara said.

He nodded for another minute and remained silent, then he reddened. "Sorry, you uh…you didn't get any of that, did you?"

"Any of what?"

Red cheeks became a completely red face. "I was sharing my aura with you. I was trying to make you feel, uh…"

"Yes?" Kylara asked, enjoying his discomfort more than she cared to admit.

Sam sighed. "We normally don't have to put this in words, but…uh, I was trying to say that you make me feel safe and our background together erm…excites…me?"

"You know what, let's pretend that I understood and that we're good now. As long as you stop acting like I'm someone different than the person who outflew you in the Straits and saved your butt later."

"Deal," he said and his old grin was back.

Maybe she could feel something of his aura because, for the first time since she'd returned from Cassandra's lair, she felt the weight she'd carried lighten.

"Hey, what did you need anyway? Or did you come over simply to save me from the asshole?" Kylara asked.

"Oh yeah, right. I intended to ask you if you've seen Tanya. I can't find her anywhere. We came through together but I haven't seen her since."

"She's probably in a pool or something," she said, but when she scanned the meadow and she counted heads, she came up two short.

"I don't think so," he said as she counted again.

"I think you're right," Kylara agreed. "I counted twice. Two students short both times. Tanya is missing, but so is someone else."

Sam's keen gaze roved the students before it flicked back to find hers. "It's Galen Stormwing, another vanilla."

"You know, you need to stop making judgments like that."

"Normally, I'd say you're right. The Steel Dragon changed the Lumos school for that very reason, but it has to be significant. I don't think Tanya would have snuck off by herself. She's, uh…"

"Yeah, you're right. She is like the definition of risk-averse."

"Exactly. Which makes me think she must have seen Galen sneak off and decided to follow him in hopes of gaining a power." His gaze had now drifted to the tree line and he searched the shadows for some sign of their friend. "There."

He pointed and she saw a form vanish into the woods—one still wearing a dress and petticoat.

"Should we tell Professor Sharra?" Sam asked.

"There's no time," Kylara replied.

"I guess I should have thought about who I was asking first." He snorted.

"Come on. If we wait any longer, she'll get too far into the woods."

The two hurried through the grass and checked constantly over their shoulders to make sure no one was watching as they went to find their friend.

# CHAPTER TWELVE

Tanya didn't understand why the pixies had forbidden her class from entering the forest. It was beautiful there. The air was cooler and tendrils of mist swirled around her feet. Every tree she moved past was as thick as the torso of a dragon. Their roots seemed like they could reach the very center of this realm and for all she knew, perhaps they did. A wide variety of beautiful plants sprouted from their trunks and branches. Vines grasped the bark and twisted up into the canopy. In the nooks and crannies, orchids and bromeliads, pitcher plants, and more varieties of moss than she had known existed created a living wonderland.

Her mother had always been partial to botany and had told her—perhaps too many times—that some plants lived far longer than humans could and were therefore worth understanding and cultivating. She had a collection of bonsai trees that was conservatively valued in the millions of dollars. Many of the trees were older than most of the world's countries. As a result, Tanya didn't feel at all out of place there. She found the plants enchanting, another beautiful mystery of the otherworldly environment.

She didn't have time to linger and admire them, however. Already, Galen was slipping away from her. He moved deeper and deeper into the forest. She considered staying where she was at the edge where she could still see the meadow, but something about the way he proceeded pushed her to follow him. He moved with purpose and she couldn't help but think he had an actual destination in mind.

So, despite some misgivings, she pursued him. They moved ever deeper, past butterflies that dwarfed those in the field, birds whose calls were so beautiful they would have taken orchestras to recreate, and the watching eyes of crabs.

Although she didn't particularly mind the humid air or the low branches of trees or dangling vines, her dress had different ideas about how comfortable her surroundings were.

More than once, a branch snagged part of her wide petticoats and she had stopped and ripped the fabric off as discreetly and quietly as she could so Galen didn't hear her. Before long, her silk shift was all that remained between her skin and the grasping vines of the jungle-like vegetation. What was more troubling to her sensibilities was that she was now barefoot.

At some point, the ground had changed from dirt to mud. It hadn't been a transition she noticed until the muck had already become so cloying that it had sucked one of her shoes off. While trying to retrieve it, she stepped in another muddy patch and promptly lost the other.

With bare feet and far fewer clothes than she preferred, she continued to pursue Galen and realized only belatedly that with her constant stops to tear her clothes, lose her shoes, and attempt to keep him in view, she was no longer sure which direction led to the meadow.

She considered simply turning and moving in the opposite direction, but he hadn't exactly proceeded in a straight, unwavering path. Plus, even if she did try to find her way back, the surface was thick with leaf litter. She didn't think she'd be able to follow any trail. That kind of thing was for humans, anyway.

Resigned to what now seemed inevitable, she pushed ever

deeper into the forest. The mud gave way to puddles, which formed slowly together into larger and larger bodies of water. Soon, she traversed a swamp rather than a forest.

Fortunately, the trees didn't seem to mind the transition of biomes. Their roots were as big and twisted, even though they now were anchored to the soil beneath slowly moving, turgid streams and thick, cloying mud. Tanya was thankful for the trees. While she kept her gaze locked on Galen, she kept her feet on their roots.

She hadn't much liked the feel of the mud, and there was something about the water in this swampy area that she liked even less. It seemed almost...opposite of the ponds in the meadow—as if those wished to give magic, while the water here wished to take it. Not that she had anything to give besides what every other dragon in the world had, of course.

Pushing the gloomy thought aside, she leapt across a pond, caught a branch between her hands, and planted her feet on a root, only to look up and discover that she had lost Galen. The young dragon looked right and left, but he was nowhere to be seen. Had he seen her and was hiding? Or had she simply spent too much time trying to keep her feet dry and clean and it had cost her too much distance?

In desperation, she scanned the area and shocked herself when she managed to recognize a footprint. She moved across the tangle of roots to make sure. Up close, she was even more certain. It had the unmistakable ridges of an American-style shoe, something she knew quite well. She preferred to wear sneakers under her elaborate dresses, one of their advantages being that they didn't show her shoes. Encouraged, she looked in the direction the toe of the footprint pointed toward.

Another footprint was easily identified. It looked like Galen had jumped across the stream and landed fairly hard. Tanya followed. His trail was easier to follow now as she found another patch of mud he had simply strode through. Halfway across, she found one of his shoes.

Not much farther ahead was a broken branch. The whitish-yellow wood stood out against the dark browns and greens of the wood and blueish greens of the lichen and moss. She felt reasonably certain she hadn't seen any broken branches before. What had caused Galen to snap this one?

Suddenly, a scream tore through the noise of the swamp. Whatever had made it sounded like it was in pain. Part of her brain was trying to tell her that it was fine—that it was a bird, or insect, or a predator dispatching a meal. But if that was true, why had all the insects and birds fallen silent?

It could have easily been the cry of a human or a dragon, which meant it might have been Galen. But could she find him in time?

She wasn't even sure she could find him at all.

Her heart thudding, she tried to decide which root to jump to next—whether she could find the young dragon or not didn't matter, she had to try—but saw something move through the water in the same direction the scream had come from.

It was white and thin, with too many parts—like some kind of aquatic crustacean that had come up to the surface from a subterranean cave. Only moments later, it reached the end of the pool in front of her and began to climb out. As it emerged from the water and shook, her brain was better able to grasp what it was.

Tanya stared in horror at what was unmistakably a skeleton, one about the size of a cat.

The skeleton of a dragon, to be precise, and it moved toward the cry of pain that she had heard.

Her instinct told her she had to get there before it did. She crouched and prepared to leap over the pond and crush the beast when the root beneath her foot snapped and her leg splashed into the water.

Immediately, the cat-sized aberration turned to her and yowled. When it did, answering calls came from the forest behind her. She turned as three more of the creatures crawled out of a pond she had already crossed. Non-existent eyes glowed impossibly with no light, the empty sockets locked on the intruder. Their jaws were open and their claws, although muddy, looked extremely sharp.

Tanya turned her back on them and launched herself across the pond. The skeleton that had alerted the others yowled and bared its teeth as she descended toward it but she didn't flinch. She landed hard enough to crush its skull and most of the bones of its ribcage. It shattered and lay unmoving, no longer animated.

"Bring it on, you anorexic bitches—" she said, spun to meet the other three, and realized too late that they had already begun their assault.

One of them drove into her and lashed out with hooked claws that ripped into the layer of fabric that still covered her torso. She flung it off but already, the other two were right behind it.

One of them bit her calf as the other bounded into her chest. She toppled, landed hard on a root, and rolled inches away from one of the pools of water. Unfortunately, she had a great view of ten more skeletons swimming toward her.

# CHAPTER THIRTEEN

"So…uh, slipping off is more your thing than mine." Samuel gave her his particularly appealing smile. "What's the plan?"

Kylara looked around the meadow. Dragons were in different pools, where they splashed, laughed, lounged, and flirted—everything you'd expect teens to do no matter what the setting. It seemed being in a magical realm that might have given great dragons of history their formidable powers didn't change those things. Some rules of the multiverse were more fundamental than others.

"We wait for a distraction, then move."

"How long do we wait? If Tanya's in trouble or something, I don't think we should wait that long."

"I don't think we'll need to." She sent a tendril of dark energy out from one of her fingers, down her leg, across the grass, and toward a group close by. A young dragon stood on the edge of the water in his human form and boasted about how gracefully he could dive in. Directly beside him was another boy, who did not look as if he wanted to be one-upped in front of the girls on the other side of the pool.

As the first boy was about to dive in, she snagged one of his feet with the tendril.

Instead of diving in, he proceeded to accomplish the most massive belly flop the pixie realm had ever seen.

When the boy she was trying to frame guffawed with laughter, she stopped feeling bad about implicating him. "Nice grab!" she shouted.

"I knew you tripped me!" the belly flopper yelled and the two boys began to splash each other with arms fueled by dragon strength. In moments, the entire meadow erupted into a massive splash fight. Boy, girl, dragon, and mage were all fair game in the water fight that consumed the meadow.

"Students! *Students, calm down!*" Professor Sharra shouted as she deflected sprays of water directed at her.

The two friends hurried toward the edge of the forest. Dragon powers gave more than only speed and strength. There were things a dragon could do in their human body simply because it could be pushed farther without tiring—like weaving through tall grass fast enough to make it to cover.

"Now wait a minute!" Something buzzed in Kylara's face. "There are woodland creatures who like to move through the grass of this meadow but you two are not woodland creatures."

Kylara straightened to see one of the pixies darting angrily around their heads. "We can explain!"

"You'd better, because I do not think you are woodchucks, prairie dogs, bunnies, or one of our spiny lizards."

"You're right, you're right," Sam said, stood quickly, and gave up on the charade of trying to escape.

"Well, what were you two doing?" the pixie demanded. "Because if it was looking for delicious root vegetables, all you had to do was ask."

"We were—"

"We were trying to slip away," Sam confessed and cut her off.

"Sam! What the hell?" Kylara looked at him with open annoyance.

"I knew it! I knew you were not woodland creatures," the pixie crowed smugly. "For your insubordination, I will now turn you into that which you were trying to resemble—woodland creatures."

"Maybe you should simply tell our teacher?" he suggested.

"A reasonable solution!" the pixie responded and darted toward the pools where the splash fight seemed to be subsiding.

"That was quick thinking," Kylara murmured to him. "I intended to see if I could snag her with dark powers."

"Ky! Are you serious? She's a pixie! We don't even know if your powers can work on her at all."

"I said that you did some quick thinking. That's a good thing."

"Hey, you two!" The pixie doubled back. "Come with me. I might not have said that but woodland creatures like you should know better."

They followed their diminutive escort to Professor Sharra, who was less than thrilled to see them herded by a grumpy pixie going on about woodland creatures.

"I can't believe you two tried to go into the forest." She was soaking wet but that didn't make her hands fisted on her hips any less intimidating. "That was incredibly irresponsible. To say you could get hurt is a huge understatement. If the pixies can be believed—or properly understood—your very existence could have been unraveled in those woods."

"That's why we had to go, ma'am," Sam said in his most butt-kissing tone.

"Maybe you don't quite understand what having your existence unraveled means," Professor Sharra snapped. "It's not good."

"Professor, we should have told you why we went. It's Tanya. She's missing," Kylara said quickly.

"And Galen Stormwing too," he added. "We think they went into the woods to try to get some powers."

The woman rubbed her face and mumbled with evident vexation. "You dragons—it's never enough for you, is it?" She straightened and seemed to realize that she had said this aloud. "Never mind. This is quite serious. You should have come to me." Her last comment was directed to Kylara. It seemed she knew exactly whose idea it was to sneak off.

Without further comment, she raised a hand and a glowing fountain of red sparks issued from her fingertip. The pixie chaperones immediately raced closer with dire expressions and their too-large eyes concerned.

"We think two students are missing," Professor Sharra explained to them. "Can you check the meadow while I gather the others in the center?"

The pixies immediately complied without comment. They radiated away from Professor Sharra and swooped in ever-widening loops, parting the grass as they raced through it.

"Students, I need all of you to come this way! Now! Those who are tardy will have grades dropped, be given detention, or whatever threat you fear most. Move, people!"

A group of sullen mages and dragons climbed from the pools and began to dry themselves with either dragon powers, mage magic, or—if they didn't have the specific ability to dry themselves—with the help of their friends.

A few minutes later, all the students stood in the center of the field and the pixies had completed their search.

"They're not in the meadow at all," Petalwing confirmed anxiously.

"Dammit. They must be in the forest. I should have thought about what vanilla dragons might try to do if we brought them here."

"But vanilla dragons are the ones who need to come here the most—"

"Not now, Kylara," Professor Sharra snapped in response. "Pixies, can you start to open a portal to get the rest of the students back to campus?"

Petalwing shared an apprehensive look with all the other pixies. With their huge eyes, it was hard for them to hide their concern. "I don't think that would be wise, most esteemed teacher of dragons and mages."

"What do you mean?"

"It will take all of us to open the portal."

"Which means none of us would be able to search for the students," another pointed out as if that were helpful and not completely obvious.

"Those woods are extremely challenging. If those dragons encounter some of the beings that take refuge there…well, it will not be good," Petalwing said.

"Right. New plan, kids!" the professor yelled, her frustration evident. "We'll all remain here in the field while the pixies find some of your hopefully simply plain stupid and not suicidal classmates."

Considerable grumbling and complaints followed this, but that was to be expected.

"We will return as quickly as we can," Petalwing shouted. "Remember, the forest is not safe in the least. Beings had taken refuge here long before the pixies discovered this world. Waking them would result in the complete and utter annihilation of all the people here. Do you understand?"

The students were listening at least. One of the mages began to cry.

"Very good!" The pixie seemed satisfied that they were taking her seriously. "We will be back as soon as we can. Remember, you must stay here in the very center of this meadow. Threads of magic tie this realm to itself. If any of you tug on them, very bad things will happen."

"Much worse than becoming woodland creatures, which

might seem great in comparison," the pixie who had first thought that was what Kylara and Sam were and then had later threatened to turn them into one said.

"We'll be here," Professor Sharra assured them. "Send up a shower of sparks if you need help."

"We'll return with the students," Petalwing said. "One way or the other."

"The other means they'll be woodland creatures," the second pixie who seemed obsessed with the forest beings said as they darted away.

# CHAPTER FOURTEEN

Tanya pushed to her feet. She had slipped into the pool, thinking it didn't matter, and was immediately proven wrong. Now that the skeletal creatures had chosen to attack her, the water seemed like the lesser danger, but her splashing merely alerted more of them. Already, they swam toward her while those closest to her advanced.

A skeleton lunged at her and she dodged. Another bounded toward her and she battered it in mid-air and smirked when her dragon strength effectively broke it into its constituent parts.

Unfortunately, their sheer numbers meant that there were too many for her to fight like this. Although, she thought speculatively, not so many that a blast of fire wouldn't incinerate the majority of them in one breath. She looked at the sky, but the way was blocked. The trees were too thick and their branches too big and gnarled. She didn't think she would be able to take her dragon form and reach the canopy. If the branches didn't stop her, her attackers most surely would.

Plus, if she took her dragon form, she would lose maneuverability. Not only that, but the mud was another very real problem. It had been so cloying that she wasn't sure what would happen if she put her dragon weight on it, but she felt certain that if she shifted to her dragon body, she would certainly not be able to walk only on the roots.

With a sigh, she accepted that she had to remain in her human form. Tanya squared her feet, noted that she had far less fabric between herself and her opponents than before, and prepared to destroy as many of the skeletons as she could.

One surged from the water and she was ready for it. She threw her body into a spinning kick that shattered the being into hundreds of bones with the force of an explosion. Still in motion, she drove through a vertebra in the next one's neck to sever the skull and the body bones clattered away uselessly.

She kicked the next but wasn't able to land a well-enough aimed blow to dispatch it completely. Another jumped on her from behind. She tore it off and hurled it against the trunk of a tree. A few of its ribs cracked and fell away, but it was mostly unharmed. It lunged immediately at her as if it hadn't even noticed that it had lost a few bones.

Tanya had to stop her attack and switch to defense in the face of so many of the tiny skeletons. Each time she tried to strike, another was there to snap or scratch at the extended limb. Already, her arms and forearms especially were badly lacerated. Her father had believed that—since she was a vanilla dragon— she should know something about how to defend herself, although what she knew seemed hopelessly inadequate. Still, she knew that these scratches, while they hurt, would heal.

At least six of the skeleton creatures surrounded her now, so close that she couldn't move beyond her present position, and more arrived with every moment. They couldn't do much to her besides scratch, but she was effectively immobilized. The real threat was the other dragons that leapt at her with cat-like lunges. She regretted that she hadn't practiced Aikido with Kylara—perhaps if she knew more about momentum, she might be able to catch those and use their velocity to destroy them.

But, as it was, she had no clue how to do that. Her dad's training had focused on using her dragon strength and speed to overwhelm her opponents. He had neglected the lesson in which she was supposed to survive a swamp teeming with tiny, runty, dragon skeletons.

One of those that nipped at her ankles finally managed a lucky bite and severed her Achilles tendon. She toppled and willed her dragon healing power to prioritize her wounded ankle before it addressed the lacerations on her forearms.

Pain demanded that she do something when her assailants piled on top of her and targeted her ribs.

Tanya tucked her arms around her head to protect her face and tried to buy enough time to heal her ankle so she could get up and out of the mud.

It didn't seem to make a difference. The enemy noticed that she was healing or perhaps had a hunting strategy that was somewhat more evolved than simply to rip the intruder to pieces. They sank their teeth into her now and used those holds to drag her toward the pond behind her.

She buried her hands into the mud in a desperate attempt to stay out of the water. Every time she punched or kicked, the skeletons bit or scratched. Nothing she attempted to do to them made any difference now, and it took everything she had to simply keep her arms outstretched and her fingers dug into the mud. As she wracked her brain to try to think of something else she might do, her gaze settled on an orchid growing in the crook of a tree.

It was covered in purple buds—big, fat, soon to open, purple buds. It made her think of her mom's greenhouse and of an orchid her mother had grown there. Once, when her father had fought a duel against a dragon with the ability to form and melt ice, he had almost died. He had been brought home, a bloody mess with scales ripped away and frostbite over his body. Her mom had taken him into her greenhouse because of the warmth and humidity and called for the mages to come and save her husband before his heart failed him.

He lay dying on the floor while his lifeblood dripped from his wounds, spread slowly across the floor, and trickled into the drains, and her mother had to look away. She had caught her daughter by the hand and told her to look at the orchid buds as the mages worked on her dad.

They had chanted and cast magic that made him scream and writhe in pain as they hastily stitched and cauterized wounds. The two dragons stared at the buds and her mother didn't close her eyes but focused on that flower and willed it to twitch, to pop open, and to bloom.

To Tanya's amazement, it had. When it did so, the mages stopped their chanting and declared the dragon saved. They had doctored enough of her father's wounds and given him enough magic energy for his dragon healing power to resume its natural work and save his life. She knew the flower hadn't saved him. The mages had. Yet she'd always remembered that day and always felt in her heart that if the orchid hadn't been about to bloom and her mom hadn't stayed in the room, her father would have died.

And now, it seemed the orchid's twin grew in the crook of a branch not ten feet away from her. A horde of skeletons tried to drag her into the water and kill her as surely as her dad would have died without the help of those mages.

She knew she would die and didn't have a way out of this. All her attempts to fight had failed. She had disobeyed the pixies, and this was the natural consequence. For a brief moment, she hoped Galen had done better but truly, it didn't matter.

All that mattered to her was that purple bud. She wanted it to open and somehow felt that if it did, she wouldn't feel so hopeless as she was dragged into the muddy pool and drowned.

It filled her soul with the taste of joy when the bloom burst open.

The creatures all hauled at her body, dragging her through the mud, and pulled her legs into the muddy pool behind her.

Tanya tried to stay above the water where she could still breathe. She reached toward the purple blossom, as beautiful as it was, and something strange happened.

As the skeletons tore at her skin and pulled her hair, the other dozen or so buds on the plant erupted into blossoms. She had never seen anything like that before. Stranger still, the orchid now grew visibly. Its light green and strangely plump aerial roots extended, inch by inch, out and away from the tree and toward her. It looked as if the plant had heard her plea for help and now did its best to pull her out of the pond.

But, she reminded herself, it was merely an orchid in the crook of a tree.

A dragon skeleton sunk its canine teeth into one of her wrists. To a dragon, the pain was bearable, but the damage to her muscles was not. Her hand lost its hold and the other wasn't strong enough to keep her anchored.

The creatures hauled her into the water.

She sucked in a breath before she plunged under the surface. It was instinctual rather than a conscious response and she honestly didn't think she could do much with the breath of air besides last an extra minute or so.

Her attackers tried to pull her deeper into the gloom but she tried to make it as difficult as possible for them. She kicked to propel herself upward and knock the little monsters off. Her lungs began to feel the strain and she used her arms to thrash and try to swim. She headbutted her attackers, drove her elbows into them, and tried to grasp anything she could. Twice, her fingers found the painfully sharp bones of one of the being's tails. On the third time, she found the root of a tree.

Tanya clutched it as tightly as she could and stopped her descent into the pool. Her fingers found bark on it like there had been on the roots above the surface of the water. It made it rough to the touch and provided more purchase than the mud had afforded her. The skeletons continued to pull at her, however, and the lungful of air she had managed to hold wouldn't last much longer.

Her attackers yanked hard and she felt her hold slip but by some stroke of luck, she managed to hang on. It felt as if a root from the tree had wound around her wrist and when she pulled on the hand, she discovered that was indeed the case. Better still, it was thickening. She grasped another root with her free hand, and it immediately took hold of her wrist.

*Air!* she thought desperately and against all common sense, the tree listened.

The roots she held onto raised out of the water, high enough for her to drag in a breath of air.

*Thank you,* she thought at the tree and could almost feel its response through her hands.

It had a type of aura like a dragon did—or any life form for that matter—but different. This was slower, older, and infinitely more patient. Yet she sensed frustration within it too as if the tree disapproved and even disliked something. Despite communicating with a dragon in a human body through its roots, it felt that something was unnatural.

It was, Tanya realized with a flash of clarity, the skeletons.

The tree didn't like them at all and thought—or felt?—that they didn't belong on the surface. They should be underground where they had been interred and where their energy could be used by the forest.

She couldn't agree more.

As if sensing her distaste for the vicious, bony beasts that currently tried to expose the dragon skeleton within her, the tree opened itself to her. Unsure exactly how she did it, she let her personal magic flow into its roots.

The effect was immediate.

A low branch swung down and brushed most of her assailants

from her back. She rolled, scooted onto the roots, and didn't stop until her back bumped against the reassuring presence of the solid trunk.

Skeletons surged from the pond in pursuit of their meal—or, perhaps, what they saw as one of them who had only to be freed from the flesh around her bones. If they accomplished that, she would be exactly like them, another undead creature haunting this swamp.

Thankfully, her new ally had no intention to allow that to happen.

Using Tanya's energy, clusters of rootlets grew at super-speed. In one moment, a skeleton scurried toward her with uncomfortably unnatural speed and in the next, one of its feet was snagged by tiny white tendrils, then a second.

Another tried to scurry past, only to be captured by a root and dragged to the ground as well. As soon as it touched the mud, hundreds more tiny growths emerged from the muck and grasped its spine. The dragon snapped its bony jaws and thrashed its claws as first its spine, then its ribs sank into the mire. Once it was more than half-buried and all that protruded was its claws, tail, and the tip of its nose, it stopped fighting and allowed itself to be dragged under the earth.

The tree had already yanked the first skeleton it had trapped to another patch of earth. This one was smaller but there was little more than a sliver of dank earth between hard knots of crisscrossing woody roots, so it was pulled in little by little. First, its tail was hauled into the hole, followed by its back legs and torso. Once about half its body was submerged, it ceased its struggles and allowed itself to be returned to where it belonged.

Tanya looked at the rest of her attackers. Those that weren't already entangled in a snare of roots and being pulled under had chosen to flee. They vanished either into the forest of their own volition or into the mud at the tree's insistence.

Finally, after what seemed like an eternity, the forest was quiet again.

In the calm that followed, the young dragon did little but breathe and try to focus her healing power on her wounded Achilles tendon. By the time it was healed, the enormity of what had happened had finally penetrated her mind.

She had gained a power. Somehow, she had made the orchid bloom and the tree defended her with a branch before its roots dragged the skeletons into the dirt.

Although it could be that the trees there were different and had come to her defense simply because they were strange, alien trees from another dimension. Tentatively, she placed her hand on the trunk beside the roots she sat on. She could feel its energy and its desires.

Like all living things, it wished to grow, to live a healthy life for as long as it could, and to maybe one day start a little forest of its own. It was also more than willing to take some of her magic and do with it whatever she wished. The only way she could think to explain it was that the tree entrusted her to do whatever she wished with its wooden body.

Tanya pushed some of her magic into it and the sensation was much like transforming into her dragon body or like breathing fire. Using her hand, however, it was more of a symbiotic decision. She told the tree to grow a branch for a purpose, and it responded in the best way it could.

A branch grew from where the orchid had been and brought the gorgeous chain of purple flowers to the person who had made them bloom.

She grinned and reassured herself that she now had a power —she wasn't a vanilla dragon anymore but a...botanical one? Although she had never heard of a dragon with the ability to make plants grow, she honestly didn't care. All that mattered was that she had a power. She was someone special now, and best of all, it was a power her family would be proud of. It was one she had always wanted, even before she'd known it existed. And in this moment, it had been exactly what she had needed. It was a miracle. She couldn't wait to tell Kylara about it—and to ask the diamond dragon mage to forgive her.

As she began to formulate a strategy on how to use her new power to help her escape the swamp, she was reminded why she had come this far in the first place.

Another scream issued from ahead, louder, closer, and more desperate than the last.

The young dragon stood, thanked the tree for its help, and raced deeper into the swamp to help Galen.

## CHAPTER FIFTEEN

With the pixies gone, the meadow with its stone-lined pools seemed a darker and more dangerous place. Kylara hadn't exactly watched the sky but she realized she should have as the sun had shifted from its place overheard to a little above the treetops. Instead of the electric-blue it had been painted earlier, the sky was now the bruised blues and purples of heavy storm clouds.

Kylara, Sam, Professor Sharra, and the other students all stood in the very center between three of the largest pools of water. It didn't feel like a safe place to be as there was no cover to speak of, but the pixies had been clear that they should remain there and not leave the meadow.

The young dragons and mages were clustered together in tight groups of two or three students with their backs to the forest as if they could somehow keep away the growing darkness. Despite the fact that their body language suggested that they did not wish to see what might approach them from the trees, they constantly glanced at the dark woods, even though with the setting sun, it seemed ever more all-encompassing.

"This is stupid," Kylara said and tried—exactly like all the other students—to focus on something other than how the sounds of the insects coming from the forest had changed.

"I know. We should have told Professor Sharra as soon we noticed Tanya was missing," Sam replied.

"Are you serious? What's stupid is that we're not out there right now looking for her."

He snorted a laugh. "You're wild, Ky. Tanya and I were captured by some crazy mage and you had to come to rescue us, and you already want to rush out by ourselves again?"

"I wouldn't be alone this time," she corrected him. "In fact, there'd be twice as many people. Plus, it's not like I failed to save you."

"This is true," he admitted, which Kylara appreciated after the way he had acted. "And yes, I still think it's a good thing we're here and the pixies are out there looking."

"Yeah, I suppose you're right. Still, I'd feel better if I at least—" Something twisted in her stomach and her statement cut off in surprise. She didn't know what it was exactly, but she could guess. It felt similar to how it had felt when she called on her dark or light magic. Strong magic flowed somewhere nearby.

"Did you feel that?"

"Feel what?" Sam asked, which answered the question fairly well, she thought.

"A surge of magic. It felt like…like…it's hard to put into words, but maybe like something woke up?"

"The professor noticed it too." Sam pointed at Professor Sharra, whose hands were no longer on her hips. Instead, one shielded her eyes from the glare of the sun through the thick clouds above the treetops. Her back was rigid and her gaze stared into the distance rather than at the students as she had done since they'd gathered there.

"Do you think she knows what it is?" Kylara asked and still tried to fully grasp the sensation. She felt that if she could understand what her body was saying, she might have a better idea of what was coming. As it was, all she could sense was something bad on the horizon. It was barely enough to feel uncomfortable but not enough to give her any indication about what they could expect.

"I don't know, honestly," Sam said, stuck his arms up, and waved them about as if he hoped to somehow snare a thread of magic like a fish if he only gestured exuberantly enough. "I don't feel a damn thing. Where's it coming from?"

"I can't tell," Kylara conceded. "It feels like it's coming from all around us."

"Well, isn't that dandy? If you had told me that you being a mage meant you would get pangs of dread about creepy hidden magic, I might not have been cool with it."

"I thought you said you were cool with it."

"I am. I said if you had told me. The way I see it now, you're stuck with me. I already got you away from a shirtless Karl."

"You were shirtless too."

"Did that work in my favor?"

Kylara only had time to turn to focus on his handsome, grinning, flirtatious expression before a student began to yell and point.

The moment ruined—not that she knew if she wanted that moment to happen in the first place—they turned to see what was causing all the ruckus.

"Did you guys see that? There was some kind of a light!"

"Yeah, yeah, you made us look. Good one, Donnie," another dragon said.

The boy didn't respond but began to walk toward where he said he had seen the light.

"Professor Sharra!" Kylara called a warning.

The professor turned to the group and saw the student moving slowly through the tall grass. "Donatello, you get back to the center of this meadow this instant unless you want to be shipped home the second we leave the pixie realm."

When the student didn't respond, she called up gusts of wind that blew from both hands in two directions. Each blast coursed through the tall grass, knocked it aside as it moved, then circled abruptly to slam into the kid's chest. With a grunt, he stumbled back, tripped, and landed on his butt.

He wiped his eyes as Professor Sharra hurried to him. "I told you to stay in the center of the meadow, you dolt! Do you think we would have warned you about how important it was if something wouldn't try to get you to leave?"

"I…what? Why is it so dark?" he asked, looked at the sun, and seemed to have the same reaction Kylara had at the way it had moved overhead so quickly. "That last thing I remember was seeing something in the woods."

"You mean like a ball of light?" Kylara asked.

"Yeah, exactly!" Donnie replied, pleased that someone could corroborate his story.

"Why do you say that, Kylara?" Professor Sharra asked.

She didn't answer and simply pointed to a glowing orb that emerged slowly from the forest. It wasn't quite a ball of light, she realized when she studied it. Something else seemed to hide under the radiance and looked like a moth mixed with a jellyfish. That was her first impression, but it was hard to make details out because of the odd illumination. One thing was certain, however. It was beautiful. She felt an urge to go to it and follow it into the woods.

"I see one too!" another student shouted, and Sam put a hand on Kylara's shoulder and whispered, "Look," in her ear.

His touch broke her focus on the glowing orb. She turned and frowned at dozens more that appeared as if from nowhere. Everyone could see them now and the forest was thick with them. Moments later, however, they began to enter the meadow.

"Are those pixies?" he asked.

She shook her head. "I don't think so. They have a different feel than these."

"You mean their magic feels different?"

Kylara nodded and realized that it was indeed their magic she could sense.

More of the gleaming spheres winked into existence in the forest. They followed the others and drifted slowly into the meadow like fireflies, jellyfish, or a red tide.

# CHAPTER SIXTEEN

Still in her human form, Tanya raced through the swamp. She found it easier now but it wasn't that the terrain was any less treacherous. The mud was still hungry for wayward wanderers, pools of cloudy water hid unknown creatures in their murky depths, and other beings moved through the trees around her, but she now had a power.

As she bounded forward, she kept to the roots of the trees as she had before. Now, however, it was as if they wanted her to succeed. She was moving too fast to see them actively growing or moving to help her, but she landed constantly on solid footing. No roots tripped her and no branches surprised her in mid-leap. Any time her feet came near a mud puddle, a root slid underfoot to support her. She didn't feel like she was controlling the plants, exactly, but she asked them for help and they were more than happy to oblige.

Traveling at this new pace, it didn't take long before she caught up to Galen, although it still appeared to be too late.

He was under attack by the same cat-sized dragon skeletons she had fought, only he seemed to have drawn their attention even more effectively than she had.

The young dragon stood in human form on a muddy island made of little more than craggy plants. Water surrounded him, and skeleton after skeleton erupted from the murky depths. He had already dispatched some of them and their broken bones and shattered skulls lay around his feet. Unfortunately, it was a tiny fraction of the assaulting force.

"Galen!" she shouted, which proved to be the wrong thing to do.

Distracted, he glanced at her for only the briefest of moments but a dragon skeleton seized the opportunity to launch itself from the water and drove into his neck. He stumbled back and three more surged onto his legs and lacerated his jeans. Blood soaked into the torn fabric.

Galen screamed as he toppled back and landed hard but he continued to fight with desperate determination. He hurled the skeleton that had struck his neck off him with sufficient force to shatter it but was now on the ground and in these nightmare creatures' domain. They sank their teeth into his shoulders, arms, and legs, his torn clothes, and anywhere they could find purchase. Despite his efforts to resist, they dragged him inch by inch into the pond that surrounded the tiny island on which he'd made his last stand.

Tanya reached out to the scraggly plants that grew on the island he was being dragged from. They responded immediately, eager for her attention, hungry for her magic, and happy to please. Fresh growth burst from their old, twisted trunks and snaked through the rib cages and wings of the dragon skeletons. The new shoots were green and pliable and the beasts hardly noticed them, not that they should. They were too weak to bind them and too flexible to do anything but be brushed aside.

She waited for an agonizing few seconds for the young tendrils to thread into the creatures' bodies. Once she judged that they were good and tangled within the beasts, she told them to build in strength. Leaves proliferated from the spindly stems to choke the skeletons with a flush of green color while the rapidly-thickening stems dragged them to the ground.

Through her magical connection, she felt the leaves pull carbon dioxide from the air, strip the carbon from the molecule, and use it to thicken the green growth into woody, gnarled bark. Those parts of the branches that touched the soil sank roots into the mud and began to haul the enemy under the surface.

Exactly like those that had attacked her, once the creatures were mostly underground, they ceased their struggles and acquiesced to their forced burials.

Galen was free.

He stood, darted a wild look of thanks at Tanya, and crouched as he prepared to jump to her. Before he could launch himself forward, he was hurled off his feet by another assailant.

This one was twice the size of the others—more like a bobcat than a housecat, with bones that seemed far thicker and more robust than its smaller counterparts. Galen pummeled it in the ribs but none of them broke. The skeleton roared and its bones rattled ominously before it slashed the young dragon across the face so deeply that Tanya glimpsed his skull before blood welled up and his dragon healing went into action to close the gory wound.

Before she could puke from the sight—her first and purely instinctive reaction—she forced herself to act. She told the plants to secure the larger skeleton. Branches reached out to grasp this leader of the undead but they were unsuccessful. Every one that grew was intercepted by another of the smaller creatures. She directed her vegetative helpers to yank each of them to the ground, pull them into the earth, and bind them.

More arrived as quickly as she could trap them and all worked together to keep her from attacking the big skeleton. Their interceptions of her vines were successful. She couldn't grow the scraggly plants fast enough to stop the larger beast from savaging Galen. It scratched his chest and left horrible wounds. His skin was torn and healed repeatedly.

He punched its left humerus with enough force to fracture the bone. It didn't break completely and it didn't so much slow its attack as change its tactics.

Instead of trying to lacerate more of his flesh, it caught him by his shoulders and sank its hooked claws into his shoulder blades while its back legs dug into his thighs. The two fell together with the skeleton on top, its claws digging into his flesh, and he struggled beneath it.

The young dragon grasped his attacker by its head. His muscles bulged as he tried to crush the skull with his dragon strength. The skeleton, not intimidated, dug its claws deeper into his shoulders and thighs. Their faces grew closer and closer together until his forehead—still bloody from the earlier injury—touched the skeleton's snout.

Suddenly, the creature flapped its wings, released him from its hooked claws, and flew away.

"Enough!" Galen shouted. His cry echoed across the swamp. The water—teeming with skeletons only moments before—stilled.

The big one that had inflicted so much injury on him beat its skeletal wings that—despite the lack of any membrane—nevertheless propelled it in flight. It was a not so subtle reminder to Tanya that all dragons were magic. A creature of their size should not be able to fly at all. Magic allowed them flight, exactly like it was magic that animated this skeleton and let it fly despite not having any way to catch the air.

"Don't let anything hurt her!" Galen shouted and the big skeleton's eyes locked on Tanya. It flew in a circle around the pool and it scanned the swamp behind her. It circled while the other dragons clambered out of the water and launched to join it in flight around the pond.

Tanya, not entirely sure if she could believe what she was

seeing, nevertheless knew she had to act. "Tell them to land and I can make the plants pull them into the mud!"

He looked at her with surprise at first but he nodded. She assumed he must have seen the plants pull the skeletons off him. While it was hard for her to accept that he could somehow communicate with these monsters, it looked like Galen attempted to process the relationship she now had with the plants.

"Make them land!" she repeated urgently.

"No," Galen said and looked from her to the swarm of flying bones. "I...I don't think I need to do that." His gaze found the larger one in the group. "Go! Go away from here!" he ordered, and the dragon skeletons obeyed.

They scattered in a dozen different directions and vanished into the swamp, lost from view in the tangle of branches and vines.

Tanya, sensing the danger was over, waded through the water to his island. As she stepped carefully through the water, the only movement she saw was the subtle shift of tree roots that grew in the bottom of the pond. They moved and expanded as they grew under her feet as if they didn't want her to touch the muck beneath them. She had to admit she didn't mind their help.

A few moments later, she stepped out of the water and onto the muddy island. She extended her hand and pulled him to his feet. "Are you all right?" she asked and tried and failed to not stare at the three slash marks on his face. One ran from the top of his nose to his hairline and another slanted up in a parallel gash that started at the corner of his eye. The third connected the corner of his mouth to the top of his ear with a bloody mark. The wounds on his chest had already healed, but the face wounds didn't seem to have sealed nearly as quickly.

"I'm fine now, thanks to you," Galen said.

"I guess!" Tanya laughed nervously. "You ordered those skeletons to leave. You did do that, right? They left because you told them to?"

He nodded hesitantly. "I…uh, I think so. I mean…you're right. They left when I told them to."

"How did you do that?"

The young dragon shrugged. "I don't know. When that big one attacked me and it scratched my face and I felt its claw touch my…my bone, I guess something changed. I could feel this…this energy running through it—like Professor Sharra explained in class. It's crazy. I always thought she was full of crap, you know?"

Tanya laughed and nodded, so relieved that they were no longer under attack by undead dragons. "I know what you mean. I think I've always been able to feel my magic running through me but never knew what it was until I felt it inside something else."

"You mean the plants, right?" he asked.

"Right."

Galen nodded. "I thought I was done for. I think I would have been if you hadn't shown up and…what did you do exactly?"

"I made the plants grow," she said, still a little disbelieving herself. "I was attacked by some of those skeletons back there and somehow communicated with a plant—an orchid—and now…" She laughed. "It's like they're an extension of me. I can feel the plants even now."

Her companion seemed to understand, judging by his expression. "I know exactly what you mean. I didn't know what was happening when I…I linked to that first skeleton. But once I did, I could feel the same type of magic in all of them. Talking to the first one seemed like learning a new language or something, but once I did, it was like I could immediately communicate with all the others."

"Well, it's a good thing you did. I didn't realize they could fly. If they had tried that when I was alone…" She shook her head, reluctant to think about what might have happened if she hadn't seen the purple orchid.

"What were you doing out here, anyway?" he asked.

Tanya blushed despite her efforts not to. She knew he could read her embarrassment in her aura, so there was no real point in lying. "I was following you. I thought you knew something about this place, that you were trying to get a new power."

Galen chuckled and shook his head in disbelief. "I was trying to get a new power, but I didn't know what I was doing. I merely saw something move in the forest and followed it. I can't believe you followed me the entire time."

"I'm sorry."

"Don't be. I think…I think I'd be dead if not for you."

"You're welcome," she said, "But hey, I'm glad it happened."

"You are?"

"Yeah! We have powers now! Okay, I wasn't exactly thrilled at the time to have to fight for my life, but now that I know I can control plants… This is all I've ever wanted."

He grinned and it didn't quite reach the wounded left side of his mouth. "I know. I can't believe that wandering out here worked! I never imagined I'd be able to communicate with… with…well, whatever they were, but it's so cool."

"It is not cool, Galen Stormwing!" A pixie burst from the thick jungle growth in a shower of sparks.

"Oh, thank goodness, Petalwing. We're so happy to see you!" Tanya exclaimed.

"Do not attempt to dissuade my fury with your compliments, Tanya Fastwing!" the creature yelled in her high-pitched, squeaky voice. "But thanks. It's nice to see you too."

"Alive, I might add," another pixie shouted and joined Petalwing and the two students in the clearing.

"Also, this is not cool," yet another pixie said and hovered beside the others. "This is warm. Or hot. Whatever the bad temperature is? This is it."

Three more pixies emerged so now, six of the glowing, vibrant creatures flew laps above the students and the clearing came alive with glowing sparks.

"You will come with us or you will find there is much worse in this swamp," Petalwing warned.

"Worse than a horde of dragon skeletons? I doubt it." Galen's voice was thick with bluster.

"Those were but runts. If we do not hurry, we risk awakening the creature that gave them life. Come along! Come along right now," Petalwing ordered.

"Or we'll turn you into toads," another pixie threatened.

Tanya and Galen, still elated from gaining new powers and at the same time terrified by almost being buried under the mud and filth of the swamp, followed their chaperones to safety.

# CHAPTER SEVENTEEN

"What are those?" a student screeched and her voice rose to a somewhat stressed squeak.

"Trouble," Professor Sharra replied and seemed the only one capable of maintaining a cool head. She whipped swirling tornados of wind and launched them into the field one after another. They collided with the floating blobs of light and scattered them. Each provided a moment of reprieve, which was about as much as they could hope for.

"I'm going out there again!" Esme shouted, took her dragon form, and lunged into the meadow to blast the approaching orbs with fire and lash out at them with poison-tipped claws.

Like every other dragon who had ventured out of the protective winds conjured by the professor, she was attacked mercilessly.

Or maybe it wasn't an attack at all. Kylara couldn't be certain. Was it considered a jellyfish attack if a swimmer deliberately swam into a swarm of them? What did one call the actions of wasps that defended their home after having rocks hurled at it?

But the motivations of these beings were inscrutable. What

was clear was that every dragon who had moved into the field had been rebuffed and sent back to the center of the meadow by dozens of stinging bolts of electricity from the balls of light.

She had already tried—against the wishes of the professor, of course—and had failed to make any noticeable difference in the encroaching wave of tentacled orbs. Her diamond scales had offered little protection against the stings and jolts they delivered.

Esme fared no better. She flew out and drew the creatures to her as if by magnetism or like they were carried on currents in the air. They stung her and she screamed. They stung her even more and she retreated.

"I said stay back!" the professor snapped, although it became increasingly clear that staying where they were wouldn't be a viable option for much longer. There were simply too many of the electric, airborne jellyfish. As they left the forest and approached the students, they crammed together and soon, none of the mages or dragons could see past them. Now, they were surrounded by a wall made of glowing blobby beings rather than bricks. Kylara would have preferred bricks. She could punch through those.

"If anyone wants extra credits, now would be the time!" Professor Sharra shouted as she continued to hurl the beings back with great gusts of wind.

"We can't take our dragon bodies as they swarm us," Esme whined. "It's like they can sense it."

"Which means we can't use our dragon bodies at all," Samuel said and grinned as he ignited his hands with light energy. He launched a blast of luminous energy from each hand and directly into the wall of glowing jellyfish.

It accomplished nothing. In fact, it did less than nothing. The attackers seemed to like his light energy. Those he had targeted surged hungrily toward this new source of energy.

Before they could reach and savage him with their painful shocks, tendrils of black rose from the ground and whipped at them. When the black tendrils connected with the blobs, something about them changed. Like a balloon with a hole in it or a deflated tire, they shriveled where the darkness touched them, then streaked into the sky and floated into the darkness.

"Kylara, I could use some help here!" Karl grunted with effort.

She nodded and moved to the other side of the group of students. She didn't have his control but she thought she could do something against these unnatural electric balls. Ten tentacles of dark energy emerged from her ten fingers. She focused and called upon the river of magic inside her to strengthen each cord. That done, she split each one in two. Now, twenty lashing whips of solidified inky darkness thrashed in the space in front of her. It took only the touch of one of these whips to send one of the glowing lights into retreat.

"Move between them, students—now! If any mages have secretly harbored dark magic, now would be the time to reveal it!" Professor Sharra ordered.

Kylara took a step forward as the others huddled between the two wielders of thrashing dark whips.

Something caught her wrist and she almost panicked. She frowned at the dark tendril of energy. Was Karl trying to hurt her?

"Now you grab me with one," he shouted from the other side of the students. "We'll make a perimeter."

"Right. Of course." She wished she had thought of it, not that it mattered. The only priority now was to protect the other students against being electrocuted.

She sent one of her tendrils to Karl. It found him and immediately, she felt it strengthen and divide. In moments, the students were surrounded by webs of dark energy. She didn't have much to do with this, however. Most of her energy was focused on driving the balls of light back. Karl defended the other students and allowed his still shirtless chest to be shocked while he protected the people he usually spent so much time talking trash about.

Kylara pushed herself and let him maintain their defense while she focused on offense. She willed more of her magic into the twenty lashing whips of energy, divided them again to make forty, then in half to make eighty.

It no longer felt like she was controlling individual threads of energy but a kind of spinning vortex. She only had to think an instruction and the tendrils hastened to obey their master. With her dark weapons strong and active, she sent more filaments down from her feet. They dug into the earth and lifted her slowly. She rose above the other students and directed her vortex of snapping tendrils to lash and strike at every group of jellyfish she could.

Those that slid past were met by Karl's dark web wall. Any that touched either his or her magic were summarily deflated and sent into the darkness from which they had come.

She had no idea how long the battle lasted. Five minutes? Thirty? An hour? The sky was no help as far as time was concerned. She glanced up and saw that the sun had set. Instead of the blues and purples of the late evening, the sky was now black. It was filled with stars that twinkled in every color of the rainbow and were grouped in constellations she had never seen before.

They continued their barrage of attacks until finally, the vortex felt like overkill. Rather than lashing out with so many wild strikes, she now used a more focused attack. She looked for dense pockets of the glowing spheres—there was no longer a wall of them and only a few clusters—and sent a thick ribbon of dark energy toward them. Once it was close enough, she used this thick growth as a base for a bunch of thrashing tendrils. After a few minutes of her and Karl working together using this tactic, the orbs were all gone.

"Karl, Kylara, well done," Professor Sharra said after she drew a ragged breath.

"Seriously," Sam agreed.

Kylara turned to where Midnight pushed through the group of students with a big smile on his face.

"You did it!" she exclaimed.

"We did it," he said and seemed to notice that he was smiling for the first time and that he had helped people. He lowered his mouth quickly into a frown and furrowed his brow, but the gleam of pride lingered in his eyes. His cold exterior had returned but now, she knew there was more to him than that. If all he had cared about was power, he would have let the powerless suffer for their weakness.

"I'm not so sure about that," she said and looked past him to where six glowing points of light moved toward them through the forest. "It looks like we're not quite done yet."

"No, no—those look different," Professor Sharra pointed out. "See the way they move from side to side and leave trails of light? Those are pixies," she said with a sigh of relief.

Six bright, sparkling pixies emerged from the forest. Kylara held her breath until Tanya and Galen stumbled out behind them.

"Tanya!" she yelled and ran toward her.

"Ky! Oh, my God. I have so much to tell you!"

"Yeah, my first question is why can I see some of your skin?" she joked as she hugged her friend.

The girl immediately reddened as she looked at her exposed legs. She smiled awkwardly and moved her hands to cover herself as if her shins were the most scandalous thing the campus had ever seen.

"Where were you two?" Professor Sharra demanded.

"Off earning new powers," Galen said with well-rehearsed suaveness.

"I don't care if you learned a dozen new powers!" The woman caught both of the returned students by their ears with her telekinesis. "You disobeyed the pixies' instructions and almost endangered the entire group."

"Wait, those skeleton creatures showed up here too?" Tanya asked. "They attacked us in the swamp."

"Skeleton creatures?" Samuel voiced the question most of the students wanted to.

"We were attacked but not by skeletons," Kylara explained. "I don't think these even had bones. There were thousands of glowing, floating, jellyfish creatures. Karl and I barely held them back. It was close."

"You speak of the will-o-wisps?" Petalwing asked.

"They look like little blobs of light with tentacles, are impervious to most dragon powers, and shock with some kind of stinging electricity," the young golden dragon said.

"Indeed! But the will-o-wisps cannot kill." She laughed so hard that sparkles shot out her nose. "They are harmless."

"That's not true," said Esme, who still nursed her wounds.

"They zap and shock, but they are not a great danger. Any time they have confronted us in any number, we simply fly away. It is great fun." Petalwing smiled.

"And what happens to the individuals who cannot fly away?" the professor asked, her tone a carefully controlled calm.

"What do you mean? All pixies can fly. It is one of the wonderful things about being a pixie. We are never bound to one place and never forced to trudge across the earth like a centipede."

"We were not able to fly away," the professor said tiredly. "Do you have any idea what would have happened if two of our students had not been able to drive these…will-o-wisps back?"

"I…er…that is…I think it would probably have been fine,"

Petalwing stammered. The question had no doubt never occurred to her.

"If you could open the portal to take us home, I'm sure the students are ready for dinner and bed."

The pixies nodded. It was hard to tell because they existed in a way that was so different from the human or dragon experience, but Kylara thought they seemed embarrassed.

Tanya moved closer to her. "Hey, Ky, can we talk?"

"Young lady, if you think you deserve to chat with your friends after wandering into the forest of a goddamn magical realm, you must have swallowed too much swamp water. You'll be in detention for a long, long time." Professor Sharra flicked her wrist and pulled the two delinquents to her.

"I was only in the forest because I saw him go in there and didn't want him to get lost," Tanya sputtered, her eyes already welling with tears.

"That's not true. You said you followed me because you thought I would earn powers."

"And did you?" Professor Sharra asked through teeth clenched so tightly they could likely crush Kylara's diamond scales.

"Yes, ma'am, we did," she admitted to their teacher.

"Cataloging what happened in perfect detail will be the first part of each of your detention. Now go. I want you two through the portal before anyone else."

Despite Kylara's sense that hours had passed in the pixie realm, it had been less than an hour on campus. It was a profoundly unsettling experience to go from somewhere she had seen the sun move from the noonday position to late afternoon, to full darkness and return to the noonday sun in the blink of an eye.

If it bothered their Magical Theory professor, she gave no indication of it. "Everyone needs to go to lunch, then afternoon classes. I'll see you tomorrow, and I expect at least two pages from each of you on what you experienced and learned in the pixie realm. Tanya and Galen, I'll expect at least ten times that from each of you."

"When?" Tanya asked.

"I already said tomorrow." Professor Sharra's icy smile did not reach her eyes.

## CHAPTER EIGHTEEN

After a few minutes and a short walk through a disturbingly normal campus, Kylara had all but pushed her strange experience in the pixie realm from her mind. She entered the dining hall and took a moment to appreciate the beauty of the space.

It was easily the most beautiful room on campus, more glorious in its construction than even the magic library. The floor was a mosaic of marble with a pattern so large it was difficult to make out. It looked like the interplay of black, white, and gray tile was some kind of fractal tessellation until one tried to piece the entire image together in their mind.

If seen from the massive chandelier that hung from the center of the room, one would discern the shape of a dragon rendered in silver where the sun caught it and black where it was in shadow. It flew through a great bank of clouds, the white tiles that made up much of the exquisite work. Although the staff claimed the mosaic had been there for centuries, she couldn't help but think the silver-scaled dragon with an ax-blade tail depicted looked startlingly similar to the dragon form of the Steel Dragon.

From the floor—but never on top of the dragon image—great

pillars of wood rose, each made from the trunk of a single tree and carved into a thousand branches, leaves, and vines. Gold leaf and rich paints covered these pillars and glowed in the light of the chandeliers that orbited the large central one. The ceiling was done in frescos, a hundred scenes from important moments of dragon and humankind's shared history. Times of both blood and peace were represented there.

The walls on both sides were mostly windows, the exception being brass bars that rested between the plates of glass. Kylara had almost completely centered herself when she looked out one of the windows and saw that the sky was not the oversaturated tones of the pixie world but the familiar distant blue she'd grown up under. She told herself it was good that she'd only been in the pixie realm for an hour, even though it had felt like much longer.

She walked through the crowd, around wooden tables, and to a sandwich bar that had been set up in the back. At first, she was surprised by the simple fare. To call the Lumos School dining hall 'gourmet' would be an understatement. Then she saw that the mages who prepared the sandwiches did so with telekinesis. She chuckled and wondered if there was any other place in the world where one could order a BLT and have someone fry the bacon with fire magic and slice the tomato with their mind.

Her plate stacked high with said BLT, plus a pheasant and avocado with alfalfa sprouts and a roast beef, mountain cheese, and smoked cabbage sandwich she had seen another dragon request and been unable to resist, she went to find a seat.

The room was crowded with dragon and mage alike, the conversation loud and often about her class's recent experience. It seemed others saw the members of the class as magical astronauts who had boldly gone where no dragon had gone before. She smirked when she didn't hear much from the dragon astronauts about how they'd spent most of the time lounging in hot tubs and had finished their trip by cowering behind her and Karl Midnight.

He noticed her looking around and sent a waving tendril of black energy above his head to call her to join them. It split in two, then two again, thickened, and split again and finally, once more. The other dragons around him stepped back and looked almost revolted by the black filament above him that looked like some kind of diabolical coral reef. She couldn't help but chuckle at their reaction.

It wasn't Karl Midnight's fault that he had a power that was less than visually appealing. Perhaps part of the reason he could come across as rude was because other dragons judged him on the appearance of his power. It wouldn't be false to say that part of why it was so easy to be nice to Samuel Lumos was that his smile could light up a room and shaking his hand could cure any bruises you had. Maybe Karl was the way he was simply because that was how he felt he had to react to others. It made sense because it was much like how her diamond scales meant she naturally put walls up and distanced herself from others.

But no.

That wasn't true anymore. She wouldn't let it be. Her mother had been like that. Hester Diamantine had hidden inside a fortress in the desert that made her feel safer than any shell could have. She had lived much like her power, but Kylara intended to push against that mold. Not that it was true anymore. If she could absorb any dragon power that was used on her, what did that make her? Someone who could accept anyone? Or someone who needed to be careful about their influences? What did her power mean about her and Karl? Was it dangerous to hang out with someone who so flagrantly disregarded the feelings of others simply because people had been mean to him in the past?

And then there was the fact that when the school had found out that she wasn't a dragon but a mage, Karl had been one of the only people, outside the over-eager faculty, who had shown her any kindness.

She wouldn't pretend he hadn't done bad things. He and his

cronies had bound Tanya with his power and would have chained her to the ground like she was nothing but a dumb beast if she hadn't intervened. Could someone be forgiven for that? She thought that yes, everyone could be forgiven. It was what she had tried to tell her mom her entire life. Hester was still alive because the woman who had hunted her for all those years showed her mercy. Surely that was merely another form of forgiveness?

People shouldn't be forgiven for no reason, of course. They had to prove themselves, but Karl had done so. If it hadn't been for his quick thinking in the pixie dimension, they'd all have been —well, the pixies said those will-o-wisps wouldn't have killed them, but still. He hadn't known that and so had technically risked his life to save the rest of the class. Had he only done that because of her influence? Maybe she owed it to him to sit with him so she could continue to influence him.

Or maybe it was arrogant to think it was her.

"Ky! Oh, my goodness. I've looked all over for you."

"Oh?" She looked at Tanya and realized sheepishly that she had frozen in the middle of the cafeteria, completely paralyzed by the simple decision of where to sit. She doubted regular teenagers ever had this particular problem.

"I was serious when I said I wanted to talk."

Kylara didn't know what to think. Even though it was the middle of the day, she felt like she'd been up for days. Fighting the will-o-wisps had been exhausting and there was still the afternoon classes to worry about, plus Jasmine Patel's ice-cold reception when she returned to her room for the night. "Maybe we should talk later?"

"No—please, Kylara, you have to sit with me!" Tanya pleaded.

"I want to talk, Tanya, I do..." What she wanted to say was that she didn't have the energy for the drama but saying that might, of course, lead to more drama.

"I only want to say I'm sorry," the young dragon blurted loudly enough to make those at the closest tables stop their chatter and giggle at them. "Please? You deserve more than that. Come on. I don't want anything to build up between us."

"Yeah, sure." She relented. It wasn't like she could say no to all that. She did glance at Karl, though, who had puffed his oily coral reef into a thousand motes of black snowflakes that blew all around him in an angry burst before they dissipated into nothing.

Tanya led her through the cafeteria and threaded between tables crowded with students. They passed mages using telekinesis to handle their cutlery and dragons eating far more food than strictly made sense given the size of their human bodies, even if they were growing teens.

At the far side of the large room, they sat against one of the walls at a table beneath a window framed between two potted Ficus trees, their branches gnarled with growth.

"Ky, first off, thanks for sitting with me."

She tried to say it wasn't a problem, but Tanya held a hand up to shush her. It was one of the unintentionally rude gestures she made all the time and that perversely, Kylara had missed.

"No, Ky, let me go first. I was an absolute jerk after we got back from your aunt's creepy, weird ice lair. I don't know why I reacted that way—no, I do. I was jealous. And yes, it's seriously dumb to be jealous of the person who saves you. Because if it hadn't been for your powers—which I was utterly jealous of—I might be dead. So yeah, I messed up. When I found out you were a dragon from nowhere, I treated you like a total charity case, and finding out that you were a crazy chameleon mage or whatever was too much for me."

"How do you think I felt?" she asked and tried not to derail Tanya's heartfelt but rambling apology.

"I know. *I know.* I can't believe you risked your life, found out that your aunt burned your home down, and that you were adopted, and that your mom had lied to you your entire life. On top of that, I treated you so badly. I was supposed to be the good person in your life."

Kylara couldn't help but laugh. "You have been a good person in my life. Honestly, Tanya, you being my roommate has colored what I think about dragons in a good way. I think that was why, when you turned me out, it hurt so badly."

"Ky, I'm so sorry, truly—"

"No, let me finish. It hurt when you did that but I overreacted too. I've tried so hard to not think about my mom...Hester...whatever she is to me. She's still a captive, still Cassandra's prisoner, and it's eating me up. We should have simply gone to sleep. I didn't need to leave."

"It's fine, though. You should get to know some mages, and if we're okay, I don't care where you sleep. As long as we're friends. How's your roommate, by the way?"

"Ugh, she's terrible. Do you know Jasmine Patel?"

Tanya shuddered visibly. "The Patels? Everyone's heard of them. They're so prestigious they look down on vanilla dragons, even though they're only mages. She's your roommate? I'm surprised she doesn't have a villa nearby and a helicopter to fly her in every morning."

"Well—and I don't think you should spread this around—but I don't think her family can exactly afford helicopter flights after the Steel Dragon changed how the dragon and mage world worked."

Her friend nodded and chewed a mouthful of her cucumber sandwich. "Do you want to move in again?"

"Yes! But I don't know if I should yet. I don't know."

"Well, if you do, I hope you're okay with more potted plants in our room," Tanya said conspiratorially.

"Uh...that's fine? It's more like I don't know what's best to do about Jasmine. I don't want to turn her into an enemy."

"Ky, whatever you think is best is fine. If you want to take some time, that's cool. But I have something to show you."

"Oh yeah, what happened out there in the forest anyway?"

"I'll let you read my homework if you want, but Ky—look." She gestured to the ficus tree behind her and to Kylara's surprise, it sprouted a new branch. It extended and pushed out smaller branches that in turn, popped out a multitude of leaves.

"Tanya! Did you do that?"

The girl nodded excitedly.

"But Tanya! That means you got a power!"

"I know! It's crazy but I can control plants. Well, kind of. I think. Honestly, I need to practice. I don't know if I can make them grow or…maybe I can make the trees walk around and use their roots like feet? I'm not sure yet. It was too intense back there to try anything other than stay alive."

"Tanya, stop talking."

"What? I thought you said you wanted to know what happened—"

"I do! But I can read your homework like you said. Tanya, we have sandwiches for lunch."

It was her turn to be confused. "Uh-huh?"

"You know what sandwiches are good for, right?"

"Getting crumbs in all your layers?" the girl responded. Kylara noticed that she had replaced her torn dress before coming to the cafeteria. She hadn't realized before because her brain thought the default for Tanya was overly elaborate dresses with too many kinds of fabric and lace.

"No, they're perfect for picnics. Let's go outside, finish lunch, and put your power to the test."

"Oh, my goodness. That sounds like the best idea." Her friend beamed. "Oh, Ky, I'm so glad we're talking again."

"Me too, Tanya. Now come on. Let's see if we can make a tree or two walk into the part of the forest the fire elemental burned down."

# CHAPTER NINETEEN

"And did you want mustard on that as well?"

"Sure…yeah, whatever," Galen replied. He had managed to escape the Magical Theory professor and reach the dining hall. While the mage behind the piles of sliced bread, cured meats, chopped vegetables, and jars of condiments whipped up a tornado of ingredients that spun adroitly and assembled themselves, the young dragon considered what had happened to him.

As far as he knew, what he had done was completely new to dragon kind. He had never heard of a dragon raising the dead, let alone controlling them. Was that what those skeletons were? He could not be certain as he had never been to the pixie realm before. There was good reason to determine whether those beings were the bones of something that had once lived or something else entirely. Professor Sharra had been less than helpful in this regard.

He had demanded that she tell him what she knew about the powers he had explained to her but she refused. That wasn't right, in his book. She was a mage, which his family had always said meant she should submit to his will. Attending this school made him question that, but whether her place was below him or not didn't matter right now. What was important was that she was his teacher and had refused him knowledge. She said it was because she wanted to read a full account of what had happened before she tried to guess at the extent of his abilities, but that seemed like unnecessary delaying tactics to him.

The only thought the young dragon could focus on was that he had to know what he was capable of, and he wanted to know immediately.

"Will there be anything else, sir?" the mage fixing his sandwich asked.

"No, that will be all, thank you." He took the proffered sandwich, wrapped it in a napkin, and hurried out of the cafeteria and ignored his brother's catcalls demanding he come back and tell him whether he was still a pathetic vanilla or a real dragon now.

Relieved to have left unhindered, he stepped onto the green field that made up the central U of the campus. He was restless and beyond curious to discover what he was capable of. Was the essence of his power that he could control other creatures and the skeletons in the pixie dimension had simply been the only others around?

Galen scanned the grounds and finally found what he was looking for—a couple of crows. He reached out to them and felt for their energy with his own. Disappointingly, he felt nothing at all. So little, in fact, that it might as well have been less than nothing.

"Okay, so it's not all animals then," he murmured. He looked furtively around him. It was a nice day and a fair number of students had chosen to enjoy their lunch on the green. A few crows flying overhead wouldn't have made anyone curious, but what he wanted to attempt next most likely would.

He set off briskly, eating as he went, and strode out of the U, past the three main buildings, and into the woods that separated the school from the training fields deeper in the valley.

Much of the forest was still a burned ruin. He wondered if

that might make his task easier but decided to enter the section that was still standing. There was cover that way and more privacy. He moved deeper into the underbrush and pushed past thorny trees and prickly plants, all of them intent on denying any intruders from gaining access to the water they held inside them.

Almost absently, he wondered if Tanya would be able to speak to a cactus like she had to the trees in the pixie dimension. He couldn't believe she had saved him and knew he would have been dead meat if not for her appearing and manifesting her power. While he had driven their attackers back with his command at the end, it had been more luck than anything else. He needed to know if something like that happened again that he would be able to help.

Distracted by his thoughts, he pushed past a particularly thorny mesquite and earned some bloody gashes on his arm that healed almost instantly. He finally reached a clearing completely hidden on all sides by thick vegetation.

After a deep breath to settle himself, he thought back to what he knew of anatomy and the skeleton inside his body. Once he felt reasonably certain that he had the shape of a human skeleton in his mind, he took another breath and tried to channel his inner magic to create a skeleton.

He focused on giving shape to the skull, the shoulders, the spine, the ribs...the uh...femur? Galen opened his eyes and cursed. This wasn't working. He didn't feel his magic growing into anything and certainly didn't feel it taking any kind of shape.

And besides, he thought as he took a bite of his sandwich and frowned at the sharp acidic taste of mustard, that wasn't what had happened in the swamp. He hadn't made anything appear and had instead made those skeletons obey him.

Was that truly what his power did? Did it give him power over the bones of the dead?

Impulsively, he reached out now and felt for bones. He wasn't exactly sure what he should look for. Did they need to belong to a dragon? A sentient being? Be imbued with magic? He continued his attempt to feel for any and all of it but found nothing.

Despondent, he sighed and took another bite of his sandwich. He remembered that he had said yes to the mustard, so it was his fault it tasted gross.

Why couldn't he use his power? Was it simply that it worked in the pixie realm and wouldn't work there? If that was the case, he wasn't sure if he'd be able to bear it. Growing up in the shadow of the legendary Stormwing had been hard enough. His grandfather had been so powerful, he could make tornados and hail and control lightning. He could make hurricanes and guide them to destroy cities of his choosing if the season and the conditions were right. By all accounts, he had been a powerhouse who had done more to ensure that dragons kept their rightful place at the top of the social hierarchy than any other except perhaps for Lord Boneclaw himself.

Galen's brother had some of his powers and with practice, their parents thought Hubert might one day rival his grandfather in his abilities. They had even taken to calling him Tempest instead of by his given name. Meanwhile, he remained Galen and always would.

It has always been an unspoken fact that he would amount to something far less spectacular. While his brother was expected to one day rule the world—or at least a continent—he had been expected to not make an embarrassment of himself. The only reason he was even at this school was because the Steel Dragon's revolution had given mages and vanilla dragons like him a place. It was a cruel irony that his parents hated how the Steel Dragon was remaking the rules of dragon society, and yet it was only because of her destroying the status quo that he was allowed to go to the same school as his brother Hubert.

He had tasted what it felt like to be special and to be someone with real powers, someone who could do more than simply fly and breathe fire. But how had he accessed those abilities?

After a moment's thought, he tried to put himself in the same state of mind he'd been in when he'd made the first skeleton obey. It had shredded his flesh in its attempt to kill him and came damn close to succeeding. He tried to remember if he'd been thinking about Tanya and her plant powers but no, he hadn't.

Galen had been thinking about his grandfather Stormwing and what he must have felt like in his final battle. He wondered if his grandfather had been afraid. Probably not, he decided. He would have faced Lumos with courage and bravery and wouldn't have thought of his death as a waste but as part of a larger fight. The young dragon had tried to channel this same energy, to use his grandfather's resolve even in the face of death to somehow survive the attack by the dragon skeleton.

He had looked into its eyes and seen death—his grandfather's death as well as the those of the animals he and so many other dragons ate to survive. In that gaze, he had seen that death was always hungry, that it was a force like any other. It had a flow to its power, as clear as any flow of energy in the universe.

Death was an unraveler. It worked inexorably and always pulled on life to force it to lay down and never move again. Yes, that much was true, but it also forced it to fight for survival and to try its best to thrive. Death wasn't evil per se. It was merely a force. He had seen all this and accepted his death as inevitable.

In that moment, the magic flowing through him—magic he had been willing to sacrifice like his grandfather had—poured into the creature. Galen had accepted that he would die and in doing so, found that death was energy.

And he could feel it now in these woods and in this desert. It was faint but it was there. He narrowed his eyes to focus and realized it was everywhere. Tentatively, he moved his hands as he had seen professor Sharra do. He swept them through the air in an attempt to sense if any place around him felt different than any other.

At first, he felt nothing, but when he tried again to accept the energy of death as merely a function of the universe, a pulling sensation responded from somewhere nearby.

Galen stumbled through the woods, desperate for this to work and terrified that it wouldn't. He wasn't entirely sure what it would mean if it did. Mindless to thorn and spine, he followed the tugging sensation without wavering and thrust past plants and branches as he had in the swamp.

What he discovered almost broke his heart.

It was a dead squirrel, although it wasn't that it was dead that hurt him. It was the idea that he had controlled over a dozen dragon skeletons in the pixie realm and now, he had crashed through the woods in wild desperation in hopes of finding something. A dead squirrel seemed incredibly disappointing after all that.

Galen sighed and scowled at it for a moment.

Still, the Magical Theory professor said that all magic started small. One couldn't make an inferno without first making a spark.

With this in mind, he knelt beside the squirrel and tried to reach out to it with his inner magic.

Once again, he felt nothing at first. It irked him that he didn't feel the immediate conflicting flow of energy the skeletal dragons had possessed, but maybe that was simply because the squirrel had yet to be animated? The young dragon looked at the little skeleton and flecks of fur that were all that remained of the creature. He tried to use his magic and his aura to make it understand that although it was dead and gone, part of it could still live on. If he gave it some of his magic, it could walk upon the earth again in return.

The bony tail twitched in response.

It would have been almost impossible to notice if he hadn't stared so intently at it. The scraps of fur seemed to puff and the very tip of the tail popped out, then withdrew, lifeless once more.

This was more than enough encouragement for the desperate young dragon who was hungry for power—any power.

He tried again to infuse the skeleton of the dead creature with his stream of inner magic and it twitched.

Galen grinned. He could do this. It might take considerable work, but he was sure he could do it.

The thought encouraged him and he focused on it again. This time, he gave special attention to the vertebrate-like pieces of bone in the tail. Instead of thinking, *Move, please move,* he thought about how exactly he wanted it to move. He decided this was for it to pull itself from the last pieces of desiccated flesh and tangled fur, extend into the air, and wave from side to side.

To his utter amazement, it did exactly that. The bones from the tail seemed to pulse as a ribbon of energy moved through them, connected with them, and animated them with a force as real and as invisible as gravity.

The young dragon couldn't stop now—and not ever. He thought about what else he wanted it to do. *No, it's not a skeleton but a squirrel.* Giving the body this intention was enough to suffuse it with energy that pulled all the bones together. He had to concentrate as some of the ribs—out of place from whatever predator had killed it—jostled for position and tried to find their right place. Galen didn't know much about squirrel anatomy but he was certain that a skeleton would not need all its ribs since it had no internal organs to protect.

No sooner had he thought this than the bones responded. Some of them simply fell while the other nestled in more cohesively.

"Good," he whispered to the reanimated squirrel. "Now, on your feet, little guy. You can do it." He spoke in the tender voice he wished his parents had spoken to him with more often. Patiently, he coaxed the little creature to pull itself free of the fur that covered its once-living body. He encouraged it to flick the maggots and ants away that had hidden beneath it to eat the scraps of meat it still possessed. Then, he gave it his will and his desires, and the creature took his magic and made them real.

It pushed up, trembling on all four legs, then slowly leaned back and sat on its haunches. While he watched in fascination, it held its little squirrel hand bones in front of it and nibbled the air with its surprisingly large front incisors.

He had achieved the impossible and had brought the skeleton to life. Or…well, animated it. He wasn't sure. Now, he needed to learn if he could give it specific commands.

"Climb that tree," he said and gestured at a nearby trunk.

The squirrel obeyed as soon as he thought and spoke the command. It raced to the tree and scaled it as easily as any living counterpart ever had. The young dragon watched in joyful amusement as it climbed ever upward from trunk to branch to twig.

"Wait, stop!" he said hastily before the creature climbed past the highest twig.

It froze at his command.

"I guess its bones are back but not its brain," Galen murmured. "Come down and sit next to me."

The creature obeyed and swung down from twig, to branch, and finally, the trunk before it raced across the ground and sat at his side.

"All right, jump!"

It obeyed and continued to do so until he instructed it to stop.

"You truly don't think for yourself, do you?" he said before he realized that wasn't quite right. The squirrel skeleton could do many things without specific instructions but it followed his commands to the letter.

But that was an easy fix for a boy who had grown up with servants.

"Squirrel, race into that tree, knock three acorns down, then jump to that one, knock two more down, then return to my side."

It did exactly as he requested. Galen grinned. He hadn't merely learned a new power but had mastered it.

"Now, climb up my leg and rest on my shoulder. We'll show my brother Hubert that I'm no longer a vanilla dragon."

---

When the dragon boy entered the woods, it watched curiously.

He found the dead body of the furry creature, and it continued to watch him.

As he gave life to the bones in the same way Cassandra had given life to the earth spirit, it wondered.

But when the boy ran to the school it had been told to monitor with the bones of a squirrel on his shoulder, it decided.

The earth spirit—not visible as anything more than a lump in the ground—sank into the soil. It was not certain if this was the kind of event its master had tasked it with reporting, but it was far more interesting than anything else that had happened thus far.

It hoped this piece of knowledge might convince her to free it from her control and let it return to its dimension.

Not that it feared being in this one. It was merely inconvenient and not its first choice.

# CHAPTER TWENTY

Kylara couldn't quite believe how very different the Lumos School campus felt now that she had Tanya's friendship again. She hated to admit it but before, when she had seen groups of students clustered in tight groups around the grounds, she couldn't help but feel excluded. It had felt as if they had all been talking about her and about the weird dragon from the desert who had been lying to only not all of them but also to herself.

The perception seemed so foolish now that she saw everyone outside enjoying an unseasonably warm autumn day. There was no reason to think that any of them had been discussing her. Why would everyone care, anyway? Admittedly, she was a little different being a mage rather than a dragon, but everyone there had their particular quirks.

"Yo, Diamantine, can I put some ice in your drink or are you gonna steal my power?" a dragon shouted at her from a group of friends who all erupted into laughter.

Okay, so some of the conversations were about her rediscovered mage power.

"Ignore them. They're jealous," Tanya said before she had

mustered any type of response. "I should know. I was jealous too and that was before I knew what you truly were."

"But do you honestly think any dragons will be jealous of me being a mage? It feels different somehow."

Her friend shrugged. "You sat with Karl the other day. If he can accept that you're a mage, I'm sure anyone can. Why did you sit with him, anyway? I know you were mad at me. Did you do it simply to spite me? Because if so, it worked." She laughed like it was a joke, but Kylara knew that there was truth to her concerns. Karl had bound the young dragon with his powers and intended to leave her chained until someone discovered her.

"No, it wasn't to get back to you," she admitted.

"Then what? Did he threaten to steal your powers back or something? Not that I think he could, of course. Or—oh wait, of course. He asked if you wanted to serve him as a mage?"

She sighed as they moved from the grassy fields into a section of the woods that had been burned by her aunt's fire elemental attack.

"Honestly, Tanya? If you truly want to know—"

"I do."

"Okay…well, the reason I sat with him is because he was nice to me. He offered me a seat at his table and was more or less polite, at least for Midnight's standards."

"He did insult you, though." It almost sounded like Tanya had asked her a question but not quite.

"Uh…yeah. In a way, although he insults everyone. Blaming him for that is like blaming Sam for flirting. It's what he does."

"Ha-ha, yeah…" From the girl's quickly coloring face, it was clear that this was a characteristic of their mutual friend she hadn't failed to notice.

"So yeah, he asked me to sit with him. We talked. He thinks it's…not cool but important, I guess, that I'm a mage."

"Do you think he only wanted to take advantage because he knew you were in a vulnerable place?"

"I was only in a vulnerable place because you and Sam turned your backs on me. He didn't."

"I know, I know, I know," Tanya said as if the mantra could somehow change her behavior over the last few days. "I'm merely wondering what his motivations were."

"I don't know if he necessarily had any nefarious plans. Oh, I guess you didn't see him in the pixie realm."

"What happened there?"

"Well, while you were out learning to animate plants or whatever, the rest of us were attacked. Karl stepped up and helped out. If he hadn't been there to use his dark magic against the glowing light blobs, we would have been toast. Maybe. The pixies were unclear on that."

"Ugh. They are unclear on everything," her friend agreed. "But you have dark powers too, right? You could have saved everyone."

"Not without his help. It was his guidance that gave us the edge we needed."

Tanya nodded. She looked jealous, concerned, and guilty as if all this was somehow her fault.

"But hey, it's not like he's my best friend or anything," she said and tried to pull the young dragon out of her woolgathering. "My best friend had run off in the pixie dimension and has now promised to show me what she can do with plants."

"Yeah, of course," Tanya said, smiling and nodding.

"All right, then. So, let me see what you got."

"Right. Here goes," Tanya said, planted her feet in the dirt, and reached toward a tree that had only been half-burned by the fire.

Nothing happened and she frowned.

"Wait, let me…" She shuffled her shoes a little and dug them deeper into the dry dirt and ash. With a small frown of concentration, she extended her fingers, waggled them, and made odd shapes with them. None of it worked. "I don't understand."

"Maybe that tree is too big? The branch you grew in the cafeteria was…uh, smaller."

"Yeah, I guess. The trees in the pixie realm were huge, though, and I could make them grow, no problem."

Kylara looked around their environment. Most of the trees were still standing, even though the majority of them had been burned and were dead. The underbrush had fared far worse. It was all blackened and charred to nothing. She knew enough about New Mexico ecology to know that seeds waited in that ash and dirt for sufficient water and although the trees' outer bark was burned, many of them would grow again.

She was about to ask what the environment was like where her friend had used her powers but didn't manage it before Tanya blurted, "How can you think that Karl's not trying to manipulate you? You saw what he did to me."

"Tanya, I thought we were going to focus on your powers."

"We are, but…well, I don't know, Ky. It's weird. He is such a jerk and now, you're defending him?"

"Well, what about you and Galen? Why did you follow him into the woods? He's not exactly friendly."

"He never used his powers against me," she retorted.

"Yeah, because he doesn't have any powers," Kylara pointed out. "You can't blame Karl for using his powers. What he did to you was messed up, and if he ever tries that again, I will one hundred percent kick his ass. But Galen and you going off into the woods endangered so many people. I guess I don't see the difference."

"For your information, he does have powers," the young dragon said.

"That's cool. Good for him. It doesn't change the fact that he's rude."

"So is Karl."

"I'm not saying he's not, Tanya. Truly."

"Then what are you saying?"

"That there's more to him than merely being a jerk, I guess. He saved people and that means something to me. And this may be crappy, but I promise you that if you learned a new power, he won't mess with you again."

"I guess it's too bad that I can't use my powers then."

"I wondered about that. What was the place like where you controlled the plants? You were covered in mud when you came back. Was it wet?"

Tanya looked at the burned, desiccated forest all around them and laughed. "Oh, my God, Kylara, I am so sorry. I thought I was over everything but I guess not. I was here thinking about you and Midnight and blaming that for my powers not working, but you're right. The place where my powers manifested was a swamp. This is as opposite as can be."

"Keep trying. Maybe the plants here have deeper roots or something," she suggested. "It might take longer."

The girl nodded, calm again and hopefully finally over Kylara talking to Karl.

"When I was in the swamp," she said, her eyes closed, "I saw an orchid that reminded me of one my mom grew. That was how I first accessed the power. I made that plant grow and realized that I could feel the same energy growing in the trees."

"Reach out and see if you can feel that same energy now," Kylara said.

"I can, I think, but it's not as strong. Not even remotely as strong."

"It won't feel that way at first. The magic in this realm is different but keep trying." In all honesty, she didn't know what the magic in the pixie realm was supposed to have felt like. She had spent her time there talking to Sam and fighting the balls of light. But that didn't matter as she'd had an idea but didn't want to say anything. She knew her friend well enough at this point to know she lacked self-confidence. Her hope was to give her a big boost of exactly that.

While Tanya kept her eyes shut and continued to reach out with her hands, she tried discreetly to summon a storm.

She knew she had to be careful and didn't want to attract undue attention to the school—even though part of her wondered if there could even be a bigger threat out there than her Aunt Cassandra, who already knew exactly where it was.

That wasn't a reason to be sloppy, though. She had seen hundreds of storms form in blue skies in the desert and clouds were present today—a rare occurrence—so she thought she could make this work.

Kylara reached out and poured her inner magic into the air around her. It traveled on the wind to find water drops too tiny to be perceived by anything but magic or perhaps the thirsty leaves of plants. She focused on the sky above them and slowly drew in more and more of the microdroplets of water. A tiny puff of cloud appeared and began to grow. She watched it expand carefully, anxious to not let it get so large as to create lightning.

"Ky! I think I feel something! The plants feel...different somehow."

"That's great, Tanya. Keep your eyes closed and see what else you can feel," she replied through clenched teeth. It was surprisingly difficult to make a cloud big enough to create rain yet small enough to not create lightning. Her efforts seemed to be working, though. The one above them grew heavier and darker until— a few seconds before she could feel it condense into actual drops —she made the wind blow the entire cloud to the ground.

"Kylara, something's happening! Seriously."

She nodded and continued to push the dense, moist air toward the parched earth. It formed beads of dew on the charred twigs, which then clustered together into tiny rivulets of water that seeped into the earth.

"Keep going, Tanya. See if you can focus on any seeds. Many plants in the desert wait for fire to regrow. See if you can find some of them."

"I can feel them," the young dragon almost shrieked and in the next moment, beneath the mist created, a thousand seeds burst into life. Kylara had seen such a profusion of life in the desert before, of course. Whenever it rained in any substantial amount on the land where she'd lived for her entire life, the plants responded by growing as quickly as possible, producing flowers, and going to seed all in a matter of days. She had always thought it was like fast-forward—that compared to the rest of the world, the desert plants were remarkably swift, if only because they understood that they'd have to return to a long wait for more water after they bloomed a single time.

But what she saw now shattered any preconceived notions she had about how fast plants could grow.

A thousand seeds erupted with tiny shoots and leaves. The new growth struggled through the mist, collected beads of moisture, and channeled it through themselves into the soil where their roots grew unseen. With this water plus Tanya's magic to fuel them, each tiny sprout grew a pair of leaves, then another, then doubled that, onward and upward until instead of tiny, almost defenseless seedlings, they stood in a circle of blooming wildflowers.

"Tanya," she said, "Open your eyes."

The young dragon complied. "Oh, my God. Oh, my God, Ky. Can you believe this?" She spun slowly in a circle and gaped at the ring of lush green growth that surrounded them. At least a dozen different kinds of wildflowers all bloomed in as many colors. Tiny tree sprouts appeared too—pine, mesquite, and even a few oaks. No longer was there any ash or dried dirt beneath their feet but a wonderfully moist carpet of fresh growth.

"I don't know what happened." Tanya's eyes glistened with tears of excitement. "I reached out like you said. It took a minute, but I felt their energy."

"What did it feel like?" she asked.

"It was weird. This was different than the swamp—very

different. Everything there was already growing when I touched it. It was like that entire place tried to grow as large as it could as quickly as it could. Here, though, it felt like the plants were waiting for something. Water, I guess. Kylara! You made it rain, didn't you?"

She blushed. "Only a little, yeah."

"Thank you. That must have made the difference. The plants in the desert didn't want to grow because they knew they couldn't, not without water, but once you supplied some..." She threw her arms around her friend and squeezed her in a big hug.

"I thought it might be something like that," she said. "We had cactus on my land where I grew up that wouldn't grow a single needle for years. Then it would rain and suddenly, it was like they had new branches."

"Of course! Ky, you're a genius. That's why the ficus in the dining hall worked. It's watered all the time. Thank you so much. Do you mind, if I...uh, practice?"

"No, Tanya, of course not. Honestly, it might be good if you could give some of the trees here a head start."

"That's a great idea. Um...which ones are the trees?"

They spent the next few minutes moving through the circle of green growth while Kylara pointed out which plants were tiny trees and which were wildflowers that would go to seed within a few days and vanish until the next rainstorm came.

Tanya made a few of the mesquite sprouts grow. Their compound leaves were fascinating to watch at the speed she could give them with her magic. A tiny green thread emerged from the central stem of the plant first, followed by a dozen green leaflets that grew rapidly into the wilting, almost fern-like leaves of this desert denizen. Watching the spines was even cooler and a reminder that the young dragon's power could prove to be incredibly versatile.

"You seem to have regular plant growth down. Do you think you can focus on certain parts of the plant?" Kylara asked.

"I don't know. What do you mean?"

"Well, when I use my storm powers, it's almost like I can feel different…uh, streambeds of magic? Okay. If your magic is a river, imagine sending it down different parts of the plants. Instead of giving it to the whole thing, can you direct it more specifically?"

"Yeah. I think I should be able to. In the pixie realm, I made the roots of the tree grow. I don't think I made any branches appear."

"Try on that mesquite. The one that's mostly burned." She pointed to a big one that had been reduced to little more than a black stump with a couple of wounded limbs trying to cling to it.

Tanya nodded and turned to it, extended her fingers, and dug her feet into the now moist earth.

Nothing happened but still, she cheered. "I did it, Kylara. I did it."

"Did what?" a new voice asked.

Kylara turned to see Samuel Lumos approaching from campus.

"Hi, Sam!" the young dragon beamed. "Kylara's been helping me master my power."

"Yeah, I can see that," he said and looked at the ring of green plants all around their feet and the few improbably large trees she had worked on.

"I made that mesquite tree grow." It was cute how proud she was—so cute that Kylara almost felt bad bursting her bubble.

"But Tanya, that mesquite didn't grow."

"Sure it did. I made its roots grow exactly like I did in the swamp."

She smiled when she finally understood. "That's very cool, but I imagine it already has well-established roots, given how it must have grown here for at least a century."

"Can you make it grow leaves?" Sam asked.

Tanya flushed, obviously embarrassed even though Kylara

didn't think she needed to be. She was starting to realize that embarrassment was one of her friend's go-to emotions and wondered what it would feel like if she could sense her aura like a regular dragon could.

"Yeah, I think I can." The girl squared off against the plant. This time, she wiggled her fingers toward the sky. At first, nothing happened but scant moments later, a single green bud pushed from the charred bark of the seemingly dead tree. It uncurled into a leaf that grew as quickly as the little mesquites had.

But that wasn't enough for her or this ancient, wounded tree. The central stem of the leaf hardened and new buds formed along it. These exploded into more leaves, which grew quickly, hardened, and in turn, pushed out more leaves. In less than a minute, the three of them were as shaded by the canopy as anyone could ever be under a mesquite, which wasn't much.

"Tanya, that was amazing." Sam grinned at her.

"I know, right." Tanya hopped around in triumph. "This is so crazy."

"I'm so relieved that some good came out of everything that happened in pixie land. I was worried we'd never get to go back," he said.

"Do you think they'll let us go back?" the other young dragon asked. "Even though Galen and I snuck off?"

He chuckled. "I do. In fact, I think they'll take us there precisely because you and Galen snuck off. No one else gained any powers except for you—and him, I guess."

"Oh, he certainly has powers," Tanya said.

"What can he do?" Kylara asked.

"I...I don't know if I should say yet," her friend responded and looked at her with pain but also certainty in her eyes.

"What? Why not?" Sam asked. He'd perhaps not seen the communication between the two girls.

"Well, let's say it's a little different from flowers blooming and

I wouldn't want the whole campus to start judging him on what his powers are instead of what he can do with them."

"Oh, come on!" he protested.

"No, Tanya's right," Kylara agreed. "But back to you. You mentioned making a plant walk. Do you think you can do such a thing or are you simply talking shit?"

"I can try." The girl smiled and returned to her finger-waggling while her friends laughed.

The trio spent the next hour in that ring of lush green growth. Tanya practiced incessantly, although she never quite learned how to make a plant walk. Of course, that might simply have been because she was laughing too hard at her companions' antics.

When they left the forest, Kylara could genuinely say that it was better than when they'd entered it. Instead of burned under-growth hoping to one day make a comeback, a smattering of wildflowers brightened the landscape because Tanya had felt compelled to use every trace of the moisture her friend had produced to help the plants grow. Fresh branches sprouted from many of the burned tree trunks with the promise of more leaves instead of simply rotting away. The young dragon had even learned to make the bark flex when it grew, which went a long way to shaking loose much of the charred outer layer of the trees.

Kylara felt much like these burned and blackened trees. She and her friends had been through something traumatic. It had hurt them and would no doubt leave scars that they would forever have to deal with and yet, they were still growing. They continued to reach for new heights and tried to establish them-selves in places that could give them what they needed to thrive.

CHAPTER TWENTY-ONE

"So what are you anyway—some kind of mage-lover?"

Cassandra sat on a chair formed from the cave rock itself. She had made her most powerful earth elemental build it for her before she sent it on surveillance. It was positioned directly across from Hester Diamantine, so all that was between her and the imprisoned diamond dragon was a pool and the water elemental that lived in it.

"Excuse me?" her captive asked and raised her head to look her in the eye. The mage had loosened her chains so she could now sit. She had begun to feel uncomfortable when the woman had been forced to sleep standing up, supported by nothing but the chains connected to her magic-dampening wrists.

"I saw how you behaved toward those mages before your partners slaughtered them," she said, knowing the events of that night were never far from the front of the dragon's mind.

"I didn't want them to die," Hester said. "No one deserves to die simply for being who they are."

"A sentiment most of your kind don't share."

The prisoner shrugged weakly. "I suppose not enough of us, no."

"Is that why you named Kylara after the mage who used to serve you? Because you're a mage-lover?"

"Lara did not serve me," she all but snarled with surprising savageness.

"She wore a cuff similar to the ones you wear now. Is that not true?"

"Of course it's true." The savageness had left her voice like a tiger upon waking and realizing it was still imprisoned in a zoo.

"So she was your servant. She could not harm you and had to do as you said."

"She wore a cuff because if she didn't, she would have been slaughtered. I cared far too much for her to let that happen."

Cassandra nodded. It was not something she could disprove. Before the Steel Dragon had come along, free mages were slaughtered or enslaved. There was no middle ground for their kind. Things were finally changing for the better, but there remained a long way to go, in her mind.

"So you are a mage-lover, then?"

"I loved Lara, yes," Diamantine responded and her breath caught.

"Oh…I see." She was disappointed by the heartbreak she heard in the dragon's voice. "It was…intimate then? Between you and her? That's why you named Kylara after her—because you saw her as a…a what? A lover? A concubine?"

"Why is this any of your business?" Hester moaned.

"I am simply trying to ascertain the reason that compelled you to protect a baby mage for almost two decades. If you were a mage-lover, it would imply that there are others like you in the dragon world. And if a member of Dragon SWAT—the most ruthless dragon agency there is—could love mages, then why not anyone?"

"I don't see what me being in SWAT has to do with loving mages."

"I don't think it does," Cassandra said sadly. "I think you were merely in love with this one mage. It's not completely unheard of. When she died, you transferred those feelings to the baby."

"It's more…complicated than that."

"Is it? I hope so. Because if you only saved Kylara because of some misplaced sense of guilt, I don't see much point in keeping you around once I bring her to the side of the mages."

"Cassandra, why must there still be sides? Hundreds of dragons and mages died fighting a war about this very issue. Why can't we try to live side by side? I understand that horrible things were done to your family, but you've had your revenge. You won't be punished for it."

"There are still sides as long as dragons live for millennia while the rest of us are lucky to survive a century."

"But there's nothing to be done about that. Don't you think I've thought about it? About how much it'll hurt to watch Kylara grow old and die in what to my kind is but the passing of a day? If I could give her my longevity, I would!"

"Ah, but maybe you already have," the mage replied. "Maybe Kylara will already live for thousands of years."

"And that's a bad thing?"

"If she refuses to share that gift with her fellow mages because the woman who stole her from her family brainwashed her against us? Then yes, it is a grave injustice for which you are responsible."

"Cassandra, I will do anything to make sure Kylara is safe. You can't expect me to apologize for making her as strong as I possibly could."

"I don't expect an apology. I want you to make things right."

"How am I supposed to do that when I'm chained?" Diamantine demanded.

"I'm working on it," she said.

As if on cue, an earth spirit rose from the ground.

Cassandra didn't know what the earth spirits looked like when they moved beneath the earth in their preferred habitat. She knew they could shrink and expand the amount of space they took up and that they were incredibly fast and able to move through the soil instead of with it the way air elementals did.

When it emerged to speak to her, it brought earth and stone with it and formed it into the rough shape of a human. The one that now stood before her was made up of a pile of stones held together with mud and grit. It had no legs and instead, its core extended into the soil as if the earth itself animated this crude puppet. After working with her for so long, it had learned to form a reasonable simulacrum of a face. It used gemstones for eyes and a mess of stones for a mouth that moved and shook while it vibrated itself to speak.

"I have found something of interest, my master," the earth spirit said.

"Excellent! What has young Kylara learned now?"

"It is not your niece who gained a power in the pixie realm but another. A boy," the being intoned.

"And what power has he learned?"

"I observed as he gave life to the bones of a dead creature. It had lain quietly and added its remains slowly to the earth beneath it, but when this boy gave it his energy, it gained the ability to move at his command."

"That's unnatural!" Diamantine blurted.

With a gesture, Cassandra ordered the water spirit to rise out of the pool surrounding the dragon and soak her with a violent splash of water.

"Don't forget to get a drink," she said and made no effort to look at her prisoner. "Would you recognize him if you saw him again?" she asked the earth spirit.

"Yes, master. Yes, I have learned human faces at your command."

"You have done very well. You may have an hour to yourself," she said to it. The entity nodded and sank into the earth to leave nothing behind but a small pile of stones and the crystals it had used as its eyes.

"You're not serious, are you?" Diamantine asked. She rose, still damp from her soaking. "You can't think this boy can somehow be of use to you?"

The dragon rarely managed to anger her captor. It was hard to feel much of anything when someone was chained and so obviously at one's mercy. But anger flared in her now and rose like bile into her throat.

"How dare you claim to know what is best for my life?" she yelled and called on the elements as she spoke. Flames surged from her fingertips, wind blew at her hair, the water before her churned, and rocks fell from the roof of the cavernous lair. "You, who have taken everything from me! You took my sister, my father, and my niece—the only family I ever had and the only people I ever loved. Then, you showed Kylara mercy and in doing so, took away the only thing I still wanted in the world —revenge."

Diamantine was speechless. She stood against the stone pillar and tried to look brave but mostly cringed like the human Cassandra had forced her to become with the magic-dampening cuffs.

"Planning your murder was all that fueled me for years. It was why I developed these powers when most mages shirk them or brand them dangerous in their ignorance. Learning that you cared for Kylara drained my life of its final purpose."

"Then why keep me here at all? Why not simply kill me and end yourself?"

"Have you listened to nothing I've said?" She sucked a sharp breath through her teeth in disapproval. "Discovering that Kylara can turn into a dragon has changed my entire purpose in life. When I first realized who she was, I wanted only to teach her what she was. But even I didn't fully understand the implications of her gift. Her taking the form of a dragon changes everything."

"Then why worry about this boy and his…necromancy?" Diamantine asked

"You must first understand what I've been through," Cassandra said and paced around the pool now while her gaze remained fixed on her captive. "I watched the technomages gain power for over a decade and I watched their weapons grow in potency and lethality. They tried to recruit me more than once, of course. I said no every time, even though that made me an outcast not only from the dragon world but also this new hidden one of mages as well. An outcast of outcasts, you could say."

"But why not join them? You have no love for dragons," Hester asked while she tried to crane her neck to see the mage and failed. Her captor liked the fact that she had lost the will to follow up on her questions. She wanted to know Cassandra's machinations for this skeleton boy, but she knew she would answer her in her own time. So, for the time being, she simply paid attention to what she had to say. It was a simple thing and if more dragons did so, it might have made a different and even a better world.

"I never wished to focus my energy on their tricks with dead dragon bodies. It was a living dragon I wanted—you. While they worked and the world kept spinning, I focused on learning to summon spirits from the different realms. You have met my spirits, but have you ever met their equal?"

"No…no, I have not. They're very powerful."

Cassandra chuckled. "Yes, thank you. I am quite fond of them as well. They have put me worlds ahead of other mages and yet… in a few decades, they will return to their dimensions when I pass. I am human and will die as one."

"That's what you want from Kylara," the dragon said. "You want to take her power."

"Don't be so naïve, Diamantine. It doesn't become you. I don't wish that power for myself but for all mages. With it, we could live as long as dragons, and only then would we truly be equal. We too could look at the centuries ahead of us, not in wonder but with a plan. It would change the world."

"But what does this have to do with the skeleton kid?"

"I was getting to that, thank you," she said. "You did quite the number on Kylara's belief system. Because of you, I don't know what she thinks about me or even about being a mage. I fear she'll never forgive me for kidnapping you. Even though you and I both know that your continued existence is a mercy, she may not see it that way." She shook her head. "I should already be teaching her how to summon the spirits but instead, she returned to that dragon school. But all is not lost. Not anymore."

"You're after a dead mage, then?" Diamantine asked.

"A mage...yes," Cassandra chuckled at the simple-minded guess Diamantine had ventured.

"But how can you be sure this kid's ability will bring back anything about their essence? He might merely be a...a kind of bone wizard." The dragon curled her lip in disgust.

"Ah, you dragons. You have your beliefs and you stick to them. I guess there is nobility in that, even if such beliefs can be stifling to fresh growth."

"But you have to admit there's a risk that he can't bring back anything of this person's knowledge. In which case, you're out of luck."

"You have spent so much time with me and yet you have thought so little about these beings I control," Cassandra said pontifically.

"What is that supposed to mean?" Diamantine asked. There was fear in her voice and her captor relished the feel of it.

"It means that I have already brought forth many spirits from other realms. It is a spirit from the water realm that circles you now. A spirit from the fire realm warms our food. There is a realm of the dead as well—or...a...dimension, I guess. Nothing like what the human religions imagine, I can assure you of that. But there is a place where a person's essence goes. A realm of souls, one could say."

The prisoner shook her head as if all this was too much to understand. Cassandra assumed it probably was too much for her. Dragons didn't study theory or how their powers worked. They simply took flight and burned whatever was in their path. It was such a travesty that they were in charge. The Steel Dragon had done something to change things but there was still so much more to be done, and Cassandra was on the eve of achieving all of it.

"But...but if there is some secret spell you need to give you Kylara's ability, why not simply summon the spirit?" It had probably taken every synapse in Diamantine's brain to come up with such a question.

"Spirits cannot last long in this realm—seconds, sometimes only the briefest of moments and nothing more. This realm pushes them out to make room for more. It is the way of things here. Even my spirits cannot exist without an anchor."

"*That's* why you need him!" the prisoner exclaimed.

"Very good, dragon. Very good," Cassandra nodded. "My ability to call spirits, even the spirits of the dead, coupled with the boy's ability to reanimate the very bones of the being I wish to speak to, may give me the secret I wish to have for myself and to share with the world."

"You mean the ability to become a dragon." Hester's voice was hollow with horror as if everything but terror had been scraped from inside her.

The mage threw back her head and laughed. "Exactly! A truly remarkable idea, is it not? To think that if all goes as planned, within a few weeks, I might very well have the same powers as the niece you stole from me. Then, when Kylara sees that we truly are family, she will help me spread this gift and finally make the world a more equitable place."

She turned her back on the imprisoned dragon and moved into the depths of her lair. There was so much to do and so little time. Fortunately, she had been preparing for this. She summoned some of the other elementals she had worked with and began to inform them of the beginnings of her plan.

CHAPTER TWENTY-TWO

Now that Kylara was back on speaking terms with Sam and Tanya, the semester continued into autumn in what she thought of as a pleasantly normal fashion. That was an absurd understatement, of course, for there was no normal about attending a dragon school. Plus, as this was still the first year that mages were allowed on campus, it continued to bring various challenges.

Not least of which was her new roommate. More than anything, she wanted to move in with her friend again, but she didn't see how she could and not mortally offend Jasmine Patel.

Although it seemed almost everything mortally offended Jasmine. She didn't like the dragon mage's grooming schedule, nor did she like the fact that she still socialized with dragons despite being a mage. She had asked the girl if she wanted to hang out with her a few times. The response had been colder than her aunt's lair beneath the frozen lake.

Despite this, she didn't want to simply move out. It was obvious that the young mage was going through some serious family difficulties. She fretted about jewelry and did her hair with extra care anytime she had to wear a shirt she'd worn within the last few weeks as if she wasn't used to having to wear clothes more than once. Plus, she never visited the campus store, nor did she have packages delivered like some of the other mages did.

The only thing Jasmine did do was prepare for the Halloween social. While other students hung out on the green or stuffed their faces without fear of gaining weight due to their dragon metabolism, she worked on her costume. It was a dress of some kind, Kylara knew that much, and when she'd pried, the girl had confessed that it was identical to the dress a dragon queen had worn for her coronation when… That was about how far she had lasted before she'd become bored and simply let her roommate ramble on.

Although she didn't care much for fancy dresses—one advantage about not rooming with Tanya was there was no longer any pressure to borrow the dragon's clothes—she recognized that the gown was stunning. All black lace and done in beautiful cascading layers, it truly was a work of art. Most nights, when Kylara got back to her room, Jasmine was working on it, making the fabric levitate while she sewed by hand.

"Is the Halloween Social a big deal here?" she asked one night.

"I wouldn't know as I am not a dragon."

"Right," she said and was ready to go to the library to study and forget about her roommate when Jasmine cleared her throat to keep talking.

"I hope it can be an event where we all…mingle," the young mage said.

"Sure. That would be great! Have you talked to the mages about it?"

"Not really, no."

"Then how are they supposed to know to even go?"

"I don't know, Kylara. I only know this dress has to look perfect if the dragons are going to…I don't know, see me on their terms or whatever."

She nodded. It made sense. Dragons always dressed spectacularly. If one wished to impress them, one would have to dress well. "Wait, Jasmine. Do you want to impress all the dragons? Or only one?"

The storm of thimbles, needles, spools, and thread that drove Kylara from her room was fearsome enough to make her walk the grounds for a while. But—despite Jasmine's obvious embarrassment—she thought she had a point. The Halloween Social would be a good time for dragons and mages to mingle.

Plus, it would give them something to look forward to now that Professor Sharra and Petalwing had canceled trips to Pixie land.

"You can't be serious!" Galen protested.

"I am serious—deadly serious. We will not return until we have better safety protocols in place. And yes, class, you can hold Galen and Tanya responsible for this decision."

There were groans at this and a flurry of balls of paper was thrown at both students' heads.

Petalwing giggled at the barrage, darted overhead, and swooped between the harmless projectiles.

The rest of the class passed in tedious monotony. Now that there was no chance of being able to visit the Pixie realm, learning magical theory seemed a dull and useless exercise in futility.

Kylara left the class and caught up to Tanya, eager to talk about Halloween and not the class they'd both suffered through.

"Will you get a new dress for the Halloween social?" she asked.

"Are you serious? Of course! I thought I could go as Dorothy from the Wizard of Oz. Like, somewhere over the rainbow is kind of this school. You know what I mean? Maybe you could be the scarecrow or something."

"I might wear a dress," she protested.

"As if. You haven't worn one since you got your own clothes. Instead, all you wear is jeans. Hence, scarecrow. Samuel could be the tinman. He likes to pretend he doesn't have a heart when he does."

She was about to reply with a less than stellar quip about her roommate being the wicked witch when she saw something strange moving through the tops of the trees. Without thought, she simply transformed into her dragon shape and became airborne as she prepared to use her storm powers.

"Ky! Ky, it's okay that you wear jeans," Tanya shouted after her.

Kylara didn't hear her. Her gaze remained fixed on the disturbance. It had been subtle but she knew it wasn't natural. She had fallen into the habit of reaching out with her storm powers in case something like this happened.

It was, without a doubt, an air elemental on campus.

From what she could see, it headed toward the main building.

She summoned her storm powers and threw a gust of wind into the elemental's path. To her surprise, it cursed.

"Goddammit, it got away from me!" She realized it wasn't the elemental that had spoken but one of Amy's security mages.

"I have visuals. Preparing to blast in three...two...one..."

Kylara dodged as a great ball of fire streaked in front of her. It caught the air elemental and dispersed it into nothingness or made it flee, she couldn't be sure. She pumped her wings to gain altitude while she probed for other entities—or worse, her Aunt Cassandra herself.

Instead, she was met by Amy Williams, who wore a beanie against the autumn air, a hoodie two sizes too big, and unlaced skater shoes, and rode a skateboard that featured a gorilla flipping an obscene gesture.

"What do you think you're doing up here?" she asked almost politely but still undoubtedly annoyed.

"Helping you guys stop Aunt Cassandra," Kylara replied, confused that the mage even asked such an obvious question.

"You are not helping. We had tracked that elemental since the moment it entered the area. What you are doing is earning yourself detention for being late to your next class."

"You're joking," she pushed. "You wouldn't have seen it if not for me."

"Uh-huh," Amy said, her voice flat and unimpressed. "And what about the earth elemental that tried to break in last week? Did we need your help with that one?"

"The…earth elemental?"

"And then there was the water elemental that tried to gain entry through the pipes. Remind me again about how we needed your help to stop that one."

"We…fought an elemental that came out of the pipes," Kylara said and scrambled to make sense of what she'd been told. "That's what stole Sam and Tanya. If one of those was on campus, I would have heard of it."

"Oh, would you?" Amy asked sardonically and gestured firmly at the ground as she led her to earth. "Because the only people who were informed about it were the mages on my security detail. Maybe you didn't hear because you were in class, learning like you're supposed to do. Because, you know, you're a student."

They swooped low and she spread her wings to slow her flight before she transformed into her human shape and tucked into a tight little front-flip to cut her momentum before she landed. "I may be a student, but she's my aunt. I should be helping."

"We haven't needed it thus far, my young mage. What exactly makes you think we needed you for this one?"

"But isn't that a little weird?" she asked and hoped it didn't seem like she was changing the subject.

Amy sighed and smiled indulgently. "What is a little weird?"

"That you've been able to stop them so easily. Think about it. The water elemental that came before took two dragons and was able to fight off several others plus mages."

"Mage students. Dragon students. There's nothing unusual

about children being overpowered. That is one of the main advantages of attacking them." Amy scoffed.

"But—"

"Kylara, look, I understand that you went through some serious…stuff. I was impressed then and I'm still impressed with you, but it's not your job to defend this school. The best way for you to help is to keep your nose in the books, focus on your radical ability to learn new powers from dragons, and stay out of our way. We're getting better at fighting these. It's as simple as that."

She nodded, not wanting to risk the wrath of Kor if she was late, but the next few weeks passed with an uneasiness bordering on dread. She couldn't help but think there was more to Cassandra than these weak attacks. While she had to admit that it was possible Amy and her team had grown stronger—especially given how little she knew about mages— she didn't think that was the case.

When a week passed and another elemental attacked—one made of fire this time—Kylara didn't hesitate to jump into the fray. Again, she used her storm powers in the hopes that she could drown the spark that floated seemingly out of nowhere to land in the top of a nearby pine tree.

"Kylara? Are you hot or something?" Tanya asked. The three friends were spending time together near the woods.

She ignored her, took her dragon form, and launched toward the upper branches of the tree as more and more of them burst into flame. She activated her dark powers—she'd managed to practice with Karl once or twice, to Tanya's undisguised displeasure—and attacked.

Entirely focused, she lashed out with tendrils of ropy blackness to sever branch after branch in the canopy and deny the fire elemental its fuel source.

The blazing core of the creature from another realm tried to ignite and burn brighter, but the rain made it difficult. She flew closer and readied a final web of dark energy to snuff it out.

Before she could, a gush of water sprayed from the ground and extinguished the flames so thoroughly that the tree didn't even smoke.

Kylara wheeled, ready to face the water elemental that had stopped its ally for some reason, only to discover that it wasn't a one at all but one of Amy's mages.

"Kylara, right?" the tattooed man asked in a deep, slightly accented voice.

"Ha-ha, yeah. I didn't see you there," she said.

"Thanks to you, we now won't get to see where that fire elemental was trying to run to," the mage said and made no attempt to hide his annoyance.

"Kylara was only trying to help," Tanya said to him.

"She could help more if she'd let us do our job," he replied sharply. "These elementals are easy enough to stop. We're trying to determine where they're coming from."

"My aunt, obviously!" Kylara snapped.

"Obviously indeed," he said and wiped his brow dry from her continued rainstorm. "We are trying to ascertain the location of the mage Cassandra. Please, do not interrupt our work again."

"But…you wouldn't have been able to stop that elemental without rain from my storm," she complained, unable to help herself.

"We had followed it for over an hour," the mage replied and gestured to a jug of water that hovered behind him. "I was prepared."

"But don't you think it's odd that it let you follow it for that long?" Sam asked.

The mage took a slow, deep breath and sighed. "It is a being of pure fire from a realm so different from ours we could never hope to comprehend it. I do not think it is capable of leading us on a merry chase around campus."

"It could with Cassandra's help," Kylara pointed out.

"Spirits are not so tied to their masters as you seem to think," he replied. "It is obvious you do not have the theory to be of assistance with these intrusions on campus. Please, let us do our job. I wish to go home and visit my family before this winter, which will not happen if you continue to disrupt our attempts to protect you and your fellow students."

"But we don't need protection," she said forcefully.

"I'll be sure to include that in my report to Mage Williams and the headmaster," he said as a way to excuse himself.

She watched him go, more frustrated and confused now than when she'd battled her aunt and the elementals she'd controlled in her fortress of ice.

CHAPTER TWENTY-THREE

The next day, the three friends were outside again, enjoying lunch in the brisk fall air. Halloween was fast approaching and thanks to Tanya, the school buzzed with excitement for the social. She had told everyone how great it would be and how no one should be caught dead missing it.

Kylara wished she could get excited about the event since she had told her friend about Jasmine's hopes, but she couldn't stop thinking about the attacks by the elementals.

"They have to be from my aunt Cassandra. There's no other explanation." She interjected her summation between her friends' conversation about costumes.

Samuel sighed. They'd been over this before and more than once. "Yeah, we agree that it has to be your aunt, but that doesn't change the fact that Amy and her mages are working on it."

"And you're fine with that?" she demanded. "Being protected by mages?"

"Whoa, listen to the separationist," Tanya joked. "Maybe you have spent too much time with Karl Midnight if you think it's a problem to have adult, professional mages guarding dragon students."

Kylara stood and began to pace. "I know they're missing something. The few elementals I faced are nowhere near as strong as those she used to capture you two. Why would she send weak elementals when she doesn't have to? There has to be a point to it."

"Point, yeah, like a sword," Samuel said and rubbed his chin.

"Make fun of me all you want but I know something is up," she said and spun on her heel to wipe the grin off of his face with her scowl.

"No, no. I'm serious about a sword. As in what if it's merely a feint? Part of fencing—a big part—is testing your opponent's defense. That means attacking with strikes that are weaker than you're truly capable of."

"You're not entirely making sense, Sam." Tanya groaned.

"No, he is," Kylara exclaimed. "What if she's sending in these weaker elementals to see how fast the campus security reacts and how strong they are?"

"But if that's true and she's still after you, Ky, it makes more sense for you to not engage at all," he said and sounded firm but apologetic.

She stopped, her hands on her hips. "What? No way!"

"Think about it. If she's after you, it's better if you don't show her what you're capable of."

"Sam's right, Ky. If Cassandra had known about your shadow powers when you came to rescue us, we'd probably still be there."

Kylara resumed pacing, her back to both her friends.

"You hadn't thought of that, had you?" Samuel asked.

Finally, she sighed and sat again. "No. No, I hadn't. Goddammit, Sam. That makes so much sense."

"Also, what? Do you fence?" Tanya asked.

Sam blushed. "I...no. I tried when I was younger and was horrible at it. I always lunged at everyone's feints."

They all laughed at that.

"Well, I don't like being benched but I guess it makes sense—for now anyway," Kylara said.

"Besides, it's not like we don't have stuff to do." Tanya grinned.

"Tanya, if you talk about the Halloween social one more time, I think I'll lose it," she said.

"No, not that. I was talking about my powers. I've made so much progress."

"Is that right?" Sam asked.

The girl nodded. "Observe." She pointed at a tree above her. The leaves on one branch fluttered and buds on it swelled until they burst into flowers.

"Wow! That was cool!" He congratulated her with real enthusiasm.

"If I get lucky and something pollinates them, I can get only one branch to make seeds too."

"Is it harder to make only part of the plant do something?" Kylara asked.

"Yeah, much harder," Tanya admitted. "Getting them to do anything besides grow toward the sun is always difficult but I'm getting better. I'm working on sap now."

"Thrilling," Sam said sarcastically.

"And you can do better?" the girl demanded.

"Well, I too have worked on a new trick," he said formally.

"Oh, is that right?"

"Indeed. Observe." He held out his hand and it began to glow. The palm shone brightest and the fingers and thumb less so. But, as he furrowed his brow and focused, his thumb went dark, then his pinkie, ring, and middle fingers did the same thing, so only his index finger and palm were glowing.

With a final grunt, he extinguished the light in his hand and forced all the energy into the single digit. He pointed it at a tree trunk and a narrow beam of light streaked forward. He used it to burn his name in the trunk of a tree and gasped for breath when he finished. "I'm still working on it but yeah, I have a finger laser."

"They don't like that, by the way," Tanya said.

"Who?" Sam asked.

"The trees don't like being used to note that someone loved someone here once or whatever. They don't mind being trimmed but they do not like to be written on—with lasers, carving knives, or anything else."

"Huh. That's good to know," Kylara said.

"What about you, Ky? Have you picked up any new powers yet?" he asked.

She shook her head. "I wish. Ever since it became common knowledge that I can absorb powers, no one wants to use them on me. I even won a match in Kor's class simply because my opponent wouldn't attack me."

"That sucks," Tanya said.

"Yeah, although I get it. Dragons like being special. Having a mage take your powers doesn't exactly leave you with an edge." She sighed. "Still, I wish I could pick up more, especially if Sam's right and Cassandra is only testing the school. It would be best to have as many as I can to keep her off guard."

"Well, what about plant powers?" Tanya asked. "They might take some work but I bet your aunt won't suspect that you'd use an oak tree to attack her."

Sam laughed. "That's something I would like to see."

"What do you say, Kylara? Do you want to try? It's the least I can do after all you've done to help me and how crappy I was to you. Or you could move into our room again." Tanya stood, spread her legs wide, and worked her feet to dig them lightly into the soil.

Kylara smiled. "I want to move, Tanya, I truly do, but if I do, Jasmine will hate me forever."

"She already hates you forever," the girl pointed out.

"I know, but...never mind. Plant-power me or whatever."

Tanya nodded. "The first thing you have to understand is that plants always have some water in reserve. You can use…that water…to make them…grow!"

The tree roots closest to the young dragon mage exploded with new growth and caught her around her ankles. She tried to stand and pull herself free but before she could, more appeared and grasped her wrists.

Instinctively, she pulled against them with one of her hands and tapped into her well of dragon strength. She was able to snap the roots and her hand jerked across her body, suddenly free and able to move. But she had underestimated how hard they had held her, and the force of the sudden release launched her hand across her to touch the dirt.

This was a mistake because as soon as her fingers encountered the soil, more roots emerged and lashed across her hand. Now she was in an even worse position than before. Her right arm was pulled across her body and she was half-seated. This wasn't exactly something she could explode out of.

She glanced at Tanya, who looked a little too proud and way too smug, so she continued to fight to pull free as more roots crawled up her legs and arms. One of the grasping roots poked her and she winced. It drew blood before recoiling.

Her friend stopped immediately. "Sorry. They do that. Although they don't want to drink the blood—my guess is it's too salty—they can sense moisture and always try to reach it."

"No problem," she said, completely immobilized.

"Plus…well, I know you seem to absorb powers when they're used on you, so I thought…uh, that if the root drew blood…" She shrugged.

"You stabbed her on purpose!" Samuel grinned.

"She has dragon healing powers." Tanya's expression was one of extreme guilt and embarrassment.

"It's fine, Tanya, seriously. In fact, it's awesome." Kylara praised her friend which was well-deserved. "Now if you could release me, that would be great."

"No problem," the young dragon said, and the roots loosened and retracted toward the earth. Once they found the soil, they buried themselves and in moments, it was like nothing had happened at all.

"All right, Ky's turn," Sam said. "I have to admit, I'm excited to see you steal someone's powers besides mine."

"You don't like that I can heal you?" Kylara teased.

He shrugged and tried not to blush. Before she could stretch the small victory, Tanya began to instruct her.

"So, the most important part is to feel for the plants. They have desires and needs, exactly like us. What you have to do is give them some of your magic and tell them what they must do in exchange for it."

"You talk to the plants?" she asked, spread her feet wide, and worked them into the dirt as she had seen the other girl do.

"Not in words, no. It's simply something you can feel if that makes sense."

"Nothing about anything we can do makes sense," she said, but she tried to do as instructed. She closed her eyes and attempted to focus on the trees around them and their needs and desires. After a minute, she thought perhaps she felt more…thirsty?

"Do they want a drink of water?" she asked.

Tanya giggled. "No, not at all. You made it rain here a week ago, remember? For these desert plants, that's more than enough water."

"Right. That makes sense." Kylara felt somewhat embarrassed, given that it had been her idea to give the plants water in the first place. She assumed it was foolish to think the same solution would solve her problem with the plants.

"Like I said, feel for the plants. They want to grow and your magic will let them do exactly that."

She nodded and reached out with her magic. Her eyes closed in concentration, she tried to send it into the plants—to give it to them and to cover them in it.

"Uh…Kylara?"

When she opened her eyes, she immediately saw what had triggered Sam's slight concern. She had completely covered a tree in tendrils of her dark energy.

"It doesn't like that," Tanya said matter of factly.

"Right, sorry." She tried to not let herself get frustrated and failed. After a long, slow breath, she tried again, but from the moment she closed her eyes, she knew it wouldn't work. She was too impatient and exasperated to focus beyond the negative emotions.

"Maybe I've absorbed all the powers I can," she said and lowered her arms as she opened her eyes and stepped out of the wide-legged stance she had adopted.

"You mean like you're maxed out?" Sam asked. "Does your inner magic feel full?" he added in a surprisingly accurate impression of Professor Sharra.

"Yes, the river of magic has been dammed," she replied in her much poorer attempt at mimicry.

Tanya sucked her teeth at her fellow students for making fun of their teacher. "Remember what you told me when I first tried to do this. Sometimes, it takes a while."

Kylara nodded. Her friend was right. Her other powers hadn't been immediate. They'd all taken practice. But with Cassandra possibly testing the defenses of the school, time was one thing she didn't feel she had much of.

# CHAPTER TWENTY-FOUR

The day of the Halloween social dawned. Predictably, the school was abuzz with chatter and gossip about who would dance with whom, who wouldn't dance with whom, and exactly how much dancing might happen.

Kylara was excited. Jasmine had certainly talked about it enough, but the young dragon mage also had other priorities. Top of her list was the field trip for her History of Magic class.

They had made no more visits to the pixie realm. It seemed Professor Sharra and Petalwing were close to establishing some type of safety procedure that might make going there possible again, but that hadn't stopped the other professors from planning other excursions.

"I would like to say that all of you should consider yourselves lucky," the professor said. Josue Perez was an exceedingly drab man who wore brown robes that might have once been a more interesting color and unlike so many of the other mages, had no tattoos to augment his magic. He didn't even have an interesting haircut.

Most of his history of human and dragon classes consisted of him monotonously reading about events he had already assigned to the students to read. The only good thing about the class was that the tests, homework, and lectures were almost identical. Kylara didn't have to worry about homework from him at all.

But it seemed as if someone had spiked Professor Perez's coffee with something more interesting or perhaps released an insect inside his cloak. This morning, as they prepared to step through a swirling portal to another part of the world, his heavy mustache twitched with excitement.

"There was much talk of canceling this trip because of these elemental attacks," he explained, "But I pushed back strongly against that. We can't simply shut our education system down and cave to this rogue mage terrorist."

"Is the history of magic that important, sir?" Galen asked. He still had the skeleton of a squirrel on his shoulder. Tanya had repeatedly told Kylara that it was not creepy and she had repeatedly argued that yes, it was.

"If this class had been taught as something more than an elective fifty years ago, we wouldn't be in this mess with a rogue mage." Professor Perez snorted indignantly. "The Steel Dragon's entire war might have been irrelevant if people only paid more attention to the history between us."

The young dragon mage conceded that was a good point, although it might have been more strongly made by a man who didn't spend his lectures trying to put entire classrooms filled with students to sleep.

"Your teacher's right," Amy Williams said, her hands on her hips and the hood of her top bunched around her neck. "School is real important—which is why I expect you all to be on your best behavior. I don't think this trip is a good idea, but I and half my team will work as chaperones so you can all have the education your headmaster thinks you deserve. I expect you to behave as if this field trip is as boring as the professor's regular lectures. Do I make myself clear?"

Professor Perez didn't know what to say about that. He sucked his mustache in and blew it out a few times like he was some kind of bottom-feeding fish that hadn't worked out what it had swallowed.

"Do you think half of your team will be enough given the elemental attacks?" Kylara asked, which earned an elbow in the ribs from Tanya.

"Half of the team is more than enough. The most recent attacks have been light and we'll all be staying together—right, Miss Diamantine?"

"Yes, ma'am," she replied quickly. She didn't particularly like Amy's answer but had no idea what else to say. The thing was that the mage was right. The attacks had been less frequent, and Kylara had barely noticed them. Generally, by the time she even saw a battle, it was already over. The mages won every time and often single-handedly. She wished that reassured her but instead, it made her think about how Sam might be right and these were all merely feints.

"You kids will enter our portal, follow the professor for his tour, pay attention, and not ask stupid questions, and we'll be back for lunch. Got it?"

"Yes, ma'am," the class grumbled.

They all lined up to enter the portal. Amy went first, followed by the professor. The students proceeded through one by one and finally, the rest of the security team brought up the rear.

Kylara was near the back of the line, so when she stepped through, the other students were already poking around what appeared to be an abandoned and blackened castle. They stood outside the structure in a field of tall grass littered with dozens of gravestones. Copses of trees stood here and there, some kind of oak or something that was way larger, thicker, and greener than any of the trees she had ever seen in the desert.

The old ruin stood about a hundred yards away. Professor

Perez was already walking toward it and pointed gravestones out as he went.

"Your professor is teaching. Move it," Amy snapped at Kylara, although it wasn't mean-spirited. She got the sense that the mage knew exactly how the students felt about this boring field trip and simply played the role of hard-nosed chaperone.

With a shrug of acquiescence, she beckoned to Sam and Tanya and the trio hurried to catch up to the rest of the class. She stole a backward glance at Amy. The last security mage came through the portal and the four of them closed it behind them. Their leader gestured at the ruin of the castle and in two other directions, and the mages separated. The first elevated abruptly and landed on the top of the castle—no doubt to serve as a lookout— while the other two stayed closer to the students with Amy, shepherds for wayward learners.

"This is the place of the first battle of the Second Mage War in the New World," Professor Perez gestured behind him at the castle and overgrown grounds with the trees in need of a trim. Nothing else cluttered the landscape. An old dirt road led to the keep, but it was barely discernible as anything more than a line in the tall grass.

"I thought the Second Mage War was mostly fought in Europe and Asia," a bookish mage commented.

"That is a common misconception. It's prevalent because the mage wars were fought before the modern nations of the New World were officially founded. That is, of course, quite different than being fought before the New World was officially 'discovered' based on the tips given to humans by dragon kind." The man punctuated this with a dry, wheezy laugh. He must have slain at history conventions. "Many of the most famous battles were fought in the Old World and considerable blood was shed there, but many dragons and mages died here as well."

"You mean we're not in Scotland or something? This blows!" a dragon shouted to a chorus of giggles.

"Indeed not," Professor Perez responded, although from his tone, it wasn't exactly clear if he knew what "blows" meant in this context.

"This is the estate of a dragon known as the Prairie King. He wished to set up his fiefdom here, much to the chagrin of the local humans and the Dragon Council of the Old World, who used North America as a kind of experiment on what humans would do without dragon intervention. The Prairie King came from South America, installed himself here, and made the locals build this castle out of stone."

"I didn't know there were castles in North America," Karl Midnight said and earned a snicker from Tanya that edged toward nastiness.

"Which is an example of why a quality education is so important," the man snapped in what might have been his most assertive exchange with a student ever.

"What happened to the Prairie King?" Samuel asked.

"He was murdered—in his sleep, in fact." The professor said this as if discussing the importance of tariffs. "A number of poor European immigrants, slaves from Africa, and native people of this continent worked for him. All of this was forced labor, of course, as was common on this continent at the time. In his arrogance, he assumed that none of these…erm…lesser humans would be capable of magic. He discovered how erroneous his hypothesis was when the mages broke through their language barriers by using the shared communication of magic. They collapsed the tower he slept in on top of him, overwhelmed his dragon healing power, and killed him in the process."

"But the castle still has a tower—or most of one anyway," Samuel pointed out.

The stronghold stood behind a stodgy rectangular wall that was about twenty feet tall. Inside, a slightly less stubby keep poked up, its only nod to elevation being the mostly standing but still burned round tower at the back of it.

"Indeed it does," Professor Perez responded and seemed to have warmed to his topic. "The mages who led the rebellion worked out how to communicate and set up a type of collective among the people the Prairie King had captured and forced to work. They decided to stay here and survived with a mixture of simple agriculture, hunting, and gathering—all of which was augmented by the mages' powers, of course. Many historians believe it to be one of the first sites where mages from North America, Europe, and Africa all worked together in a more or less democratic society."

"If it's so important to historians or whatever, how come I've never even heard of this castle?" Karl asked petulantly.

"Because the people who lived here were wiped from the earth," their teacher replied grimly. "When the South American dragons discovered what had happened—you must remember, this was long before electricity and that no one particularly cared what the Prairie King did to the humans—they became enraged. They contacted their compatriots in the Old World who were, at the time, engaged with the mage rebels and the pixies the mages had created to fight in their second war."

"So, they came and annihilated the community?" Galen asked and sounded as proud of the bloodshed as if his family had had some part in it. Kylara realized it was possible that they had. The thought made her stomach turn and his tone didn't help.

"Oh no. Well…yes, the mages here all died, but it was not an annihilation. The message was intercepted by the rebels, who sent their people to defend against the dragons. The ensuing battle was quite epic and bloody. Many lives were lost on both sides, a true tragedy of ignorance. We'll walk through the major stages of it today."

"I'm afraid not, teach," Amy strode through the students to the professor. She whispered something in his ear which was enough to make his mustache and bushy eyebrows almost leap off his face.

"Come along, students. Come along! We need to get inside the walls of the castle as quickly as possible. No dawdling now!"

"What's going on?" Kylara asked and remained where she was.

"Nothing you need to worry about," Amy snapped. "Get inside with the other children and let the professionals handle this." She winked as if that would take the sting out of what she had said.

The mage turned away and faced the south. A great swirling dervish of wind approached—not quite a tornado but a mass of fast-moving air that looked as if it could lift a human or three off the ground with ease.

"I can help."

"I know you can. Get inside. The other students will follow you," Amy replied shortly.

"This one looks stronger than those on campus. It's huge." Kylara didn't move.

"All the more reason for you to get inside." The young woman's jaw was set but there was a gleam in her eyes. She was excited about this fight.

"Come on, Ky. Look," Tanya said and pointed away from the swirling air elemental.

Confused, she looked to the east and saw the prairie burning as a ball of fire rampaged through the tall, mostly dead grass. She wasn't sure what was more troubling—to see the familiar face in the flame or the fact that this elemental only burned a tiny path through the grass and left the remainder as fuel.

"There's another one over there too." Sam pointed to the west. The ground swelled as if an enormously large mole or a whale that could swim through the dirt approached.

"I'll bet a water elemental is coming from the North," Tanya said. "Let's get to the castle so we can see." She darted a look at Sam that Kylara understood to be about her. Neither of her friends wanted her to rush into the fray.

"We can help in this fight," she protested.

"Maybe, but we don't know if they need our help." He put a

hand on her shoulder as if to stop her from running off. "Let's get to the castle and prepare to help in case they do need us."

# CHAPTER TWENTY-FIVE

The elementals pounded into the walls of the castle in a terrifically powerful synchronized strike.

Amy and her mages were ready for them, however.

The fire elemental was met by a mage wielding the water from the bottom of the well to slow the beast of flame. The mage facing the water elemental used tight slices of telekinesis to sever arms of water from its amorphous body. Amy battled the wind elemental herself and used her wind powers to suck and push the elemental back so it couldn't simply fly over the wall and into the students. Her colleague battling the earth elemental used augmented strength to weather the rocks and waves of earth it threw at him, but the entity was too clever. It threw a rock, then another, followed by another, and when the defender fell into a rhythm, it rocketed a plinth of hardened earth from beneath his feet and hurled him away.

"We can't let him get hurt!" Kylara shouted, took her dragon form, and lashed out with a messy dark energy web at the end of a rope of power. She managed to catch him before he made impact with the hard earth.

"Thanks," he shouted as he landed and immediately leapt into the fight against the earth elemental, as futile as it seemed.

He wasn't the only one who was outmatched, though. The mage battling the fire elemental suddenly found herself impotent when the water being got a rivulet of water into the well and repositioned itself in the center of the courtyard inside the castle walls.

The mage fighting this elemental redoubled his efforts to slice the arms and limbs from the creature, but there was now an almost limitless source of water for it to draw on.

Only Amy seemed capable of holding her own against her opponent. That in itself was evidence of how powerful they were, as she was widely known to be the most powerful mage in the world.

"I won't let these beings steamroll me!" Karl Midnight shouted to no one in particular, transformed into his black dragon body, and lashed out at the earth elemental. He made a web of darkness over the point in the ground where it tried to rise into the courtyard.

"He's right," Kylara shouted. "There are more of us than there are of them!"

"Ky, don't!" Tanya protested.

"We have to! If we don't fight now, the mages will be overwhelmed and we'll have to fight without them," Sam said and although he remained in his human form, he ignited his hands with bright yellow light.

"That won't happen," Kylara said and dive-bombed the earth elemental. It had moved away from where Karl had tried to block it but before it was able to emerge fully in the courtyard, she drove into it with a diamond-encrusted shoulder. Diamond was harder than stone, and the entity retreated into the earth again and this time, it roared with the sound of an earthquake.

It began to rain as Tempest took to the sky and called a storm that dampened the blaze of the fire spirit.

She added her power to his and created a great gust of wind that thrust the air elemental Amy fought out into the grassy field.

"To the keep!" the lead mage yelled to the students and the wide-eyed professor. "If you don't know how to fight, get inside the inner keep. Those who think they can handle themselves, choose an elemental and support my mages!"

The battle became harder to follow as the attackers pulled on previously untapped wells of energy. The water elemental wasn't able to attack quite so enthusiastically. Every time it launched a liquid arm, Samuel sliced it with a blade of light. The water that fell to the ground was then absorbed by Tanya—whose new power had progressed considerably—and she fed it into the plants that pushed upward into the courtyard.

The earth elemental tried constantly to break through Karl Midnight's dark energy. He tried to keep it contained, but the creature fired tiny spikes of rock from the earth that were only a couple of inches wide. These were able to penetrate his web and already, the young dragon was bleeding in multiple places.

The fire elemental had weakened in the growing rain until a dragon blasted it with fire. It raged to life, latched onto a tree inside the courtyard, and engulfed it branch by branch as it grew in intensity. Tanya tried to make the tree shake it loose, but the invader was too tenacious. The movement only gave it more oxygen and it burned brighter.

Amy, Kylara, and Tempest faced the air elemental, but even between the three of them, they were able to do little more than hold it at bay. The two students took turns to throw messy gusts of wind at it, while the mage used her telekinesis or wind power to haul its spinning form away from the students running into the castle.

Galen Stormwing watched all this in mute terror, his back to the interior side of the wall around the castle and his body half-hidden by debris from a wall that must have fallen centuries before. He wanted to help his brother but he didn't have storm powers. All he had was the skeleton of a squirrel, which wouldn't do a damn thing against creatures made of the elements.

Some of the dragons managed to consistently thrust elementals back so they had to continually reform themselves. He didn't know if their enemies would tire, while some of the students were already out of breath. Currently, the battle was a stalemate, but if the dragons and mages didn't win the short game, he put his money on the elementals.

What they needed were allies who wouldn't tire any more than the elementals would. He looked at his squirrel. It never tired and never slept. It had even lost a few bones but continued as it had before. Unfortunately, a squirrel wouldn't help against these massive beings.

Galen reached out with his power and felt for dead bison or deer, although he hoped that maybe he'd stumble across a bear or a mountain lion.

What he felt resting beneath the surface of the soil was far more impressive. The professor hadn't been lying when he'd said there had been losses on both sides of this battle. He could feel all of them. There were well over a dozen dragons inside the courtyard itself, plus many more outside the walls.

Between their massive bodies were perhaps a hundred humans. Many of the bones were broken or damaged, but he could sense one dragon particularly close to him that was almost intact. It had a single snapped rib that bent inward. He wondered if its heart had been punctured.

It didn't matter, though, he reminded himself. The dragon had been dead for hundreds of years and how it died was irrelevant. All that mattered now was that its bones were still strong and it might be able to push these damn elementals back and away from him, his brother, and the other students.

He reached out and sent his inner magic toward the skeleton, then inside it. It surprised him how easy it was to infuse the long-dead corpse with his magic.

"I guess practicing with you helped, huh, buddy?" Galen muttered to the squirrel as he forced more magic into the buried dragon. It was different than the tiny creature, however. For one thing, it took considerably more magic to fill the bones, but there was something else too. After a moment, he realized that the bones had inherent magic to them. He accepted that it made sense as he knew dragons couldn't exist without magic. It would have been impossible to fly if not for the power that flowed through their bodies. He hadn't expected that to last beyond death, though.

The youngster began to sweat as he focused on filling the bones of this dead warrior with his magic. As he tried to raise the skeleton, the castle seemed to come apart all around him. Despite Tanya's best efforts, three of the trees in the courtyard were burning. The earth elemental had pushed past Midnight's web of dark magic and currently battered the young dragon's head repeatedly against a stone wall. Karl used his dark magic to make a snarl of webbing around his head to protect himself, but it took all his energy to maintain this life-preserving defense.

The water elemental now extended arms of water from the soil itself, which made it much harder to defend against.

Amy Williams was hurled aside by the air elemental. She pushed to her feet, but her nose was bleeding—not a good sign for mages, Galen knew.

He focused and released more of his energy into the skeleton until he felt so weak that he collapsed against the wall and slid to the moist earth.

"Come on…" He grunted as a flash of pain in one nostril served as a prelude to the trickle of blood that followed.

Finally, the dragon's skeleton shifted. It was a small movement, so slight that the surface of the soil above it didn't so much as tremble, but it was all the encouragement he needed.

He pushed to his feet. "Rise," he stammered as he stood slowly. "Rise! I tell you—rise!"

The dragon thrust from the earth. First, one massive claw drove out of the soil. It dug in and used the anchor point to shove up against the dirt. The shoulder, neck, and wings pushed through and the other front arm came next. It immediately stabbed its talons into the ground to provide purchase for the long-dead skeleton to rise.

The rest of it followed quickly. Ribs that had been loose popped into place. The tail tightened and became a solid line of bone, then loosened as it swung into the bulk of the water elemental and a few of its arms disintegrated into nothing but harmless droplets of water.

Galen was elated. He had hoped that the dragon could help, but it was already proving to be more powerful than he'd imagined. The water elemental raged against it, but the skeleton felt no pain and its body was mostly empty space. The gouts of water that the attacker tried to blast at it went through the hollows where its body would have been if it still had flesh.

The being retreated into its well and the dragon lunged on top of the hole in the earth like a fox chasing a rat down a hole.

But the water elemental wasn't alone in this fight. Its earth ally pushed from the soil with a great thrust of stone that cracked the massive skull and the skeleton toppled into a wall.

The dragon righted itself, but the earth elemental and the water elemental joined ranks for a united attack aimed at trying to crack the bones that comprised its arms and legs.

The dragons and mages who had fought the two invaders watched the spectacle in open-mouthed shock. They didn't rush into battle because they were wounded or out of breath—or perhaps didn't want to get caught between the adversaries.

"One won't be enough," Galen murmured and reached out for another of the skeletons. He focused on a smaller one this time and infused it with his magic. Oddly enough, it was easier and he realized that the first was no longer draining his powers very much. It seemed like once he charged the beast, its latent magic was more than enough to sustain it.

Soon, the second crawled from the earth. He ordered it to focus on the water elemental and it bolted to the well and drove the being from sight.

No one seemed to have associated Galen and his skeleton squirrel with these new dragons, but that was fine. There would be time for congratulations later. Right now, he needed to raise more of them.

With effort, he managed a third, then a fourth. These two threw themselves at the air elemental. They weren't able to do much to it, but they jumped and lunged constantly through its wind currents to disrupt them, which made it difficult for the entity to strengthen its attack enough to do much damage.

But it still wasn't sufficient. It was nowhere near enough.

So Galen, growing drunk on the power he felt coursing through the dragons, raised a fifth, sixth, seventh, and eighth in rapid succession. He sent these at the earth elemental before he summoned another four to fight against the other attackers.

With twelve skeletal dragons fighting, those gathered there were finally given a reprieve. They raced to the castle and rushed inside while the mages and Kylara stood at the door to guard their retreat.

That suited Galen perfectly. No mages or dragons involved meant he could see what these skeleton dragons could truly do.

Already, he'd narrowed the fight to only three elementals. Since the water one had crawled down the well, there had been no sign of it. He focused on the earth one next.

The first dragon he'd summoned—the largest of them—turned its attention to the earth elemental while the others supported it by preventing its quarry from escaping. The dragon simply reached its massive claw into the dirt and scooped it out like a raccoon snatching a crawfish from a stream.

Yanked from its natural habitat, it was bizarre indeed. If it resembled anything at all, it was a ball of roots, but rather than wood, it was made of filaments of dirt, stone, and even slivers of metal. It thrashed and clawed at the hand bones that held it captive. The dragon simply swung its bony arm and hurled the entity over the wall in a great arc that catapulted it through the sky.

The dragons turned on the fire elemental next.

It lashed out with blazing arms of flame, but these found no purchase on the dried bone. The defenders pressed forward in a united assault to deny the being the trees it used to fuel itself. It became smaller and smaller until, in a great roar of sparks, it launched an ember high above them.

The dragons leapt after it and flapped the bony appendages that had once held the membranes that granted them flight in life.

But the ember was in the domain of the air elemental. It caught the tiny flame and whisked it away, over the castle wall and in the same direction that the earth elemental had been thrown.

Galen smiled. He'd done it. Against all odds, he'd saved his classmates, his professor, and even the security team. He couldn't wait for the Halloween social and was sure he'd be the talk of the evening.

"Rest now, friends!" he said to the dragons and walked out from his place of safety behind the boulder near the wall.

The dragons turned to him. They stared at him with empty eye sockets as if appraising him. He welcomed their stares and wondered what they thought of him. Did they see him as a father? A savior? Did they have thoughts at all?

"You've done well. Now, return to your resting place," he said.

The dragons ignored him.

Confused, he tried to revoke the magic he had given them to animate their bodies.

This, however, was the wrong thing to do.

The creatures roared and somehow vibrated themselves to make a horrible, rattling sound that shook his bones.

"Can you control them or not, kid?" Amy demanded from her doorway.

"I can!" he shouted, a little offended by what she was insinuating.

He rushed forward and tried to get closer to the undead dragons in the hopes that might help him regain control. Once he thought he was close enough, he tried again to take their power but the dragons didn't like it. They roared in response.

In the next moment, they attacked the mages guarding the students.

# CHAPTER TWENTY-SIX

Kylara thought they were all dead. She simply didn't see how a couple of mages and a handful of tired dragons with less combat experience than her could possibly stand against a dozen dragon skeletons.

But the mages were more prepared for the assault than she gave them credit for. They formed a wall of telekinetic energy and whipped wind, fire, and stone that the dragon skeletons hurled themselves against but did not break. At least not on their first strike.

They were so large that they couldn't all attack at once. When the first barrage of tooth and claw clattered against their defenses, Amy used her powers to force the dragon skeleton at the forefront of the vanguard through his allies and against the back wall. Bones broke and fell away, but the skeleton didn't stop its attack. It would take more than a few fractured ribs to stop these reanimated bones of the dead.

"We're missing a student!" Professor Perez chirped, although he didn't make any effort to run out the door and through the gauntlet of undead skeletons.

"It's Galen!" Tanya shouted over the sound of another dragon skeleton driving into the mages' rapidly crumbling defenses. "It has to be him who summoned them. He took control of dragon skeletons in the Pixie dimension as well."

"Yes, it is, but do you have any idea why he's attacking us?" Amy grunted as she used her telekinesis to rip a huge stone out of the castle wall and crush a dragon arm that had pushed through the barrier.

"They were attacking the elementals first," Kylara interjected. "Maybe he thinks one of them is inside here with us. Come on, Tanya. We have to find him!"

"No, Kylara. Dammit, that is not a good plan!" Amy shouted but she ignored her.

She caught her friend by the hand—both had taken their human forms inside the castle—and raced toward the door. A dragon attacked, she paused, and when it was forced back by flames cast by one of the mages, they raced out into the courtyard.

All the while, Amy continued to yell. "No, Kylara, do not go out there! I am serious, young lady! You will get detention or not get to eat a whole cow or whatever teachers do to punish dragons." As soon as it was clear that the young dragon mage did not intend to obey, she cursed and changed her tone. "Cover them, dammit! Cover them!"

They ducked past the barricade and dodged beneath the whiplash strike of a dragon's skeletal tail.

"Galen!" Tanya shouted as Kylara threw up a web of black threads to catch a dragon's claw before it impaled her friend. The dragon—even denuded of its meat and skin—was still so strong that she had to anchor the webbing to the side of the castle behind it to stop it from hitting them.

"This way!" she shouted and pulled the other girl along, who looked frantically for Galen.

"Dragon forms!" she ordered.

"Right!" Tanya said and transformed.

Kylara was faster, though, which was a good thing because the skeletons had now focused their attacks on these new intruders in their funeral grounds. Claws and the spiky, bony appendages of raw tail bones hammered into her. It hurt but her diamond scales were tough and didn't allow the bone to draw blood.

But she had been in enough duels by now to know that even if she wasn't made to bleed, too many bruises could essentially render her dragon healing power inert while her enemies pulverized her and the squishy organs inside.

"Galen!" Tanya shouted again.

To their immediate relief, he replied.

"They won't listen!"

Okay, so there were admittedly better things he could have said, but it was progress. At least their classmate hadn't transformed into a fully murderous individual with his new powers over the dead.

"Where are you?" Tanya shouted as Kylara blasted a skeleton in the face with a beam of light that flaked some of its bone away but did little else.

A blast of fire answered their question—something the undead had yet to prove themselves capable of.

She fought toward the crumbled part of the wall the flames had come from. Skeletons attacked and scratched her flanks as they tried and failed to crack her diamond scales. She kept herself between them and Tanya, knowing the other dragon didn't have the same defenses.

They almost made it through the courtyard but one of the beasts swung its claws under her and managed to inflict some gashes between her diamond scales. The blood seemed to focus the other dragons and she knew her advantage had lost much of its potency.

But they'd reached Galen. He had transformed into his human form to make space for the two girls. Tanya did so as well and clambered into the alcove made of debris and the wall from which it had fallen.

"You have to make them go back into the ground," she said as Kylara tried to protect the human-shaped students from the barrage of bony claws and teeth.

"They won't listen to me. It's like once I empowered them, they stopped needing my magic. I can still feel them but it's like they can't feel me."

"Shit," Kylara said as another skeleton raked her across the face. It managed to jab her in the eye, so half her vision was suddenly only blood.

"This is bad. Shit, this is seriously bad, Kylara. We shouldn't have come out here," Tanya said in agitation.

"Yeah, well, we're here now. I'd love to go back too."

"They won't let us!" To Galen's credit, he continued to try to control the skeletal beasts even though his efforts were fruitless.

Kylara could see through the maelstrom of bones that the mages attempted to fight to reach where the three students were, but every time they made any progress, the dragons attacked them with renewed vigor.

"Should we run?" he asked and sounded completely panicked, which prevented her from slapping him across the face right then and there.

"We're not leaving them," she snapped.

"No, we need to stay and fight," Tanya said, her gaze not on a dragon but one of the trees in the courtyard.

"Tanya, I don't mean to be rude, but I don't see how a branch will exactly—" She stopped talking as the nearest oak tree leaned forward to intercept the dragon that had lunged at her.

At first, she thought the skeleton might simply be blown to pieces by the force of the impact, but it struggled under the weight of the trunk. Fortunately, it wasn't only the tree trunk that held it trapped. The roots extended from the soil. Already, they'd grasped one of its front claws and its tail. It thrashed and fought, but it had to put down another claw to get leverage to break free.

Exactly like Tanya had done when Kylara tried to escape, she used her roots to entangle the beast's other foot. The roots began to sink into the ground and hauled two of their captive's legs and its tail into the soil itself. The dragon struggled and thrashed and bucked as if trying to dislodge an invisible rider. Its skull was forced to the earth by a thwack from another branch and the moment it touched the dirt, more roots immediately wound around its jaw. As soon as the massive head was partly submerged, something changed. Instead of fighting and resisting, it seemed to accept its return to being buried. It was swallowed and fought no more.

"All right, new plan!" Kylara shouted to the mages. "Bind the dragons as close to the ground as you can and let Tanya finish them off!"

Fearing they might need an example—or worse, that Amy might not want to listen to the strategic advice of a seventeen-year-old—she leapt out to intercept the closest dragon. They collided painfully and the skeleton lashed at her with its claws. She grimaced but made no real effort to stop it. While it struck, she directed dozens of ribbons of shadow through its ribs and around its spine and tail to drag it down. When they landed together, she rolled aside and threaded these ribbons through the dirt to drag the captive to where it could be trapped effectively.

A tiny sapling exploded with growth. Its trunk—not more than three feet high—extended vertically and thickened as dozens of ropey roots wound around the downed dragon and pulled it to a place of rest.

"I gotta say, plant powers are way better when not in the desert!" Tanya exclaimed. "That storm you and Tempest made earlier was a good call. I feel like I can do anything."

"Stay focused. You might have to do everything," Kylara replied, although she beckoned to the clouds above to increase the drizzle to a stronger rain. If Tanya needed water, she would give her water.

She ducked as one of the undead dragons rocketed overhead and bulldozed into the far wall of the keep. Before it could move, a huge boulder careened after it and followed the same trajectory until it shattered the creature as if it were a fly swatter hitting a particularly leggy and segmented insect. Broken bones clattered to the earth, and whatever energy had animated the dragon was no more.

"Mages, brute-force them or bind them. They need to be destroyed or buried!" Amy shouted from the doorway to the castle.

Another boulder elevated sharply. By Amy? Kylara wasn't sure but it must have been because the other mages used wind and fire to force a skeleton back and the floating rock crushed it.

A blur of darkness raced from the castle that she recognized as Karl Midnight wrapped in a net of protection. He must have seen what she had done and now tried to use his powers in the same way.

Sure enough, one of the dragons that advanced aggressively toward the keep tripped and fell when its ankles were lashed with ropy darkness.

"Tanya! You got it?" Kylara pointed.

"No problem," the girl replied. This dragon was already near a partially bent tree. Its roots reached out hungrily and sucked the beast into the earth, straightening the trunk in the process.

Karl cursed and the lashings holding the last of the skeletons vanished as one raked its claws across his back and knocked him off his feet.

Kylara roared and a blast of lightning sizzled from the sky and struck the beast with such energy that some of its bones simply exploded. While it tried to pull itself together, Tanya struck and the closest tree responded and began to drag it into the dirt. The dragon—already wounded—barely fought. It looked as if the ground wanted to swallow it—as if the bones being unearthed was somehow wrong.

The rest of the battle blended in the young dragon mage's head. By the time it was over, she wasn't exactly sure how many of the dragons had been dragged underground and how many had been destroyed, but she did know that without the mages and Tanya working together, she and all the other students would have been dead.

The courtyard looked completely different. Instead of a mostly grassy space with a few large trees, it was now overgrown with oaks of a variety of sizes. The earth was almost completely covered by the woody growth of tree roots that had woven together in an elaborate carpet. If Kylara had walked into it without knowing what she did, she would have assumed that it had taken hundreds of years for the trees to grow to such heights and for their roots to fuse into an almost continuous piece of wood. In reality, it had been less than twenty minutes.

It had been the most exhausting battle of her life.

# CHAPTER TWENTY-SEVEN

The transition through the portal didn't seem strange this time because Galen had wanted to leave so badly. His mind still struggled to comprehend what had happened. He had never had any issues with the squirrel and the first dragon he'd summoned had worked great. It was the other eleven that had been the problem.

All he wanted to do was return to his dorm, take a shower to wash away the flecks of bone and dirt that covered every inch of him, and go to sleep. He'd lost his squirrel in the battle and wanted to try to practice more the next day. It seemed important that he determine if all the things he reanimated could survive without his magic.

"Tanya, thank you for your quick action," Amy said. Although she spoke directly to the young dragon, her words were loud enough for the entire class to hear. "It was disgusting to see the dead turned into weapons like that."

"The first two saved us," Galen protested.

"No, sir," the mage snapped. "The first two interrupted a battle. We could have come out of that."

"It didn't look like it to me." He couldn't believe that Amy blamed him for the dragons and forgot what they'd achieved. The only reason they had all even been alive to see the creatures turn on them was because they had saved them in the first place. "We needed them and you know it."

"I agree with Miss Williams," Professor Perez said from behind his mustache. "Many of those dragons were heroes—flawed ones, but heroes all the same. It was not right to desecrate their memories and that place by tearing them from their resting place. You ought to be ashamed."

Galen reddened. These mages were impossible. While they looked only at him, the entire class was behind him. All the other dragons now stared at him like he was a freak. If they hadn't realized the loser with no powers except the weird ability to reanimate a dead squirrel had been the one to raise the dragons that had almost killed them, they knew now.

It seemed that the professor knew the damage that had been done to the young dragon's already lousy reputation. He turned hastily to the rest of the class and sent them to their dorms or the cafeteria. When the boy tried to follow, his shoes wouldn't move. For a moment, he thought he was being sucked into the earth like the skeletons had been before he realized it was the bossy mage, Amy. It seemed she wasn't done trying to embarrass him.

"That was completely irresponsible of you," she said, her voice low now that the other students were gone.

"I—"

"Please listen. There is no reason to ever push yourself past your ability to control. You should have realized that a dragon was a level way beyond a squirrel."

"Furthermore, those bodies belonged to sentient beings!" the professor added indignantly. "Your squirrel was…unsettling but acceptable. But to do that to a thinking being is completely unacceptable."

"So you're saying it's wrong to use my power?" Galen tried to control his voice, but like his powers over the dead, it got away from him.

"Of course there are wrong ways to use your power," Amy snapped. "Any mage knows that. It's high time dragons learned it too. When my powers first activated, I killed two dragons with my telekinesis. I lost control and it hurt people. That was wrong."

He felt the blood drain from his face. He could not believe that this mage had spoken to him that way. "Are you…are you threatening me?"

"What? No!" she replied as if he were a complete and utter moron for even standing up to her. "I'm only saying you need to learn how to control your powers before you go and do something stupid like that again."

"Or what? You'll control them for me?"

"Galen, I know you come from a well-respected line of dragons, but that does not mean you get to talk to the Steel Dragon's ally this way," Professor Perez said with a frown. He seemed uncomfortable with the direction of the conversation. "Perhaps this should be addressed privately instead of in front of the—"

Galen cut him off. "Oh, I get it. She can threaten to kill me with her telekinesis, but I can't make a mistake one time? I only need practice!"

"You cannot truly be considering practicing with more dragons," the man said to him as if it wasn't a total insult.

"How else am I supposed to learn to control them?" he demanded, furious now.

"It's not your place to control the bodies of thinking beings," Amy said.

"But that's exactly what I can do!" he roared and took his dragon shape without meaning to. Amy didn't step back, though, even though he could have crushed her. She remained in place and used her powers to make the air between them shimmer with off-blue energy.

"What you can do is march your butt to the headmaster's office, where you, me, and Amythist can have a discussion about how you will learn about control and respect."

"Respect?" Galen laughed. "You want to talk to me about respect? I am a Stormwing. I know about respect—like the fact that you have to give it to earn it and—"

She cut him off. "Exactly. You showed no respect to those dead dragons and the lives they lived."

"You show no respect to me!" he yelled. "All I need is practice. I'm new at this and already saved everyone, but you yell at me in front of everyone about learning to control it? Well, guess what? I'm in school to learn how to control these powers. Although I guess there's not a point if my teachers don't even want me to practice."

"The boy does have a point about being dressed down in front of—"

Galen didn't hear the rest of whatever weak comment Professor Perez intended to make. He pumped his wings and took to the sky to give himself some space to think and practice.

"Galen! Galen, don't make me stop you!" Amy shouted—the nerve of her.

"No, no, let him go," the professor mumbled. "He merely needs to calm. He'll be back for lunch."

The young dragon heard nothing else as he flew from the campus and out into the desert. He couldn't believe how rude the two mages had been and how badly they'd treated him.

But maybe part of what they said was right. It was irresponsible for him to use his power without being able to completely control it. When he had been able to control all twelve of the dragons, the fight against the elementals had been a breeze. If he could only practice, he would show people what his powers could do.

He couldn't wait to show the world what he was capable of.

# CHAPTER TWENTY-EIGHT

With so many students tired, wounded, and terrified by the attack of elementals and skeletons of the dead, the Halloween social was ruined.

Kylara still attended for Jasmine's sake, but it quickly became apparent that she hadn't needed to. Hardly anyone was there, but her roommate managed to convince a dragon to dance with her. The girl had never looked so happy, she thought as she slipped away. Then, she slept for about twelve hours.

When she woke, she discovered Jasmine was already awake and that the mage had prepared tea.

"It was very kind of you to have your friend tell everyone about the social," Jasmine said, completely without sarcasm. "I don't think I would have had such a good time without your help."

"Uh…you're welcome?" she stammered, wiped the sleep from her eyes, and reached for the tea, hoping there was caffeine in it.

"That's why I think you should move in with her again." The girl smiled over the rim of her cup.

"You're…happy so you want me to move out?" She hadn't had enough sleep for this.

"I know you and Fastwing made up and that you've only stayed with me because you were worried I would have been… upset if you had moved out."

"No way. I…uh, like it here."

"You were right," Jasmine said. "I was waiting for you to move out and turn your back on your rightful place among the mages since day one. You didn't and I respect that, so you can move out with no hard feelings."

"Just like that?"

"Well, I also heard that everyone was almost killed by that loser Galen and that it was you and your friend who led the charge and saved everyone. Being a leader is a sign of a dragon. Plus…well, you demonstrated that mages and dragons do need each other. If the rumors can be believed, that is."

"Oh yeah, they can be believed and you know what? I think you're right. You probably want to have your space to yourself anyway, so I'll get out of your hair if that's cool."

Kylara had tried so hard to get on Jasmine's good side that she wouldn't waste this opportunity. If the girl seemed happy and she wanted her to move in with Tanya—no hard feelings—why would she argue?

"Let me gather my things," she said and slid out of bed.

"Here—allow me, Lady Diamantine," her roommate said with mock formality. She used her telekinesis to pick Kylara's things up, including her toothbrush, her notebooks, and her pens. She opened the drawers where her clothes were kept and whipped them above her head. The mage then took this cloud and packed everything neatly into a piece of her own luggage her roommate hadn't noticed until it was closed and zipped.

"Uh…thanks?" she said weakly.

"You're very welcome. I'll see you around, all right?" Jasmine smiled and Kylara made her exit.

The walk to the other dorm was surreal. It continued to feel that way until she knocked on Tanya's door—her old door—and waited for the girl to answer. With bleary eyes and a hastily pulled-on but still extravagantly unnecessary bathrobe, her best friend yanked the door open.

"Ky?" was about all she managed to say without yawning. "What are you doing up at this hour? Didn't you go to the social last night?"

"I did and it sucked."

"Sorry?"

"No, it's great! Jasmine was super-happy about it because she got to dance with a dragon."

"Which dragon? No, never mind, it's way too early. Is the cafeteria open? Have you had coffee? I want coffee."

"Tanya, you're a dragon. You don't need coffee. Flush your system with your healing ability and you'll be fine."

Her friend grumbled but she straightened and her eyes widened, evidence that she'd done as suggested. "You know you can't do that every day, right? Dragons still need sleep like we need oxygen. Now, can you please tell me what on earth you're doing at my door?"

"It's our door, Tanya."

"Wait—you mean you're finally moving back in?"

In response, she lifted the piece of luggage Jasmine had packed for her and thrust it into the dragon's arms.

Tanya promptly tossed it behind her and onto Kylara's old bed and wrapped her arms around her friend in a hug so tight it only could have been achieved with dragon strength.

A few weeks passed in relative ease. Now that Kylara was back living with Tanya, school felt like a home instead of a place where she had to survive for as long as she could. Jasmine was true to her word and remained polite although not exactly warm. No more elemental attacks came, not even the small testing feints.

Sam and Tanya believed that this was because Cassandra's attack on the Prairie King's castle had been such a failure, but the young dragon mage wasn't convinced. Still, it was pleasant to not watch the defenders race off to combat her aunt's elemental spirits every few days.

The only thing that was out of place was Galen Stormwing. No one had heard from him since he'd left after the field trip. The mage security team searched for him multiple times and the Steel Dragon had even sent in a team of dragons to try to locate him, but there was no sign of the skeleton summoner. This was a constant point of rumor for many of the students at the Lumos School.

Kylara had been pulled into a conversation about him more than once, but the fact that no one had found him didn't surprise her. The desert was vast and he could fly. He could be hiding almost anywhere in the desert or even beyond it. The Rocky Mountains weren't far, nor were the endless fields of the Midwest. It didn't stretch her imagination to believe that one dragon could escape being found. After all, Hester Diamantine had managed to avoid detection for years, and she hadn't even moved around.

One positive change was that Petalwing and Professor Sharra had finally agreed on some rules to make travel to the other dimension possible again. The pixie was extremely hesitant to allow any more travel. She simply didn't want any lives to be lost to the forces there and had made it increasingly clear that the realm didn't belong to the pixies. They had not created it or anything like that.

Rather, it was a place of almost pure magic, a kind of pocket dimension that the pixies had discovered and expanded. They'd brought in many of the plants, insects, and creatures that abounded there. But there had been accidents. Creatures that died there didn't exactly stay dead, proof-positive being the cat-sized dragon skeletons that had attacked Tanya and Galen.

Petalwing would not risk any dragon lives being lost, both because she detested the idea of a dragon dying and because she knew that in the pixie realm, they might not stay dead. If she had her way, they might never have returned at all, but Professor Sharra had argued for another attempt and often in front of the class.

"We have five other pixies besides you who are willing to help. What if we took only six students at a time? That way, no one could wander off," was the crux of the professor's argument, delivered again and again in a dozen different ways.

Finally, the pixie had relented and agreed to resume visits to the strange realm. The class had been ecstatic until they discovered that the professor had already divided them into groups and that they would have no choice as to when they would go or who they would travel with.

Professor Sharra more or less arranged the students in reverse potency of powers. That meant Tanya—who had already gone to the dimension and earned a power—was dead last. Kylara was in a group a few before that since she had so many powers as well. Kylara suspected that she would have been in the last group but that the headmaster had intervened. Sam had already made his trip and failed to learn any new powers, although he didn't mind. He'd worked on his finger lasers, although he was careful to not carve his name into any more trees since they would tattle to Tanya if she asked.

So when the day came for Kylara to go to the realm, she couldn't help but be excited and relatively guilt-free about leaving Tanya behind to study in class with a substitute professor while she went to a magical land to master new powers.

The six students—her and five classmates she didn't really know, which was probably another indication of the Headmaster at play in her affairs—lined up in the U between the main buildings of campus on one side of a glowing portal that the six pixies had opened.

They entered one by one and they emerged in the same peaceful meadow with its rock-lined pools filled by trickling water.

When she stepped through, Petalwing flitted over to instruct her.

"Hello, Kylara! How do you do?" The pixie bowed so deeply it became a front flip.

"I'm good, Petalwing, and yourself?" She bowed as deeply to the tiny pixie as she would have to any dragon.

"Quite pleased any time a dragon bows to me. Oh, but you are not a dragon at all, are you?" The gleam in her oversized eyes said she already knew the answer to that question.

Still, it was probably wise to humor the being of pure magic in this strange realm. "That's right. I'm a mage who can absorb powers."

"It is very curious." She flitted all around her, poked gently at her, and even sniffed her. Kylara got the sense that if the pixie had antennae, she would use them. "Your essence almost reminds me of pixies. It's as if there is somehow more magic in you than in most dragons or mages."

"Is that possible?"

"The human who invented the idea of a spectrum was very wise, young Kylara. All things exist on a spectrum—life, intelligence, love, hate, and magic too. There are beings with less magic than you and beings with more. It is your place on the spectrum that is odd, not the spectrum itself."

Kylara nodded and tried to process this. Did that mean Amy existed higher on this spectrum than most mages? And what of the Steel Dragon and her legendary acquisition of powers in this realm? Did that advance her in one direction, or did she always have that power and simply learned to access it while she was there? "Is it possible for me to move on this spectrum?"

"It is. But it may also not be necessary." Petalwing winked. It seemed pixies liked their ambiguous statements. "Come, let us train. I was hoping to teach you the power of fire!" She laughed maniacally in what the student hoped was an odd magical being's attempt at humor.

They got to work and the girl moved through a series of stances that were supposed to transform her inner magic into heat, then flame. She mastered the heat without difficulty, which her teacher praised her profusely for, but when she admitted that she had the power because she had already taken it from another dragon, the pixie was forced to try new methods.

"Perhaps the issue is not your inner magic but how you express it. Come, let us give you a target for these flames of fury."

They walked a short way through the tall grasses. Petalwing fluttered from side to side in front of her, looking for something, and finally alighted on a mostly dead bush that grew in the grass.

"This bush is almost dead. Its lifecycle nearly over," the creature explained prosaically. "It needs flames to burn it to ash and clear this space for other plants but also to free its seed. I want you to burn this little guy."

Kylara nodded, focused on the mostly dead bush, and tried to set it on fire but without success. She tried more of the stances, but none of them accomplished anything. "Maybe I should try it in dragon form?"

Petaling shook her head. "In dragon form, you will simply rely upon the mechanics you've always relied upon to create fire. It is a form of magic tied to that body. It is these assumptions we must break if you are to become awesome and rad like us pixies!"

She nodded and tried again, but with the same dismal result.

"Perhaps if you see me do it, you will better understand how it works." The creature didn't wait for an answer. She conjured a ball of fire in front of her and kicked it at the bush with a loud, "*Hi-yaa!*"

It struck the target which ignited immediately and the flames moved from dried leaf to desiccated twig to stick to branch.

"Can you sense the magic?" the pixie asked.

Kylara could feel every bit of it, but it wasn't the flames she sensed but the plant itself. "It's in pain. I can feel it calling for help."

"Oh, dear! You must help it—hurry!" Petalwing squealed as if she hadn't been the one to set the stupid bush on fire.

She reached out to it and felt its pain as her own. It didn't mind them burning its leaves or the twiggy growth at the end of its branches, but it most certainly did not want its trunk to be touched by the flame. She used her magic to help to dry out the branch that was on fire. At the same time, she made the bush thicken its bark around the part of it that it did not want to be burned.

The limb, weakened, fell away and when the bush was no longer connected to the part of itself that was ablaze, it promptly stopped caring. She decided in that moment that plants were quite weird.

"Fascinating! Your professor told me you possessed powers but did not list the ability to control plant growth as one of them. Did you learn this from the dragon who discovered that ability here?"

"I did, yes. Tanya is my best friend and she's practiced this with me. This is the first time I've been able to use it, though."

"That is perhaps because this realm is already so thick with magic," Petalwing intoned sagely. "It's why many can discover their powers here. Come, let us practice with this ability. Hopefully, you will be able to use it when you return to your world."

They set to without further discussion. The pixie made demands, and Kylara would perform them. First, she made a plant grow its roots, then another wave its branches. She moved on to leaf growth and blooming flowers, although she wondered the entire time what she'd be capable of when she went home. Tanya had practiced some of these exact abilities without success. If she came here, would she be able to transfer those skills out? She certainly hoped that was the case.

"You are doing very well." Petalwing had paused for a break after what had felt like hours, although the sun had not moved an inch from its position overhead.

"Thanks, yeah. This has felt great," she admitted. "There is one thing I've wanted to try, though."

"Oh yes, please! You humans—or human-esque beings—are always so creative. What did you wish to do?"

"Tanya has wondered if it's possible to make trees move—or not simply move so much as walk. Do you think it's possible for these powers to help a tree lift its roots from the soil and travel across the land?"

"It is certainly an exciting thing to try." The little creature glowed with anticipation. "Come, let us see if we can move one of the trees that grow on the border of this meadow deeper into the forest."

Kylara strode through the tall grass while Petalwing darted above it until they were perhaps twenty feet away from the tree line. The pixie pointed out a tree that had encroached a little into the meadow. "See if you can convince that one to go back into the forest."

She nodded and reached out with her magic to fill the tree and augment its natural strength and energy with hers. When she thought it had sufficient, she asked it if it wished to go deeper into the woods and closer to more of the swampy water Tanya had described. The tree agreed that it would, so she tried to sink her magic into its roots and urged them to lift or dig or do whatever they could to pull itself into the forest.

It shifted a few feet back before it came to a stop as if it had been snagged. After she'd prodded it gently, it shook a little, lifted a root from the soil, and swung it in the direction in which it wanted to go. It was in the process of digging the root deeper into the earth and raising another when a creature exploded outward from a knot that had been formed in the roots.

As it surged toward them, it seemed to grow larger and more

ferocious. At first, it appeared to be something like a rabbit, but as it closed the gap between them, it sprouted tusks and grew somewhat alarmingly until it resembled a wild boar with long ears and a poofball tail. It showed no signs of slowing its headlong attack.

Petalwing wasn't a fighter at all and immediately elevated to a safer height. Kylara lashed out with tendrils of dark energy and tried to anchor the creature's hooved feet to the earth beneath it. She succeeded in slowing it but not stopping it.

It shoved past her restraints and shredded some with its tusks, then powered into her. She managed to push its tusks away and avoid being gored, but in doing so took a shoulder to the chest and catapulted away.

The long-eared hog seemed to employ this strategy often and it continued to rush forward toward the place where she would make impact. Now, however, the hooked tusks that seemed to grow longer by the second were waiting for her.

Recognizing the danger, Kylara drew on her inner magic and used it to keep herself safe. Before she touched the earth, blue mist burst into the air immediately below her. In the center of it, a shimmering pane of magic formed that she plunged into.

Somehow, she reappeared about ten feet behind where she had been.

She landed hard on her butt and looked at the creature. It stared back with wide eyes but it seemed the rabbit part of its ancestry had not been forgotten. When she flashed a bright light at it, the beast squealed like a pig before it bounded into the woods on the back legs of a jackrabbit.

"Kylara! How did you do such a thing?" Petalwing seemed to be everywhere and flew in loops to circle her head and streak between where she had fallen and where she should have been gored.

"I don't know. I didn't want to hurt it and kept thinking about how I could get away. I guess the portal kind of happened."

"But that is not a dragon power!" Petalwing pointed out excitedly. "That is an ability we pixies and the mages use."

"Yeah…yeah, I guess you're right," Kylara said. "I guess that means I can get powers from pixies too? It had to come from either you or Amy, but given that it happened only now, I can't help but think it was pixie power."

"It was pixie power." The diminutive creature rubbed her tiny, pointed chin. "Mages take longer to open portals than we do."

"So…uh, you think I simply absorbed it when I came in here?" she asked.

"I believe so…" Her companion did not sound excited about this development.

"Is everything okay? It's not like I tried to steal it from you or anything like that," she said.

"Everything is fine," Petalwing said way too quickly. "But I must talk to the mage by the name of Amy. Come along. Teleportation powers and plant powers are more than enough for a young dragon to learn in a day. We must return to your school."

"But the other kids—" Her words turned to silence in her mouth when she saw that they were the last two in the meadow and that the sun had slipped from its position overhead to something approximating late afternoon.

She followed through a portal and back to school. Once the pixie had closed the gateway behind them and given her a rather long and uncomfortable look, she fluttered away and left her with her newfound abilities.

## CHAPTER TWENTY-NINE

The next day, Kylara still hadn't told her friends about her new power. A part of her wished it had been more difficult to deceive them but with her also gaining the ability to control plants, it had been easy enough to simply not mention her ability to teleport at will.

Her roommate—to her delight—had been ecstatic that they both now had plant powers. They spent the morning before Thanksgiving break practicing together. She progressed much more quickly than Tanya had, which both girls attributed to the young dragon's excellent teaching. She hadn't had to think through anything as her friend had already done all the legwork.

At noon, when Tanya's parents arrived to take her home for the holiday, the two friends talked about little beyond Kylara's need to keep practicing so she could be as strong as her.

Saying goodbye to Sam had been a little trickier.

"You can come with us for the holiday, seriously," he explained. "No one would think it's weird, I promise you."

"No one would think it's weird that you bring a mage home who absorbed your power?"

He reddened. "Well…okay, you already have light powers, so it's not like you'll take them from anyone else in my family."

"I appreciate that invite, Sam, I truly do, but it's cool. Thanksgiving was never a big deal for my mom and I. We always ate whatever we wanted and it's not like we ever invited anyone over. Go enjoy your time with your family. I'm looking forward to some peace and quiet."

"Sometimes, I wish you had an aura so I can read you like a normal person."

"No one at this school is normal, Sam," she replied.

Sam chuckled at that, then hugged her farewell and went to join his parents.

Kylara waited for the campus to clear before she used her new power. It wasn't that she wanted to keep it secret but rather that she wanted to use it for a plan she had before Amythist or Amy found a way to keep an eye on her and prevent her from using it to go wherever she wished. She would have told Tanya and Sam her plan, but she was one hundred percent certain that they would not have approved. She wouldn't have been surprised if one of them had stayed simply to prevent her from doing it.

It was with a strong sense of the clandestine that she opened a portal to the house where she'd grown up.

She waited until late afternoon when the few students on campus were all at dinner but there was still enough light to poke around.

Truthfully, she didn't know what she hoped to find. The house had been almost completely razed. It had been built into the side of a mountain, though, so the shape of it was still there, even though all the wood and fabric had been engulfed in flame and transformed to ash months before.

Had it only been months? To her, it felt like another lifetime. She considered that and decided that in some ways, it was.

The young dragon mage poked around the ruins of her home and tried not to cry over the broken glass and burned greenhouse and the wooden floors that were now little more than charred remains. The marble slab they had prepared all their meals on was still there, although it was cracked in half.

In the burned shell of her bedroom, she found what she was looking for.

Well, not exactly, but close enough.

It was a note from her aunt Cassandra.

*Dearest Kylara—my niece, and my blood.*

*I hope you can find it in you to forgive me for how our lives first intersected. If I had known that after all these years, you were not only alive but thriving under the care of Hester Diamantine, I would never have attacked the place you both called home. It was an attack driven by revenge and enacted in ignorance and I am sorry for it. If it means anything to you, I have not found it in my heart to take revenge on your adopted mother. I cannot set her free either as she knows far too much about me, but in our conversations, I have learned that she truly cares about you. It causes me no small amount of discomfort that I had to separate the two of you for you to learn the truth about your past.*

*I have seen through my spirits that your friends are safe and growing stronger. Believe me when I say no harm would ever have come to them. I am well aware of the powers dragons possess and was careful to never push them past the limits of their healing abilities. I am sure they do not feel this way, but it was essential that you came to me to learn the truth of who you are and I saw no other way. Forgive my desperation and lack of imagination.*

*I long to find a way to make amends. For so long, I had lived with nothing but pain and rage in my heart and discovering you felt like finding an oasis in the hottest of deserts. I know family and your past is important to you. Otherwise, you would not be reading this note right now.*

*My dream and my new purpose are to find a way we can think of each other as family and truly come together. I want the world for you, Kylara. I want us to show the world that the Steel Dragon's vision of unity cannot come to pass until us mages hold positions equal to those of the most powerful dragons. I had dreamed of doing this with violence and vengeance but now hope that together, we can find a better way like you being alive helped my heart find a better way than rage.*

*Your aunt forever, Cassandra.*

By the time she'd finished reading the note, her eyes were wet. It contained so much that she so dearly wished to believe.

She wanted her mom to be alive. The struggle to keep going from day to day while Hester was a prisoner drove her to distraction. She wanted to break down in tears several times a day or to fly off and find her and rescue her the way she had her friends. Unfortunately, she had no idea where to even start looking. Feeling helpless was the least comfortable feeling she could imagine, especially when it came to the safety of someone she loved.

She wanted her mom to have changed her aunt's mind.

Not only that, she wished dragons and mages could coexist without the politics and hardship and she wanted something for her aunt besides rage and revenge.

But that didn't mean she could simply forgive Cassandra for all the horrible things she had done. There was no mention of why she had sent her elementals to attack her and the other students on the field trip, just as there was no mention of why she had sent the weaker elementals to the school.

There were still deceptions there, albeit deceptions of omission. Plus, there was the fact that the woman still held Diamantine prisoner.

With this all in her head, Kylara retrieved a notebook from her backpack and wrote a note in reply.

*Aunt Cassandra,*

*Believe it or not, I am open to the idea of having a relationship with you. I want to learn more about my past, my biological mother, my father, and you. I am still concerned that you use the elementals to mess with the Lumos School, and I don't know what you hoped to accomplish by the attack on our field trip.*

*Furthermore, I am not willing to have any kind of relationship with you if you continue to hold my mom prisoner. I know that she hurt you but you ruined our life together. If you can't forgive her or at least free her, we have nothing to talk about.*

*But I also know that you have changed. I know you can find a way to contact me if you wish to talk. Please don't do so, though, until you've released my mom. I would love to have a relationship with both of you. I can't start one with you, though, until I can have one again with the woman who raised me.*

*I hope you're well and hope to hear from you soon, Kylara.*

She hesitated and almost scratched out the part about hoping she was well but decided against it. It was true, after all. As bizarre as it might seem, she didn't want Cassandra to die. She wanted to talk to her and understand her. Not only that, but she wanted to learn about her family and, if she was being completely honest, she wanted to learn about the woman's powers.

But Hester Diamantine's freedom had to come first. She could entertain the notion of making nice with her aunt but only if she could see her mom again.

She read the note carefully and once she was reasonably certain that she'd made this clear, she left her home.

From the outside, it was almost as if it had never existed. The difference between a house dug into the side of a mountain and a slightly overgrown pocket of earth being burned to nothing was slight.

Kylara looked around the landscape her aunt's fire elemental had burned. Although it had only been a few months, the land already showed signs of healing. None of the cactus or shrubby growth had fully returned, of course, but it had rained since the fire and a fresh flush of green growth had emerged around the base of many of the burned plants.

She hoped for the same kind of growth for the two women who seemed to care most about her—her mom and the woman who had abducted her.

With a sigh, she reached out for her new power. Mist formed in front of her and spread into a disc that revealed the wooded part of the Lumos school campus. She stepped through, closed the portal behind her, and went to the dining hall for dinner.

As she walked across the mostly empty campus, she couldn't help but glance toward every exposed rock and every leaf that moved in the wind. Any one of them could be an agent of her aunt, after all.

# CHAPTER THIRTY

Cassandra knew the exact moment when Kylara entered the Diamantine home. She had left an enchantment on the note she placed there that told her when someone she knew touched it. She had left a few such notes in strategic locations where she thought the girl might come across them, although she was not surprised that the first place she went to was her home.

She waited a while, though, to give the girl time to fly out rather than risk a confrontation. Still, she was disappointed when she arrived at the top of a nearby mountain via underground transport by an earth spirit and saw no diamond-scaled dragon on the horizon. Of course, it was ridiculous to even hope she might. She'd waited long enough to be sure the girl was long gone.

The mage was conflicted. On the one hand, she wanted more than anything to see her but she knew their next meeting should be on terms her niece would accept. She didn't think the girl would have left immediately after reading the note, which was why she had waited. Despite this, she still felt disappointed that she wasn't there.

The master of the elementals sighed. This was all so much

more complicated than she had thought it would be. She had assumed that the guard mages would defect when they realized how powerful she had become, but that had failed to happen when the dragon skeletons appeared.

So many pieces, she mused with a flare of irritation. There were so many pieces to this puzzle and she had only begun to see the outline form.

With no dragon on the horizon, the earth spirit created a bubble of soil around Cassandra and transported her through the mountain to Kylara and Hester Diamantine's burned home.

She emerged in front of their house and sent her air spirit to look for signs of anyone. Although she assumed the girl was long gone, she didn't want to burst in and surprise her.

The entity reported that there were no moving, breathing creatures interfering with the air currents, so she hurried inside.

She moved quickly through the charred shell. Although she knew she was responsible for the condition of it and had once even fantasized about leaving Diamantine in a burned home turned mausoleum similar to how the dragon had let her partners burn her family, she felt no joy when she saw it. If she had only discovered that Hester hadn't lived here alone—that she had taken the mage baby and raised her as her ward rather than killing her—she would not have told her spirit to destroy their home so completely.

With all these thoughts churning in her mind, she entered the husk of Kylara's bedroom and found the note where she had left. It stirred slight disappointment as she had hoped the girl would have taken it with her, but the feeling passed when she saw that beneath it was another note, this one written on white paper with faint blue lines. She took it and smiled gently. It was the paper so many students learned on. How appropriate that she would use it to learn more about her relationship with her aunt.

Cassandra went outside and ordered her earth spirit to return her to her underground lair.

By the time she reached her home, she had read the note enough times to have it memorized.

She emerged through the floor of the cave, stepped out of the bubble of stone the earth spirit had made, and sauntered toward her prisoner.

For once, the broken dragon bound in human form wasn't asleep. Still chained to the stone pillar behind her by power-inhibiting silver cuffs, Hester Diamantine watched her approach with eyes hooded with wariness.

"Something has changed," the dragon said.

Cassandra couldn't help but smile at her perceptiveness.

"Indeed. I received a letter from Kylara." She walked toward the pool of water that surrounded her captive. The water spirit that resided in the pond pushed the water away so her feet didn't get wet as she approached the dragon. She held the letter out to Diamantine and dropped it only inches away from her.

The dragon gasped and reached instinctively for the letter but was held fast by the chains. The missive slipped past her grasp and fluttered to the rocky floor. Her eyes widened as it neared the water at her feet, no doubt afraid of what it would do to the ink on the paper. She didn't sense the air elemental that pushed it to her feet. Cassandra wanted to keep Hester standing but she also wanted the dragon to read the letter.

She picked it up for her and put it in her hands.

As she read, the mage spoke, knowing that she was well trained enough at this point that she wouldn't ignore her captor's words.

"I'm quite impressed with Kylara, I must admit," she said. "She is strong, principled, and forgiving. I expected the first when I discovered that you had raised her clandestinely but never would have thought a dragon capable of instilling the other attributes. You did well with her."

"You said she wrote you this letter, but seems to be a reply to something," Diamantine said and chose to ignore the compliment. Ah, the arrogance of dragons truly was a special thing.

"She found a message I left for her at your home. She could have ignored it but she left this instead. Tell me, what was your plan with the girl? Why expend all the energy on her when she wasn't yours?" Cassandra asked.

"Because even before I found Kylara, I knew what I was doing for Dragon SWAT was wrong," Diamantine said. There were times when these conversations seemed to bother the dragon or drain her in some way, but those had passed. Cassandra had poked and prodded at her life choices so many times now that there were no more secrets and no more shame.

"Why did you keep doing it then?"

"It wasn't all bad. Sometimes, we broke fights up between dragons. At others, we stopped mages who had manifested their powers and didn't know how to control them yet."

"You killed some of those mages."

"Yes. Too many. But at the time, even then, it was always seen as a failure when a mage died. Still, stopping brawls was something I knew was good. It prevented regular people from being killed. But once I understood that success meant capturing a mage and essentially enslaving them, I could no longer do it."

"But you continued to do it." Cassandra had heard all this before, multiple times, but she was always curious to see how Diamantine's relationship with her past continued to adjust.

"I thought I could change the organization from the inside. It was arrogant and naïve, but there it was. That's why, when I got to Kylara's home—your home—I...I tried to talk to the mages there. I was so close but—"

"Yes, Kylara and I saw what happened."

"That's why I took her. I understood that I could never change the system from the inside. The entire point of the political structure the dragons had built was primarily to take power from the mages. When I saw her, I knew her life would be weighed as nothing more than an animal or a tool if the dragons discovered her. When I first saw her fat little cheeks, I knew I couldn't allow her to be raised as a ward of the state, only to grow up to be a servant. And when I discovered that she could take the form of a dragon, that changed everything. No dragon in their right mind would allow such an aberration to exist."

"That's why you ran—to protect her." It was not a question that came from Cassandra's mouth but a recitation.

"I knew there would be...complexities...with Kylara's heritage. That's why I kept her on that land and away from the world."

"A risky strategy."

"Yes, but if the dragons found me, I could claim that I had been pregnant and tired of my job. Dragons have quit positions for less of a reason than that. And then there was her pendant. It fooled me into thinking she was a dragon sometimes and I knew she was a mage. I thought that if we were discovered, it might protect her."

"How long did you think this could go on?" the mage asked.

Diamantine slumped. "I don't know. My original intention was to find a home for her when she was three or four—old enough to communicate but still young enough to make a bond with another parent—but I simply couldn't. I changed my plans and told myself I needed to teach her how to fight as a human and a dragon and that I would find somewhere for her when she was twelve or thirteen."

"And then?"

"And then puberty arrived and she began to grow into such a beautiful young woman. I could see her mother's face—the face of a woman whose blood was on my hands—and I couldn't let her go. I think that if you hadn't sent your elemental to burn our home, we would be there still. I fear that if you hadn't come, I would never have let her go and she would have eventually run from me."

Cassandra chuckled softly. "How ironic, no? To think that if I had simply let her be, she might have run away and turned her back on you. But it was my drive to avenge her death that drove her from me."

"She can forgive, though. Kylara is amazing that way," Hester said and made eye contact with her captor for the first time since they'd begun to talk. "I hope she can forgive me for lying to her for so long."

"What would you do if I released you?" It was the first time she had ever asked that question.

The dragon's answer was immediate and with no hesitation. "I would do whatever I can to continue to help Kylara grow. She's safe at the Lumos School for now, but who knows if that will last? I would think the headmaster and Kristen Hall are trying to keep her true nature a secret from the dragon community at large. If the world knew what she was, people might take advantage—dragons might take advantage."

"And mages too, yes," Cassandra said.

She left the conversation there. What Diamantine had said had given her pause. The dragon was right. Kylara's ability to absorb dragon powers was remarkable. If she could find a way to share it, mages would truly be given a position of value in this world.

Did that mean she was trying to take advantage of her niece?

She didn't know and hoped not. One thing she was sure of, though, was that she no longer hungered for vengeance. It was almost embarrassing to think about it now. How long she'd let nothing but anger fuel her and how long she'd thought that taking from others the same way she had been taken from would somehow make her feel better.

It had been a hard lesson but she knew now that it wouldn't. No joy could come from pain, not even the pain of an enemy. Joy could only come from building bonds with people you loved—people like her niece.

So what was wrong with her trying to find a way to acquire the same power Kylara had? If they were both gifted with the powers dragons commanded so effortlessly, they could live for millennia together. Aunt and niece. Hell, Cassandra wasn't picky. After everything Diamantine had done for the girl, maybe she could be a part of their lives too.

It seemed a reasonable price to pay for a few thousand extra years of life and godlike power.

# CHAPTER THIRTY-ONE

It took Galen three days to find the castle amidst a graveyard of mages and dragons but he'd finally located the site.

The ruined structure was much as he had left it. Despite all the doom and gloom spewed by the short-sighted mage who was jealous of his power, the castle was fine. No serious damage had been done by the battle. In fact, with the rain Kylara and his brother had brought and the plant growth from Tanya, the courtyard looked better than it had before he'd interfered. He wasn't optimistic enough to think anyone would thank him for that, however.

But they would when he had better control. He could admit that the mage was right about that. When it mattered most, he had lost control and that was unacceptable. The ability to control the weather itself resided in his family's blood. Part of that was knowing how far to push a storm before it would become too powerful to be managed. Though he wasn't able to personally do anything with the weather, he understood that control of one's power came from practice and hard work. It was irresponsible of Amy to yell at him for what he had done, though. If she cared about him, she would have given him something to practice on.

But at this castle, he had all he would ever need.

Now that Galen was there alone with only the dead to keep him company, he could sense how many of them were there. Most of the dragons he had exhumed from the courtyard were still there, buried again. All had lost a few bones and there was something different about their energy. They seemed less eager to communicate with him somehow as if their last foray into the land of the living had wearied them.

But there were so many more there than the twelve he had already called forth. There were hundreds of human skeletons too—perhaps as many as a thousand—and another fifty or so of the dead dragons buried outside the walls of the castle's courtyard.

He was eager to start his practice but he had been raised a Stormwing. It made no sense to try to create a tornado when one couldn't control a simple breeze.

Once he'd settled his growing excitement, he reached out with his powers and felt between the huge bones of the dragons and the familiar human skeletons until he found other creatures. There were numerous rodents, a few horses and cats, and finally, a dog.

After a moment's thought, he decided he would start there. It would be similar in size to the first skeletons he had seen in the pixie realm and might help him answer a few questions about what kind of knowledge was still left in the bones from life if there was any at all.

Galen reached out with his inner energy, redirected it toward the bones of the canine, and infused them with magic to give them life where before, there had only been decay.

They responded, dragged themselves out of the earth, and clacked together as they loped toward him. He smiled as the skeletal dog approached and wagged its tail in welcome.

This wouldn't be that hard, he thought as he tested a few different commands on the dead animal. He found he could control it without speaking and that like the squirrel, it tended to do whatever he told it to do without stopping. If he told it to dig, it continued to do so until he commanded it to stop. On the other hand, if he instructed it to dig until it unearthed the skull of a dragon, it did exactly that.

That seemed like a reasonable level of control for a creature with no brain. He tried a few more tricks, which included seeing if he could make it dissemble itself. It turned out he could. Once separated into individual pieces, the bones were inert and unable to move simply because each of them was a solid, unarticulated piece of solid calcium. But his energy remained inside. When he told the bones to reassemble, they did so with alacrity and took the shape of the dog even more quickly than they had the first time.

Galen smiled. He was already learning and gaining more control.

He now turned his attention to the bones of a long-dead human and wondered how thankful they would be to know they weren't simply dead but back in the world of the living.

---

It had taken a few weeks of careful, cautious work, but Galen was ready. He had learned so much and had raised the dog, cats, birds, horses, raccoons, and even a mountain lion. In all his attempts, he had learned that more than merely bones could be raised, but only if the parts were an essential part of the original animal's function.

For example, there didn't seem to be a way to make his skeletal dog grow fur. It wasn't essential for it to function as a dog, so the skeleton and the type of magic that fueled it remained resolute in not letting it become shaggy.

Birds, however, were different. It was impossible to completely cover one in feathers but he discovered that through continued coaxing and by pulverizing some of the bones of other bird skeletons, he could make feathers. They did not look like feathers in that they didn't have bright colors or patterns, but they acted like feathers and enabled his birds to fly.

The same was true of the mountain lion he had revived. Its claws had long since dissolved but he had been able to use powdered bone from one of its ribs to remake the claws. The skeleton did this readily, as claws were essential to a mountain lion. He didn't know enough about anatomy to understand exactly why the claws had crumbled to nothing when the bones hadn't. It was one of the many questions he hoped to answer when he returned to the school's library.

He had raised humans too—hesitantly at first and with the utmost caution. Galen's fear wasn't of the skeleton itself, of course, as he could become a dragon on a whim and breathe fire hot enough to turn the relatively slender bones of a human to ash. His fear was that he might inadvertently raise a mage. He had no idea if the mages would retain their magical powers or some vestige of who they were.

The truth was that he didn't know much about this kind of magic—necromancy, he'd heard it called in movies—but he assumed mages probably knew more. How terrible it would be to give life to one of the treacherous mages who had turned on the Prairie King, although he knew he would most likely be able to destroy them unless they had power. Mages were tricky like that. It was why his parents said the best mage was a cuffed mage.

But eventually, curiosity and a need to improve his powers overcame his caution. He had raised a human and found that his fears were completely unfounded. The skeleton behaved as simply and brainlessly as all the other revenants. It was more versatile than the animal skeletons simply by dint of the human body being more versatile. It could run, walk, climb, jump, throw things, move objects, and more.

After extensive testing, he raised another human skeleton,

then another. It took time but eventually, he raised over a hundred human skeletons. Not all at once, of course, and never more than three at a time. He knew no one was there to watch him or get hurt, but it seemed like the responsible way to go about things.

Out of those hundred skeletons, not a single one had demonstrated any unusual capabilities—no fire powers and no ability to make ice or control the wind. Furthermore, none of them had tried to turn on him or do anything he hadn't commanded. It seemed that in death, all beings truly were equal. Human bones devoid of their soul were no different than the mountain lion.

This morning, he intended to prove the final piece of his theorem. He had practiced repeatedly with animals and humans and had made the creatures behave naturally and do odd things, like making cats walk on their hind legs. Better still, he had controlled multiple revenants at once and forced every single one of them to return to its inert state.

It was time to raise a dragon.

This would be the first he raised since the catastrophe of the field trip. He was eager to prove himself and it eased his mind to know that if anything went wrong, no one would get hurt out in the American Midwest.

He walked out from the walls of the castle, his temporary home and place of refuge from the winds in the area. There was a dragon out there that he'd planned to raise since he had discovered it. He had cataloged all those buried in the area and this one seemed like the prime place to start.

It was small for a dragon—only thirty feet—and most of its bones were intact. The reason he chose it, though, was because of the ridge of spines on its back. They were the spines of an aquatic dragon, which meant that although this individual was—had been?—a dragon with a special ability, it likely wasn't anything beyond being able to breathe underwater. In other words, it wasn't a threat. He could almost hear his professor praising him for the thought and research put into the decision.

Galen approached the buried dragon and poured his magic into its long-rotted corpse. He felt it answer his summons. It drank his magic as if lying in the ground for so long had done nothing but make it thirst for this power. Like before, he felt dormant magic in the bones of the deceased magical being as well. If he could give its bones enough energy, it would activate itself like an engine being jump-started.

After a minute of gifting the dragon his magic, its bones knitted together and drew themselves closer through the dirt. Patches of earth were pushed up as they displaced the soil. Shrubs and trees that had grown through the dragon, perhaps feasting on the leftover remnants of its body over the centuries, were toppled. The head emerged from the soil first. It pushed up and the crown of the skull broke through the surface.

Spines heralded the arrival of the full head—slender and elegant like the ridge of an oceanic fish. The top jaw appeared, then the bottom, before the neck, shoulder blades, and wings broke free. Next, the arms shoved and lifted the rib cage from the dirt, followed by the back legs, and finally, the tail. Its spines still had the faintest vestige of dried skin and made it clear that the tail was not merely a weapon but had also been used to propel the dragon through the water.

"Rise, dragon, rise, then come and rest before your new master." He said these words aloud but more importantly, he felt them. He had found that with the skeletons of animals and men, his intentions were more important than the word themselves. Emotions seemed to be especially important. Telling the mountain lion to prowl was one thing but telling it to hunt because its master was hungry was generally more effective. It had taken practice for him to feel passionate enough about something like commanding one of the skeletons to simply sit but now, with the bones of an adult dragon in front of him, he felt that passion acutely. The beast obeyed.

It completed the final push from the dirt and sat on its haunches as obediently as a dog.

"Very good, dragon. Now, run a lap around the castle."

The skeleton obeyed and lunged forward on creaky bones that settled into a more comfortable gait as the revenant moved. It vanished behind the exterior walls of the castle and moved quickly to complete its circuit and make its master proud. This was a test Galen had worked on. He knew his powers would be vastly superior if he could control the skeletons even when he couldn't see them. While he had practiced this on all the others, of course, he had to be careful with a dragon.

To his immense satisfaction, it obeyed perfectly. It completed its loop around the grounds of the castle, returned to him, and sat in front of him as he'd commanded it to do.

"Very good! Very good!" Galen applauded, unable to help himself. This would work. He had put the time and energy into practicing with the smaller skeletons. This would work better than he'd hoped.

Only a few more things remained to try.

"Breathe fire, dragon. A great blast into the air."

The skeleton obeyed. It leaned back, opened its jaws to the heavens, and its ribcage contracted to force air out of lungs that had rotted away long before.

Nothing happened. No flames, no lightning, and no breath weapon of any kind came from the bones. He transformed and blew a gush of fire into the air, then ordered the dragon to do the same. It attempted the feat but failed again.

Galen nodded. That was as he'd expected, and it felt good to have his hypothesis confirmed. He had tried to get a hundred of the human skeletons to perform magic and none had. It seemed that dragons were also denied their more special powers now that they had died.

"That's fine, dragon. Now, I want you to fly."

It understood and extended the bones that made the structure of its wings, pumped them, and tried to catch the wind on a membrane that simply wasn't there. As expected, it couldn't fly, not without the stretchy, leather-like skin that spread between the bones of its wings like a bat.

Of course, he had anticipated this. He knew it wouldn't be able to construct feathers the way the birds could. Dragons had never had feathers, so their bones didn't have the memory of how to create such a tool, as useful as it would have been.

Instead, he directed it to a pile of deer skins he had harvested expressly for this purpose. Unsure of how many he'd need, he had kept the body of every deer he'd killed. That was quite a few —more than fifty, at least. He'd unintentionally caught a herd of them with a blast of fire and hurt more than he'd intended. Rather than let them suffer, he'd finished them all off quickly.

The dragon skeleton took one of their pelts in its mouth and gobbled it with only its teeth. Its tongue and lips were long gone. Something about the creature "eating" the deer changed how the revenant worked. It took the leather and sinews, the cartilage, and membranes and used them to create the thinnest skin he had ever seen between the bones of its wings. It was so thin that it was translucent. When it stretched its wings and one moved between Galen and a tree, he could still see the green leaves and the brown trunk. It was all merely slightly distorted like looking through wax paper.

More importantly, the wings worked. The dragon pumped the new appendage of flesh turned cellophane and great billows of wind pushed out under them. It took a few flaps to get the skeleton airborne, but it flew. The membrane was lighter and weaker than a regular dragon's wing, but the body of the dragon itself also lacked muscle and organs. As it elevated and flew in loops around the castle, it became plain that this new balance would work. The weaker wings were more than strong enough to support the skeletal remains of this long-dead dragon.

Galen grinned. This would work! Why, for that matter, it was already working. He told the dragon to turn and it obeyed. When he commanded it to fly in a loop, it obeyed. He told it to stop flying and to crash into the earth. It did so and scattered the bones on impact. He gave it no command to reknit itself and it made no effort to do so. Its bones lay there, inert and motionless, still full of magic but biding their time until their master called on them again.

By now, he grinned so widely that his cheeks hurt. He had complete control and could tell the dragon what to do, where to go, how to act, and even to cease to be.

"Back together!" he ordered and it drew itself together as if hidden strings ran between the bones that he simply had to twitch with his mind to reactivate.

The whole experience was incredible. He could not believe how much positive progress he had made. Well, he could because he had spent so long practicing but he was still ecstatic. He was a dragon the likes of which the world had never seen.

With this power, he could protect the people he loved. He could stop people who wished to harm him, his family, or his fellow students. With practice, he could imagine no limits to his power. He might be able to stop war itself. There had been a tremulous peace since the Steel Dragon had come into power, but everyone—especially the Stormwing family—knew this simply couldn't last.

But now it could. Who would dare go to war when they knew that breaking the peace would mean an army of fleshless, invulnerable dragons would put an end to such violence?

Galen paused. The only problem with that idea was that he didn't have an army yet. He had practiced raising multiple animals at once as well as multiple humans. It had all gone successfully enough. His original plan had been to practice with one dragon for a few days before raising another, but it had already been weeks. He'd been forced into hiding more than once already when he sensed the approach of humans or dragons. Even as remote as the castle was, he worried that someone would find him there before he was prepared.

Besides, the dragon presented no problems. It had no more intelligence than any of the revenants had possessed. It didn't rebel against the master who gave it life and didn't even hesitate to let its body fall to bones when he had ordered it too.

So why wait?

He reached out to another skeleton it had been impossible to ignore. This had been a great warrior, a powerful hulk of a dragon. He poured his magic into its bones and realized that he didn't feel drained despite having already given life to the other. This one, like the first, was thirsty for his power and took it into itself willingly.

Galen could feel each bone of this great gladiator of a dragon. He felt its massive skull, easily twice the size of the last one, with a pair of twisting horns like the world's most enormous antelope. Its arm and leg bones felt inordinately heavy. He could feel that one of the hands seemed different than the other. It still responded to his magic but it seemed slower and more sluggish. He ignored the sensation for a moment and knew that if he filled the skeleton to a certain threshold, it would begin to sustain itself. Thereafter, he could explore the hand without distraction.

He pushed energy into a tail that was almost as long as the entire other dragon. It had the same black, elegantly twisting horn at its tip like the world's most refined scorpion. It was a wonder that it had managed to live its entire life with such delicate-looking horns. The rest of the beast was pure brute. The horns, by comparison, looked slender, although their length was certainly longer than any he had ever seen on a dragon, living or dead.

It started to shift as energy poured into its ribs. Hungrily, it demanded more and he gave it all it asked for. It was harder than anything he had ever done in his life, yet he could do it. He had the strength for this and when he became the master of these dragons, the world would be better for it.

He screamed as he released the last of his power into this great brute of a skeleton. Finally, it was done. The beast lifted itself from the ground, truly a sight to behold. It was fully twice as large as the other one. While hard to tell, from head to tail it might have been seventy-five feet long. It flexed its massive wings and the bones in these were as big as the leg bones of the other beast. He had only heard of dragons like this. It freed itself from the earth and Galen, despite his exhaustion, forced himself to remain standing.

The undead creature appraised its new master as it emerged from the earth, limb after limb. The final piece to be revealed was the carpals and metacarpals of the hand, which he now realized were made of pure stone. That was why they had behaved differently. They weren't bone at all. It meant this dragon was one of the specials who could turn to stone, which made it that much more interesting.

Galen tried to make it use its power to turn its entire body to stone but it only stood impassively. He tried the opposite—to turn the hand into calcium—which was also ignored. He nodded. That was as it should be. The bones were all that was left of these creatures. Whatever had given them their special powers was long gone.

Now that he no longer had to feed energy into this hulking example of dragon kind, his healing power already began to make him feel better. As he let himself recharge, he gave the massive creature some of the same simple commands he had given the others. Eventually, with all tests passed, he made it "eat" some of the deer skins to grow wing membranes. It needed a few more than its counterpart—six, in fact—before it was able to become airborne. Even then, it wasn't much of a flyer, not like the first one.

But it made sense. The other dragon was a swimmer, a being that moved through fluid—be it liquid or air—more often than it had ever walked. The hulk dragon, though, was a creature of stone. It was a brawler, the kind of beast that could stop a tank.

He laughed, excited by what he'd achieved. Although he'd summoned not one but two dragons, he still felt completely fine. He hadn't even had a nosebleed like overtaxed mages were prone to do.

So many other dragons remained, however, and all of them could be raised. Why couldn't they? At this rate, it would only take him most of the morning to do so.

Driven by his success, Galen reached out with his magic into the field of skeletons and poured his magic into what he found there. Like a storm had dumped water on a field of crops, the bones sucked his magic up and used it as their own.

Dragon after dragon rose from the earth. One after the other, they pushed free and completed the training regime he designed as he went until they came to sit in front of him, their claws crossed and head bowed as good servants should behave with their masters.

It was hard, brutal work, but every time a beast pushed free, the load lessened. Yes, it grew heavier when he tried to raise the next, but once they were filled or charged or whatever he did to them, they no longer needed him. But they still obeyed. Every single one of them obeyed. It was the most exhilarating thing he had ever experienced.

Finally, surrounded by fifty dead dragons that all obeyed his commands as obediently as any dog, Galen was done.

He appraised his work and decided it was good. With only these dragons, he could protect so many people. He could stop the elementals from attacking the school or stop any mages who tried to unjustly challenge the dragons. In fact, he could stop anyone from doing anything he didn't want.

The power and the beasts he controlled were something the world had never seen.

Without a doubt, he was a force of nature—a change in the world and a new power—and people had to see it was so.

Galen knew the perfect place to introduce himself. The Lumos School was a place for special dragons. Well, there was nothing more special than this.

It was an easy decision to return and show them his army. He would show them the value of his powers and that with his help, they would never need to fear an attack ever again.

As a unit, the dragons began to travel south. Those that could fly did so and the others gobbled anything in their path until his entire battalion of skeletons had what they needed to take to the sky.

He put the hulk dragon in front and the rest fell into formation with him at their rear—their commander, their savior, and their god.

## CHAPTER THIRTY-TWO

Snow came in the first week of December. Some of the students marveled at it and left dragon-shaped footprints or used their magic to create elaborate, anatomically correct snowmen. To Kylara, it was nothing new. It snowed every year in the mountains. A couple of inches early in December was unusual, perhaps, but not inordinately so.

The staff were of a similar mind. Classes continued as usual despite the weather. Teachers of mage and dragon alike geared up for finals, which she was rather disappointed to learn didn't seem to be that different than what regular students had to endure.

They were in their Dragon Powers class with the Silver Bullet when she first saw the strangest thing. At first, she thought that it was a flock of migratory birds—sandhill cranes, perhaps, although the timing was wrong. She had always loved it when they flew over her mother's land. It made her feel less alone and so it was with a feeling of longing that she watched the flock approach the campus from the north.

Her distraction cost her, however. Karl Midnight slapped her across the face with a tendril of dark energy that almost toppled her from the top of the stone plinth. Only her dark energy enabled her to stay on.

"What the hell was that?" he demanded. "You should have seen that coming."

"Language!" the Silver Bullet snapped, then added, "Midnight's right, Kylara, you should have seen it coming."

She knew she should have, especially given who her opponent was. No one else ever wanted to battle her for fear that she would take their powers. This meant she and Karl understood each other's techniques better than most opponents. The slap to the face was a classic Midnight feint and she wouldn't have fallen for it if not for the birds.

Except, she realized now, they weren't birds.

"Look—dragons are coming through the snow." She pointed across the grounds, past the others in her class who scuffled impatiently as they waited for their turn on the stone plinths on which their duel would be graded. Beyond them, the mages practiced their bevy of powers but she ignored them and gazed past the burned forest that Tanya had partly regrown and over the ridge. It was clear now that they were dragons.

Still, they were very beautiful through the snow—all white and almost motionless as they flew.

"Are they always like that in the snow?" she murmured.

"No." Kor did not sound at all impressed, awed, or enamored with the dragons flying in from the north. He looked at them not as visitors come to see their children before the holiday season but as he looked at everything—as a threat. "Dragons are too hot to have snow accumulate on them even when we sleep. When we fly, it's impossible."

"Then why are they white?" Karl asked.

Their instructor nodded at Sam and the young dragon released a beam of light. Immediately, a flurry of activity was visible in the center of the campus as Amy gathered a team of guard mages and came toward their group.

"What is going on?" Kylara asked no one in particular.

Kor's gaze was locked on the horizon, where the dragons began to resolve into clarity. "I think Galen is back. Students, form up. If you have defensive powers, I want you in the front with everyone else behind. If you engage these bastards, you fail my class, is that understood?"

"Yes, sir!" Half of the students sounded relieved to be told to not do anything while the other half sounded as if they'd been denied their natural rights.

"You think those are—" Before she could finish, she saw that their instructor was right.

The creatures that flew toward them were made of nothing but bone. They had no scales, no muscles, and no organs inside their rib cages and a thin, almost completely transparent membrane stretched between the bones of their wings. No light shone from their eyes, and none of them looked around as they crossed into the airspace above the campus. They showed no more interest in the land beneath them than migrating birds did for the dry, barren land where she had grown up.

It looked as if they might simply pass over the campus completely until Galen, who flew at their rear, banked his wings and the skeletal dragons did the same. They followed his lead and spiraled slowly to land in the middle of the great green U that formed the very center of campus.

No classes were held in that area, but there were still a large number of students, which wasn't unusual. They were eating a late lunch, skipping class, or playing frisbee, but all normal activity ceased when what amounted to a flying graveyard darkened the sky above them. In moments, they all fled.

Kor snapped an order for the class to turn so the tougher, more defensive dragons—like Kylara with her diamond scales—were in the front and the others were behind them. The mage professor seemed to do something similar and instructed her students to get in line and spin defensive shields around each other.

"Come—come, everyone!" Galen Stormwing roared in his dragon form. "Come and behold what I have wrought."

"A little dramatic, don't you think?" Karl joked to Kylara. He had proven that his dark powers were great at defense more than once, so he had taken the position beside her.

"You've wrought a bad grade, that's what you've wrought!" Kor retorted loudly enough for the young dragon to hear.

The instructor turned to the students. "You kids, follow me. We need to get everyone inside the dorms where you'll be better warded by the spells baked into those bricks. That means we need to get past him, which means we'll have to listen to his speech. None of you are to engage or you fail my class. Is that clear?"

With another half-excited, half-annoyed chorus of, "Yes sir," the class moved slowly toward this master of the dead.

The mage class also approached, no doubt to return to their dorm as well. Oddly enough, the students who had cut class or taken a late lunch were now the safest, as they had already retreated inside. The rest of them had to reckon with the phenomenon of the kid who had once controlled a dead squirrel and now had what seemed to be fifty undead dragons under his command.

The guard mages surrounded the U and took position on top of the three main buildings, although Amy was in the very front. She stood with her hands on her hips and her feet planted firmly in skater shoes in the snow.

"I come here to ask your forgiveness!" Galen bellowed.

"There's no need to be forgiven for being such a dork." Karl sneered.

"Shut it, Midnight," Kor snapped, and the young dragon obeyed.

"On our last field trip together, I raised dragons to protect some of you but they overwhelmed me. You see, our professors had failed to teach me about my powers because they didn't understand them. But I don't blame them for their failings. I was able to master these abilities myself and I don't think I could have done it if I had not failed first.

"I'm sorry for any pain I caused anyone, but there's no longer any reason to be afraid." To punctuate this, he somehow forced every single dragon to sit at the same time. It was an impressive show of power. Kylara didn't think fifty dragons had ever been made to do the same thing like that.

"No longer do we need these mages to protect us," the young dragon continued. "Nor do we need to live in fear of someone breaking the peace. Now, with these dragons and more, we can finally live in a true peace. I can ensure that no one else has to fight. I have learned to make these dragons do that which was always thought impossible for dragons—to obey without question." The skeletons, on cue, all laid down and crossed their front paws.

Finally, it seemed that Amy had reached the end of her patience. "How dare you?" she demanded, her voice loud enough for all the students to hear. "How dare you do this? It's unnatural. We spoke about this, Galen. You cannot use your powers on sentient beings."

"Oh, but you can?" he retorted. "You can use telekinesis to knock thinking beings around or to crush them with boulders. I don't do that. These are merely bones. They were doing nothing but resting. And, unlike the people you use your powers against, they wanted my magic."

"That's because it's dark magic. You can't fuel things like this without repercussions!" she snapped in response.

"What do you know?" Galen said and his practiced imperious tone had slipped into something whinier. "You're merely a mage. You know nothing of dragon magic."

"Galen, this is not a path forward," Headmaster Amythist said.

"I have wanted to speak to you about your power since you ran off." Her voice was calm and even gentle. "Let these dragons rest. They have served their time."

"And then what? Go back to being a nobody?"

"Then we learn how you can use this power ethically in a way you can be proud of," the old dragon said.

"You're lying," he sputtered. "You want to take my power."

Something changed about the dragons. Instead of remaining motionless, they began to twitch and they raised almost to a crouch. They showed little aggression at first, but their claws began to click against the dirt and their tails flicked like agitated cats. One of the largest dragons, a great beast with curly black horns and a barbed tail, stretched its wings and sent a flutter of discomforted activity through the nearby dragons.

"What happened to your perfect control?" Amy demanded and threw up a massive wall of blue energy behind Galen but in front of his dragon skeletons.

This proved to be the wrong thing to do. They did not seem to like being cut off from their master at all. Some of them stood and roared, a horrible sound of grating bone and claw. Others scratched at the earth as if they begged to be released to attack this interloper.

Amythist saw the danger and attempted to intervene. "Amy, stand down and remove the shield. I will handle this."

"Galen, make them lay down," the mage snapped and ignored the headmaster in her anger.

"Make me!" he responded, the perfect vision of petulance.

"Fine," she replied.

"No, Amy, don't!" The headmaster said hastily but young woman ignored the protest. Her authority wasn't granted by the school, after all, but by the Steel Dragon herself.

The world's most powerful mage faced the self-proclaimed world's most powerful dragon. She raised her arms and wind whipped up and raced toward Galen. It surrounded him so now, anything he said was lost in its roar.

The undead dragons liked this even less. A few of those closest to him lunged forward and against the shimmering wall of energy like dogs barking at someone walking too close to their fence line.

Amy ignored them.

She swirled the wind even faster around the young dragon.

It was difficult to see exactly what she was doing to him—for that matter, it was hard to focus on anything except the dragon skeletons—with the wind and the magic and the students who had now begun to panic.

It was a genuine surprise to Kylara when Galen fell to his knees, gasping for breath.

"Will she kill him?" She was shocked.

"No way. She is too smart for that. My guess is she'll knock him out so his skeletons crumble," Karl Midnight said.

Sure enough, the young dragon clutched his throat before he fell on his side, unconscious.

Only then did Amy stop the swirling winds she had controlled with such deftness that she had been able to make an actual vacuum around him.

But knocking Galen unconscious did not have the desired effect.

The skeletons became enraged. Those closest to the wall of magic lunged constantly at it—mindlessly, tirelessly, brainlessly, as if they would destroy themselves before they entertained the idea of Galen being kept away from them.

Kylara wondered what the boy had told them to do.

The other undead dragons—there were possibly fifty of them —didn't all press toward Galen. Most of them became airborne and headed around or over Amy's wall, ready to attack the mage herself.

Kor flicked his silver tail spines and managed to knock holes in a few of their wings, but this also came with unforeseen conse-quences. The beasts divided their ranks to attack the teacher as well as the mage.

The dragon students who had been spoiling for a fight unleashed their flames and more mages threw shields up. This only enraged the creatures further.

And so it came to pass that one student truly did have the power to throw the entire Lumos School into a brawl of the living against the dead.

## CHAPTER THIRTY-THREE

"All right, kids, everyone fall in and get to the dorms!" Kor ordered and the students, even those who had only a moment ago so valiantly pissed off a horde of dragons, began to race to safety.

"Let's go!" Sam shouted but Kylara didn't follow.

She vaulted skyward and took her dragon shape. As the first enemy swooped toward Kor, she lashed out at it with tendrils of dark energy. It crashed violently and as soon as it met the earth, Tanya made roots grow through its ribcage. With a roar of blind rage, it struggled and thrashed to break free.

"Some water would be great!" the young dragon shouted.

"I got it!" Kylara replied and called on her storm powers to summon roiling masses of cloud. Unfortunately, the air was too dry to hold any moisture at all. When it had snowed, it had precipitated all the water out of the atmosphere and there was nothing for her to draw on.

"No, but I do," Sam said. He opened his dragon jaws wide and blasted the entire field in warm, radiant light. The snow melted in an instant.

Tanya grinned. "That'll do it!" With this new source of water, the grasses grew more quickly. Hundreds of thin long, spreading roots extended from the soil. It would have been impossible for the grass to pull a living dragon under the ground as each individual strand was simply too weak. But a skeleton was a different thing entirely.

Rather than round, thick limbs of flesh, it was nothing but narrow bone. Instead of a torso rounder than a tree trunk, the dragon had dozens of ribs, each of which the grass was able to wind around and pull into the dirt. It fought for a moment longer as Tanya hauled it deeper into the earth, but when most of it was beneath the soil, it ceased to struggle. She stopped yanking the now lifeless bones into the ground and simply left the dragon half-buried in the grass in the middle of the U. Kylara didn't blame her. There were other things to focus on.

Another skeleton lunged at her. It pounded into her diamond scales and she used its momentum to hurl it past her. It landed on its back, and its spine snapped in two places but that didn't stop it. The dragon simply rolled over, stood, and shook like a dog emerging from a pool of water. The pieces of broken bone fell free to bother it no more.

Unhurt by any of this, it lunged at her again. She caught it in a web of dark tendrils she had already sent across the ground toward it and toppled it. This time, she summoned a wind and a great swirling column of air spiraled around the beast and tried to rip it to pieces.

It didn't work as the bones were too smooth. The wings were shorn away but the creature continued to struggle against its shadow bindings as if nothing had changed. Kylara took a deep breath, concerned that two of her powers had barely slowed it. She reached out to the plants below the dragon. They grew quickly and whipped wildly in the wind, but they found the bones and obeyed her instruction to drag them into the earth. She lacked the control Tanya had already mastered so wasn't able to stop the plants until it was completely buried.

When it was finally defeated, she released a slow breath but sucked in another as yet another dragon surged toward her.

Before she could respond, a beam of light burst into being and her attacker's rear leg was severed. Its bony body unbalanced, it toppled past her and landed heavily where Tanya was ready for it. Although it was able to roll, it went no farther as more grass roots caught the leg with the missing foot and its tail and sucked it under.

Kylara jumped, flapped once, and landed beside her friend. She wrapped her diamond scaled body protectively around her while the more slender dragon finished her work.

"Are we all right?" Sam asked from where he flew overhead.

"Better than them!" Tanya pointed a long, dirt-encrusted claw at Amy and her team of mage guards.

It was true. The mages did not appear to be doing very well. The problem was that the only power that seemed to work with any consistency against the skeletal dragons was telekinesis. Wind blew through their hollow, fleshless bodies. They ignored the splashes from a mage who tried to shoot them with water. Without a need to breathe, there was no fear of water. One mage summoned a great ball of fire that incinerated most of a skeleton. The remaining bones fell, but the cost was great. Blood poured from the defender's nostril and he almost fainted, and he had only eliminated one dragon.

Amy Williams simply grasped the creatures, lifted them high, and hurled them as far away as she possibly could, sometimes into one of the mountains on either side of the valley that sheltered the Lumos School.

Even this did not seem terribly effective. The dragons struck a rock face or a boulder and cracked a few bones that would fall free, but it caused them no pain and seemed to cost little in locomotion either.

"Try their skulls!" a mage shouted desperately to Amy.

The world's most powerful mage twisted her hands and

wiggled her fingers at the nearest skeleton, and its skull simply imploded. A single bead of blood dripped from her nose when she did this, but it stopped the dragon—for about thirty seconds.

Another lunged forward and plowed through the wreckage of its recently dismembered compatriot from beyond the grave. As it traveled through the mess of bones, some of the pieces flew up to rejoin this new skeleton. It replaced missing ribs and a wing that had been shorn away to make it as good as new.

"We have to lead some of them away from Amy," Kylara said.

"Are you crazy?" Tanya demanded but she was laughing, probably high on adrenaline.

"You must be if you stopped to talk."

From the corner of her eye, she saw another beast hurtling toward her. She didn't know how it had come so close but she reacted reflexively and called the teleportation power she had recently acquired in the pixie realm.

Unfortunately, she needed more practice and the portal didn't open fast enough. The skeleton collided with her and she sprawled awkwardly. Pain flared in her shoulder, something she rarely felt in a dragon fight with anyone but her mom. She felt like she had been cut but with no time to ponder that, she rolled across the hard earth and came to rest beneath a truly massive skeleton.

A pair of long, slender, spiraling horns rose from its head. A matching one on the tip of its tail arced over its shoulder and gored her at the base of her wing. It punctured her diamond scales like a jackhammer through the sidewalk. She roared in pain and unintentionally blasted her assailant in the face with the fire which, of course, did nothing to it.

Kylara struggled to throw it off her. Despite its huge size, it didn't weigh as much as it might have since it was missing so much flesh. It gave her no opportunity to fight free, however. Instead, it swiped her face with a claw made of the same dark material that had already cut the base of her wing. The force of the blow continued through her jaw and snapped her face to the left enough to make her snout smack the dirt of the U.

Time seemed to slow for her as she fought to stay conscious.

The skeleton's other claw rested on her chest to pin her to the ground. It was normal—or as normal as a dragon skeleton's claw could be.

Through smoke and thousands of bones, she saw students racing to the dorms as teachers tried to protect their retreat. The mages tried to change battlefields and the skeletons obliged them. Like mice, they ran to the forest and like cats, the beasts followed.

There was nothing she could do about any of this—or even about the skeleton seated on her chest. It still had its tail pinned through her wing and struggling to break free caused a tremendous amount of pain. She could only watch in horror as it brought its too-heavy claw back for another strike that would likely break the other part of her jaw and cut slices in the diamond scales on that side of her face.

Before it could strike, it was stopped by a mass of black webbing. Dozens of dark, grasping tendrils reached through the carpals and metacarpals of its claw and slowed it enough for the blow to pound into the soil beside her instead of into her face.

She was still stunned from the first blow and had no idea how she had used her dark powers to stop it. It seemed impossible. She had barely been able to think but somehow used her plant powers to bind the dragon's too-heavy hand to the ground? How? Someone yelled as if from a distance—at her, she realized in surprise. "Get up, Kylara, Karl can't hold it much longer. Kylara!"

In the next moment, she was being dragged by Samuel and his light flowed into her and she understood. It wasn't her dark powers that had stopped the dragon from crushing her skull but those of Karl Midnight. And it wasn't her plant powers that the massive skeleton broke free from but Tanya's. She hadn't yelled at herself but had suffered a massive concussion, and the only reason she was able to think again was because Samuel had dumped some of his healing power into her body and super-charged her healing ability.

As reality clicked in, she managed to move out of the huge skeleton's range scant seconds before it ripped free of Tanya's vines and lashed out at her with its tail. In doing so, it sliced through Karl Midnight's tendrils of darkness like a scythe through dried wheat. The ends of his magic were severed from their source and simply evaporated into nothing.

The vines proved to be more of a challenge for the hulking creature. It had already ripped its extra-heavy claw free, but the vines clutched at its other limbs. Not ready to go to its place of rest, it vaulted from the ground and took flight.

To see something so large in the air boggled Kylara's mind. The skeleton of this dragon alone was bigger than some planes and it didn't seem fair that it could fly with all that bulk.

It rose higher, screeched, and called other dragons to it. Then, it settled its empty gaze on her and dove.

She had no idea how to stop it. It had knocked away all her powers and demonstrated that even her diamond scales didn't provide much defense against whatever material the tips of its tail, claw, and horns were made of.

While she didn't know what to do, it didn't mean she refused to act. She dug her claws in and prepared herself to be shredded by this undead monster.

"Get to safety!" she told her friends. "Make sure the other students are all right while I hold it off."

Neither Tanya, Sam, nor Karl listened.

The four of them stared at death itself as it plunged from the sky.

# CHAPTER THIRTY-FOUR

Cassandra was deep in study when the air spirit interrupted her. It raced in so rapidly that the entrance it came in through whistled with its passage. Before she could pull herself away from the tome on spirit magic she had been studying to reprimand the being, it riffled the pages—another habit she had tried to train out of it.

"What on earth is so demanding that you would interrupt me while I am studying the secrets of the spirit realm?"

The wind spirit couldn't speak like the fire or water spirits could. Although capable of making a tornado that could rip a house from its foundation, its voice was nothing more than a breathy whisper.

When it told her what it had seen, she sat bolt upright and began to swear and didn't stop until Diamantine cleared her throat.

"What is it?" Hester demanded from her place of imprisonment. "I mean...what troubles you so, Lady Cassandra?" She rephrased the question, proof that dragons could be trained more easily than the spirits.

The mage considered not telling her anything. After all, the former Dragon SWAT member would have her mission and reservations about what young Galen Stormwing could do. But she still thought she might need her. Her spirits could be troublesome in their ways but they didn't lie. They didn't even understand the concept of lying. If the air spirit whispered fifty dragons made of bone, it meant exactly that.

"The boy who can raise the dead has grown in power."

"Well, that's good for you, right?" Hester asked. "I know you have some aspirations for the boy. Since his discovery, you've obsessed over those books."

Cassandra frowned. Perhaps she should have kept her prisoner in another part of her lair, but she did so like having her nearby where she could see her. Plus, the conversations were always interesting. "He has raised fifty dragons and brought them to the Lumos School. My air spirit stayed until he lost control of them, then raced here."

"He raised fifty dragon skeletons?" Diamantine's mouth gaped. "I thought when you last saw him he had barely managed to raise a dozen."

"As I said, he lost control of them."

The sound of the dragon rattling her chains startled Cassandra. It had been so long since the dragon had even given the impression of wishing to be free. Now, she struggled valiantly against the dampening cuffs.

"Kylara is in danger! You have to let me protect my daughter." She moaned as she pulled at the restraints.

"Why do you think I told you this?" the mage asked rhetorically. "I will not allow my niece to be hurt by the work of a boy who doesn't understand his powers."

"So why aren't you on your way there already? I know that earth spirit of yours is always nearby." Diamantine scowled as she peered around the room.

"Because the last time I faced these bones of the dead, my spirits were overwhelmed. Their powers are formidable but specific. If there is no flesh to burn or lungs to drown, the spirits of flame and air are useless. My earth spirit will be an asset but it may not be enough."

"Release me and I promise to work with you to save Kylara," her captive said.

"Do you swear it on her life?"

"I will not let harm come to Kylara. I swear it on my life and hers. You know I care for her. Believe me, I won't act against you if you free me for this purpose. Not until Kylara is safe and not after."

"Now, let's not go and make promises we cannot keep," she replied. "But I accept your offer. I'll free you and we'll fight together to save the girl we both love."

"Agreed. Yes, please—anything. We're wasting time," Diamantine said as Cassandra moved through the pool of water and unlocked the magic-dampening cuffs.

As soon as she opened them, the dragon gasped and sucked in a great big breath of air as if she had held her breath underwater for minutes. The mage assumed that without her dragon healing power, perhaps that was how it felt.

"Which way do we fly?" she asked and looked around the subterranean lair for an exit.

"We don't have that kind of time," Cassandra said as she took the hand of the dragon's human form. Hester recoiled at the touch at first but the conditioning of her training set in and she allowed the mage to hold her hand. "Earth spirits understand touch best of all."

The ground rose around the two of them. Rocks moved through it and fitted together like bricks or pieces of a puzzle. The dirt closed above them, and the two were enclosed in a bubble of darkness. Cassandra held a hand out to reveal a dancing flame.

Diamantine's look of surprise told the mage that she hadn't

seen her take an ember from the fire elemental's brazier and tuck it in her pocket to transport him.

"We'll be there in ten minutes," she said. "My air spirit cannot communicate with us while we're underground, so I have no idea what the conditions will be like when we arrive."

"It doesn't matter. My diamond scales will protect me long enough to find Kylara."

"A good plan. You protect her and I'll give us cover until we find her."

The bubble sank into the soil and accelerated as the earth spirit displaced the dirt and stone to move his master and her freed captive.

Cassandra was glad that Hester went along with her plan so willingly. If the dragon with her formidably powerful dragon scales was focused on protecting Kylara, she would have a better chance to sneak Galen away safely. That might be the only thing that would stop the skeleton dragons. Or, of course, it might not stop them at all.

If it didn't, she believed that Kylara and her mother together would be able to deal with the undead creatures. Hopefully, if everything went as she planned, she would take Galen with her, win the good graces of her niece, and would be that much closer to enacting the next part of her dream.

# CHAPTER THIRTY-FIVE

Kylara and her friends had hardly any time to act. The massive dragon with the terrible horns and claws dove toward them.

"Karl! A web!" she ordered and he obeyed. Together, they threw up a web of intertwined tendrils of dark energy.

"That won't be enough!" Tanya shouted as she tossed an acorn that landed immediately behind the mesh of dark magic. It took root and, in a moment, was a sapling. Seconds later, it was a young tree with a trunk thick enough to stop an out-of-control automobile. Shortly after that, it was a tree so large that most dragons wouldn't be able to topple it.

The skeleton dragon turned it to splinters with its claw. It was as if nothing could withstand the razor edge of that deadly tool. While the tree had slowed its attack, it didn't stop it. Instead, the dragon bulldozed through it and into the dark web. It shredded this like it had before.

They weren't perturbed, however, as that was part of the plan.

Samuel and Kylara blasted the entangled dragon with beams of light. Hers weren't yet quite narrow enough to burn through the bone but Sam had been practicing. He severed one of the bones in the dragon's leg. It stumbled forward, no longer able to support its massive weight.

Another dead dragon joined the fray and drove into her from the side. She kicked it away. This one was made of nothing but bone so was unable to cut through her diamond scales. But as it careened away, some of its bones snapped free and merged with the enormous one that had its sights on her. It absorbed the bone transplant and pushed forward on all four legs again.

She took the brunt of its attack head-on. Its massive skull powered into her and hurled her off her feet, but she managed to dodge the pair of horns which would have put a quick end to her if she'd been a little slower.

Two more dragons attacked her friends and effectively separated her from them.

It took everything she had to stand against this giant bastard of a dead dragon. Her first priority was to dodge its powerfully vicious blows. She didn't have a second priority, to be honest, as a strike from its claw, horns, or tail would end the fight.

As she ducked and parried its attacks, she noticed that Karl, Tanya, and Sam had overcome their differences in the face of their possible annihilation. Midnight worked to bind the dragon's limbs to the ground so Tanya could use plant roots to engulf the animated bones. Samuel provided the distraction and blasted light and lashed out with his claws while the other two learned how to work together to bury their attacker in the earth.

They were doing much better than Kylara was. Her primary strategy at this point was simply to retreat. She knew she had to fight. Her mom had taught her the power of her diamond scales as a defense but had also shown her repeatedly that they could be used offensively as well.

When the dragon swung at her with its claw, she only half-dodged and stayed within range of its tail so she could thrust a spiked shoulder into its ribs. Some cracked and fell away, but the beast seemed unconcerned. It let itself fall on top of her. The difference in size was such that it could trap her inside its ribcage.

With bones all around her, it was impossible to dodge the barbed tail that tucked in and out of the creature's ribs like a chef overzealously testing a piece of meat for doneness.

Each strike hurt worse than the world's worst wasp sting when it stabbed skin and flesh. Finally, its target properly skewered, the dragon pulled off of her. It drew the claw back. With horrifying predictability, it swung the black bones in an attempt to crush her face into nothing but pulp.

At the very last second, a force of blue energy shimmered into existence inches in front of her dragon snout.

The force of the claws battered through the shield but like a deer crashing into a windshield, most of the blow was stopped.

"Amy?" She gasped.

"Amy wishes she knew the secret to Patel telekinesis!" Jasmine retorted cheekily.

Kylara could not believe that her former roommate and all-around snob had come to her aid at her weakest moment.

Neither could the massive dragon skeleton. Perhaps it was reminded of the first mage that had separated it from its master, or perhaps the grudge was older still. Maybe this was the skeleton of the Prairie King himself, a dragon who had enslaved mages and used them as little more than animals. It was possible that even in death, it remembered the hatred it felt for those lesser magical beings and it turned on the newcomer as if it had completely forgotten about its first target.

"Although I must admit, she is more powerful than us Patels!" the girl shouted as she tried to run.

The dragon lunged after her. It struck her and Kylara understood that she had just seen her ex-roommate killed.

"No!" she screamed and raced after the hulking skeleton. She pounded into it with a diamond shoulder and this time, managed to crush part of the shoulder that held the extra-heavy hand.

With this bone broken, the dragon was unable to lift its most formidable weapon.

It screamed in rage and one of the smaller dragons came to aid it.

She knew that—rationally—she should stop the smaller dragon from giving it some of its bones, and that again, rationally, she should leave her dead ex-roommate where she lay but she couldn't.

Instead, she raced to Jasmine and lifted her from the ground in a claw.

"Kylara?" the girl wheezed.

Kylara managed a bloody grin. "You're alive!"

"Thanks to you." Jazmine's breathing was labored. She must have stopped most of the dragon's punch with her telekinesis but not all of it. It was crazy. If she was a dragon, she'd probably be healed by now. She poured healing light into the girl to stabilize her injuries.

"I'll get you to—"

The massive dragon had restored itself while she was checking on her friend. It struck her so hard that they careened helplessly to crash through one of the walls of the school.

She landed in the Magical Theory classroom. It was one of those that was bigger on the inside than the outside.

"What do we do now?" Jasmine asked. She did not sound good.

"We wait," she said.

They didn't have to wait long.

The massive skeleton thrust through the hole it had created with Kylara's body. It had to widen it to fit and for a moment, it merely knocked bricks away like they were nothing but cardboard.

The young dragon mage used the moment as best as she could.

"Shouldn't we—"

"I have a plan," she said and called on her inner magic.

Their attacker pushed through the hole and with one powerful lunge, hurtled across the classroom toward her.

She chose that moment to step through the portal she had opened to her left. Instinct had warned her to keep the disc of the portal perpendicular to the skeletal dragon, so if it had noticed it at all, it would have seen only a line. She stepped through it with Jasmine still in her claw as the hulk of bones careened past her and into the back of the classroom instead of the diamond-encrusted dragon it had aimed for.

Kylara stepped from the portal and into the U, where her friends were working together to bury another dragon.

"You beat that monster?" Sam asked and sounded hopeful.

"That dragon will find its way back here," Jasmine interjected. "Kylara merely bought us some time."

"We could use it!" Karl said and threw up tendrils of energy as a dragon flew past and tried to gut him with a lash of its tail.

He missed, and the creature moved on as another came in for a passing strike.

"What's going on?" Kylara asked as she moved to stand with Sam and Karl around Tanya and now Jasmine, the squishiest two of the five.

"They've changed tactics," the golden dragon explained. "They somehow understand that Tanya is the only one who can stop them."

"I destroyed one," Karl protested.

"With my help!" Sam retorted.

"Boys, focus!" Tanya pointed at an approaching dragon.

"On it," Sam said and leapt skyward.

He deflected the beast in the most basic of ways—intercepted its path and let it collide with him. It didn't seem to like it and instead of fighting, it tried to break free, but he managed to force it to the ground. Karl was ready and lashed it with dark energy as Tanya summoned plant roots to bury it.

As soon as she did so, however, the rest of the skeletons in the sky all began to attack.

"A little help on the perimeter?" Sam shouted as he raced toward Tanya.

Kylara reared on her hind legs and batted away the first two skeletons. Sam caught the third, and Karl put a web up that frightened the next two away. That bought Tanya enough time to bury the one she'd wrestled with. They had eliminated a number of the dragons since she'd broken away to lead the hulk on a wild goose chase. Their bones protruded from the ground, half-buried in dirt and grass like some kind of macabre piece of artwork.

Unfortunately, far more continued their flight than what had been buried.

"I don't get it," Tanya shouted as Sam and Kylara tracked the dive-bombing dragons. "Once they're mostly buried, they stop trying to fight. It's like they want to be buried—like they know that is where they belong. But until then, they fight tooth and nail."

"My little sister was like that," Sam said. "She never wanted to take a nap even when she needed one."

"Great, so we simply need to put down a horde of grumpy dragon skeletons for an eternal nap?" Karl asked.

"That's the plan." Kylara scanned the grounds. All the students had retreated to safety. A few skeletons harried the dorms, but the teachers and the dorm's enchantments seemed to hold them at bay. She couldn't see Amy anywhere but she could hear screams and the sounds of bones cracking beyond the buildings. They were alone, for now, but they could do this.

Sam lunged and managed to force another dragon into a crash landing. Karl bound it while Jasmine used her shielding to protect the group from the other dragon attacks. Most of them focused immediately on Tanya but this time, it was Kylara who used her plant powers to put the beast to bed.

"This can work if we alternate," she said. "If we thin their numbers enough, we'll win."

"I don't think that'll happen," Karl grouched.

"Do you always have to be such a downer?" Sam retorted.

"Only when that guy's around," Karl sent out a tendril of black energy to point toward one of the school buildings. The big dragon with the black claw and horns lumbered out of the school. Its empty eye sockets settled on Kylara.

CHAPTER THIRTY-SIX

The massive skeleton barreled into the five friends like a tidal wave.

Any chance they had of putting the other dragons to rest was washed away as the monster was simply too strong. Kylara tried to keep herself between it and her allies and in doing so, wasn't able to use any of her other powers. Karl attempted to bind it with his dark powers, but it simply ripped through them like they were nothing but the shadow they were. Sam didn't have time to launch one of his tight light beams, and it continually yanked Tanya's plants away. Jasmine was the only one of the group not focused on the hulking skeleton. She threw shields up in the paths of the dozens of other creatures that continued their assault.

"We need a plan to defeat this big bastard!" Karl shouted as it tore free from a cocoon of black webbing he had managed to wrap around its tail.

"My plan was to ditch it inside the school!" she said desperately.

"What if you opened another of those portals?" Jasmine suggested.

"Portals?" Sam asked before the dragon's tail whipped viciously to knock him off his feet and slice a nasty gash across his belly. "Since when can you portal?" he asked through clenched teeth.

"I'd need time to open one. Besides, where could I send it?"

He fixed her an incredulous look. "Anywhere but here!"

"Antarctica!" Karl shouted.

It wasn't much of a plan—merely another deferment, probably—but she couldn't think of what else to do. She called on her inner magic and tried to focus on a far corner of the land she'd grown up on. If she could get the skeleton dragon there, it might buy them an hour. The idea to send it to Antarctica—a place she had never been to and had no geographical knowledge of—was not an option.

Unfortunately, it seemed this plan wouldn't ever be put to the test to determine its usefulness in this brawl. About fifty feet away, the earth began to move.

"One of them is rising again!" she shouted.

"No—no it can't be." Tanya gasped and her horrified gaze settled on the upheaval. "If we can't put these beasts to rest…"

"We're doomed," Karl finished for her.

"That's not a dragon. It's earth magic!" Jasmine shouted as she threw a shield up that managed to stop a skeleton from ripping Kylara's tail off.

The young dragon mage wished the news that the skeletons weren't rising again from the earth was comforting, but it wasn't. Not when she knew what the alternative must be. Aunt Cassandra had most likely come to prey on the chaos of the moment. She dodged another blow from the hulking dragon skeleton, unable to even hazard a guess as to how the hell she was supposed to fight against this monstrous beast, its horde of lesser minions that constantly healed the damn thing, and now, her aunt's bevy of elemental spirits.

"We still need a plan!" Karl shouted.

It soon became clear that it wasn't a dragon but rather a bubble of earth that she suspected Cassandra had instructed her earth spirit to create so she could travel safely underground. Rather than a skeleton heaving itself out of the earth limb by limb, the sphere simply emerged. Like a beach ball from a pool, the earth parted to let it pass and reformed behind it.

Kylara stood quickly and readied herself to crash into her aunt. If the mage had enough time to properly determine what was going on, she knew that the fight was lost.

To her utter surprise, it wasn't her Aunt Cassandra who was revealed when the sphere of stone and earth melted into the soil.

The shock of seeing her mother cost her precious seconds during which she forgot her frightening attacker completely.

"Kylara, no!" Hester Diamantine blurred into a streak of blue lightning. She had always been fast—annoyingly fast to the girl she'd trained for sixteen years—and she used that speed now. She took her dragon form as she flew toward her adopted daughter and finished her transformation barely in time to get between the student and the heavy, black claw of the skeleton dragon.

She took the blow in the gut and was thrust back and left a trail of blood between her and the girl who had worked so hard to make her proud.

"Mom!" Kylara screamed and lunged toward her, oblivious to the dragon that had almost killed Hester and still very deliberately tried to kill her. The beast cracked its bony tail and rocketed the black stone stinger on the end toward her neck. She had already committed herself to her push toward her mom, and the skeleton had timed its strike perfectly. As she tried to think of a way to slow her momentum, she realized she would not be able to dodge, would be stabbed in the neck, and would bleed out on top of the woman who loved her enough to come to help her.

Desperate, she tried to increase her speed in the hope that it might make a slight difference, but a pillar of stone erupted from the soil and blocked the skeleton's barbed tail.

The massive beast roared in frustration. She ignored it and scrambled toward Hester.

"Mom—Mom, are you okay? Mom, please don't be dead. Not after all this, please."

"Ky…" Her mother coughed and blood stained her white crystalline teeth. "Don't be so…melodramatic." Hester Diamantine rolled and pushed to her feet. She was no longer bleeding and the gash on her stomach was already healing thanks to her dragon power. The diamond scales had begun to reform over the wound.

"Mom, you're okay!"

"Now that I can see you're okay, I'm fine."

Kylara blushed despite the intensity of the moment. "Now look who is being melodramatic."

"I haven't had a dragon make me bleed in years." Diamantine grinned and the girl knew the look well. It was that of someone ready to excel at a challenge. "This will be fun."

"How are you here?" Kylara asked as her mother tensed her muscles in anticipation and watched carefully so she could choose the perfect moment to join the fight.

"You aunt set me free on the condition that I save your life. Now, if you'll excuse me—"

Hester surged toward the skeleton dragon as it bulldozed forward. They collided with the sound of an avalanche and pieces of bone or shards of diamond scattered from the force of the impact.

It quickly became apparent that Diamantine hadn't taught Kylara everything. The older dragon faced a skeleton that was twice her size and had four weapons that could cut through her, and she did it with style.

The creature swung its tail at her and she dodged, then swiped it violently with hers to crush some of the vertebrae and force it to reknit the appendage, which was shorter now. It tried to pound its head against her but she was too fast. She answered its head-butt with her own and managed to get under its two long horns. Forehead struck forehead and diamond scales beat bone.

Her adversary shuddered as it took two stumbling steps back. A web of hairline fractures was visible in the middle of its forehead.

"Are you going to use the claw or what?" she demanded and smirked at the skeleton.

It roared, raised its heavy black claw, and threw all its weight and power behind the blow. Diamantine spun away seconds before the talon drove into her chest. She pivoted so quickly that she was able to batter the arm that supported the strange bone in three places and break it in two of them.

The dragon groaned and its bones rubbed against each other to echo the sound as it tried and failed to lift its most devastating weapon.

"I'll find Galen and help him stop these dragon skeletons," Cassandra shouted. "Earth spirit, aid them in defeating these aberrations!"

The sphere of earth emerged from the ground, this time in the vague shape of a human.

"It will obey you for this fight, Kylara. Use it well," her aunt said before a gust of wind from her air spirit caught her leather cloak and whisked her away.

"Earth spirit," Kylara addressed the muddy form and it seemed to listen. "Can you open a crack in the ground?"

It answered by doing exactly that and in a few moments, a thirty-foot gash appeared in the dirt beneath their feet, perhaps ten feet wide and fifteen feet deep.

"Finally, a plan! Throw the skeletons in the hole," Karl shouted.

The rest of the team sprang into action. Sam vaulted skyward and hurled another dragon to earth and the freshly opened hole. Karl snagged the creature's wings with tendrils of inky darkness and began to drag it laboriously into the fissure. Kylara and

Tanya reached out with plant powers and bound it before it could escape.

"Spirit, close this hole!" the young dragon mage ordered and the spirit obeyed and pushed the earth together as easily as a kid might have smoothed a sandbox.

While they focused on the lesser beasts, Diamantine continued to dominate the big dragon. She'd disabled its claw and anytime it called for another dragon to lend it a bone to repair itself, she lashed out with her tail to snap any offering in half.

Tired of being interfered with, the skeleton attacked her and tried to gore her with its horns. She dodged and moved so quickly it was almost hard to follow. Still in motion, she swung her tail between the dragon's ribs and lashed her diamond scales into rib after rib to fracture some and shatter most. Bones rained around her quarry.

The dragon tried to lift its tail but Diamantine moved too quickly. Instead of allowing her body to be punctured, she used her wing to block the blow. The black, stony barb pierced through the thin membrane of her wing, but she had obviously used the tactic before because she didn't cry out or scream in pain. She merely grunted and folded her wing against her side to tangle her adversary's tail with it.

It shouldn't have worked. The larger beast should have been able to hurl her aside. It should have been able to lift its tail and throw her off like a dog shaking mud out of its fur. But it was no longer a dragon and existed as only bones. It seemed to still be somewhat accustomed to its formerly formidable weight and didn't quite know what to do with this diamond-covered dragon who did her damnedest to batter it to pieces.

With another bellow of fury, it tugged, yanked, and finally, tried to rip itself free but with no success. Hester had no intention to release it. Instead, she allowed it to make a bloody mess of one of her wings while she used her tail to pound the bones of its legs.

"We have to help my mom!" Kylara shouted, and her friends all confirmed.

They finished burying another dragon and turned to help the older dragon, who fought tooth and nail with the beast. Despite having three of its legs broken, it still thrashed and tried to slice her with its head, its one good appendage, and its injured ones.

"Open a trench!" the dragon mage ordered and the earth spirit obeyed. The ground gave way beneath the giant skeleton and both it and Diamantine tumbled into the hole together.

"Bury us!" her mother shouted.

"Certainly not," she replied and whipped her tendrils of dark energy toward her mom. "A little help, Karl?"

Karl grunted an affirmative and launched his barrage of tentacles to grasp one of her wings. Together, they tried to haul her out of her adversary's grasp.

"No, Kylara, no!" Diamantine shouted.

She was right. Without her to entangle the skeleton, it was able to right itself and scramble out of the hole. It clawed to the surface and was about to surge into Diamantine again, but something held it fast.

"It'll tear that root!" Tanya shouted.

The dragon seemed to understand what was going on and it turned and tried to sever the root binding its one good foot with its teeth. It couldn't make contact, however, as a shimmering shield of blue energy was in its way.

"Let's finish this!" Jasmine Patel shouted, her hands raised as she manipulated the shield.

"Karl—"

"On it!" he replied and lashed the creature again. Now that the bones supporting its claw were damaged, it had more difficulty severing the dark energy. It became even more difficult when Diamantine launched herself at it.

Kylara, knowing better than to get between her mom and something she wanted to beat the crap out of, helped Karl bind the dragon with dark energy.

Hester attacked savagely to shatter the rest of its ribs into little more than shards, brutalize its spine, and pulverize its tail. She battered its head with hers once, twice, and a third time and finally, the plates of bone that made up its skull caved inward. No longer was she fighting the skeleton of a dragon. The specter before her was little more than an amalgamation of broken shards of calcium, vaguely representative of the shape of a dragon. It was like she was fighting one a child might imagine. There were too many missing pieces, too many broken parts, and too many slivers for the creature to regain its ferocity.

Diamantine dodged its final and now entirely pathetic blow, inhaled, and blasted it with fire. The force and the heat of the blast were such that the last few tiny bones holding it together crumbled or burned away to nothing and the beast toppled into the pit. It landed on its back, unable to immediately right itself in the tight space.

Kylara and Tanya were ready. They dumped their magic into the plants in the soil. Roots crisscrossed the fractured pieces of bone as the skeleton tried continuously to reassemble itself. It lashed out and struck a blue shield that stopped its claw. When its tail broke free, the tip was severed by one of Sam's beams of light.

"Close the chasm!" the dragon mage bellowed at the earth spirit and it immediately pushed the two opposite walls of earth together and smothered the enemy within.

Still, it resisted and tried to retaliate. As the walls pushed closer, it fought even more savagely to break the shadow bonds Karl had wound around it. It struggled against the roots that grew through it and tried to maim the dragon who had used light to burn the deadly tip of its tail away.

Fortunately, it's sheer maddened will wasn't enough. The

earth spirit continued to push the earth together to fill the spaces between the bones of the beast while Tanya and Kylara urged all the trees, grasses, shrubs, and even moss to grow as swiftly and thickly as possible.

The great skeleton remained on its back, and that was where it would stay. Between Karl's dark energy, Kylara and Tanya's root growth, and the earth elemental filling everything between the bones with dirt, the dragon was finally defeated.

It slowed its fight and finally, it stopped. Still, its horns, claw, and tail protruded above the earth as if to remind everyone of exactly how horrible the battle with the beast had been.

"We did it!" Kylara shouted, proud, relieved, and still shocked that her mom was alive and there with her.

"We're not done yet," Diamantine replied and gestured at the battlefield around them.

In the distance, skeletal dragons still engaged Amy and her mages, but it was a much closer sight that drew the girl's attention.

Cassandra had revived Galen and was speaking to him. She could not hear anything the boy said because concentric rings of fire, wind, and water surrounded the two of them. She could see he looked scared but determined and hoped Cassandra was telling him how to finally put these dragons to rest.

She would never get to know what was said, however, because suddenly, she understood why their battle with the giant dragon had proceeded relatively uninterrupted.

The rest of the skeletons were in the sky. As one, they launched themselves at Cassandra and attacked her as an almost literal storm of bones.

# CHAPTER THIRTY-SEVEN

The mage's defenses lasted all of about thirty seconds.

The dragons simply drove through the fire. They showed no indication that it had hurt them or that they could feel it at all and simply pushed through the flames while their bones blackened.

The swirling air did even less to stop them. One of the smaller dragons was pulled away, but the larger ones sank their claws into the ground and pulled themselves closer to this woman who would dare to interfere with their master.

For a few moments, the water elemental was able to hold them back but only because it could become ice. It created a ring of it around Cassandra, but it took a few dragons all of twenty seconds to power it through.

Still, she wasn't defeated. She yelled at Galen as if whatever she had to tell him was more important than them being eaten by dragon skeletons.

But if she attempted to give him directions on how to stop the creatures, he failed to understand them.

The beasts pushed closer. One reached out with a claw of bone and had almost wrapped its hand around Cassandra when a great pillar of rock erupted from the soil and punched into its jaw. The strength of the strike was such that it completely broke the bone in half. It also unbalanced the attacker and it wobbled precariously before it plunged to earth.

Another tried to break through and was met by a wall of stone.

The third succumbed when a boulder pushed through its ribcage and broke it in half.

But the fourth managed to avoid the earth elemental. It flew in from above without ever swooping low enough to come within range. The earth spirit continued to defend the perimeter around Cassandra but it couldn't save her from the sky. The skeleton stretched a claw out, snatched the mage up, and lifted her high.

Kylara could not let anything happen. She launched powerfully, spread her wings, and caught up to the beast. She opened her jaws and launched a pure beam of light that she directed through the beast's body.

Despite its speed and strength, it had no effect. The dragon continued to fly on with its captive in its claw.

Frantic now, she tried something else. She focused on the space in front of her. She desperately needed to open a portal.

Thankfully, her new ability, as unpracticed as it was, hadn't abandoned her.

A gateway appeared in front of the dragon but traveling in the opposite direction. She powered into it and fragments of bone scattered everywhere as the skeleton exploded into shards. It simply wasn't able to survive a collision with a living battering ram coated with diamonds.

Cassandra fell but this wasn't a concern. Kylara reached out with her dark tendrils, caught the mage, and lowered her to the earth while the other dead dragons circled overhead.

Her mom, Tanya, Sam, Karl, and Jasmine had all taken positions around Galen, who was on his knees and screamed at the dragons still in flight.

They appeared to ignore him. Instead, they flocked in ever tighter patterns until they grew so dense that when they attacked, there'd be no way to stop them.

Kylara had no idea how she would get past this, but she knew she'd had enough. She had already thought she'd lost her mom and Jasmine. Now, Cassandra had almost been killed as well? It was too much. It was honestly too damn much.

She opened a portal, stepped through it, and reappeared beside her friends and family.

"This Midnight kid keeps going on about a plan!" Diamantine shouted over the sound of a thousand bones clacking against themselves.

"That's because we need a plan!" Midnight shouted.

"Don't worry, I have one," Kylara replied.

She shed her dragon form with its diamond scales and stopped thinking about teleportation, or light powers, or shadow magic. Instead, she focused all her energy into what was needed to defeat these dragons.

When the first one struck, she was ready.

A thousand roots lashed from the soil to tangle the first dragon, the second, the third…the fifth…and the tenth.

Kylara screamed and willed the wind to blow through the field and whip all the snow and ice into the air, then melt it and rain it down again. With this water, she made the plants grow.

Every dragon that came within five feet of the earth was snared and brought to the surface where hundreds more roots, blades of grass, and shrubby branches twined between their bones and hauled them into the earth.

Blood poured from one of her nostrils, then the other. She thought one of her ears was bleeding too, but she couldn't tell since the blood didn't drip into her mouth. All she knew was that she could no longer hear on one side. Her head began to pound and didn't stop. With each beat of her pulse, it felt as if another nail was hammered into her skull but still, she continued. Grimly, she made her mind up that she wouldn't stop until she had dragged every single one of these unnatural undead monsters into the earth where they belonged.

She realized then—as her blood trickled and her head told her to do something nice for a change like perhaps use a chainsaw—that she could do this. Despite the strain, she had the strength and the power. She—and she alone—was able to force these skeletons to return to their place beneath the earth.

The only problem was that it would kill her to do it.

In that moment, Kylara didn't care. She didn't want to die but she wanted more than anything to protect her friends and her mom. Pushing the negative thoughts aside, she continued to pour her power into the plants. Her dragon strength evaporated and her healing power followed, then seemed to become the opposite when parts of her body seemed to shut down.

Her vision began to dim but she gritted her teeth and continued to drag the skeletons beneath the dirt. She hoped that whoever buried her had the good sense to cremate the remains first.

In the next moment, the pain wasn't so bad. Her healing power had somehow returned.

"You can do this, Kylara!" Sam shouted into her deaf ear. His hand was on her shoulder and he gave her his light energy to heal.

"Not alone, she can't!" Karl shouted and reached out with dark powers to snag more of the creatures and drag them earthward.

"Well, if anyone could do it alone it would be Ky. But she has us." Tanya sent her magic through the plants and another ten thousand seeds Kylara hadn't been able to sense burst from their hard casings. Desert wildflowers—some of which could have been there since before the school had been founded—erupted in the field and added their biomass to the great grasping mess of root and grass she was controlling.

The dragon skeletons didn't stand a chance. Those that managed to break free of the shadows found Jasmine's shimmering force field above them and were hurled into the carnivorous forest of skeleton-hungry plants.

They fought as long as they could but with everyone helping, it wasn't particularly long. Soon, the only sound that could be heard was the strangely insectile scrape of grass growing in rapid motion until finally, it was over.

They had won. Kylara had never been so tired, but who was she to complain? She was alive. Her friends were alive and her mom was free.

Kylara collapsed into Hester's arms, who transformed into her human body in an instant and caught her.

"Oh, Kylara, I am so proud of you—truly I am."

"Where have you been, Mom?" she asked.

In an extremely uncharacteristic show of emotion, Diamantine wiped an actual tear that had somehow intruded in her normally hard expression. "I'm…honored that you would still call me that after you learned the truth."

"You always cared about me, Mom. From the moment you saw me, you protected me. I would never turn my back on that."

"That means so much to me—the world, in fact."

"That being said, you have a ton of explaining to do."

"Yeah, number one being how the hell you arrived with the elemental mage?" Sam asked.

Diamantine didn't look at Sam but kept her gaze locked on her adopted daughter. "We'll talk, I promise we will. Right now, let's make sure everyone is safe."

"Aunt Cassandra!" Kylara realized that the last time she had seen the woman, she had thought she might be dead.

But the mage was gone. There was no sign of her where she

had dropped her and nothing to show where she might have gone.

"I thought that might happen," Hester said. "She freed me but only so I could help you. I told her I would spare her life after this, but she wasn't interested in making promises about anything other than your life, Kylara."

"She said that?"

"I have many opinions about Cassandra, but one thing is certain. She cares for you very much. There were times when I was imprisoned that I wished it wasn't so, but I won't deny her feelings for you."

"Then where is she?" Tanya asked. "If she loves Ky so much, she should have stuck around."

"She'll be back," the older dragon said with a chuckle. "Something about the boy raising skeletons appealed to her. She won't be able to stay away knowing he's here."

"But he's not," Karl Midnight said flatly.

"Pardon?" Diamantine turned away from Kylara for the first time, her brows furrowed.

"He was in the middle of all of us." He pointed to the ground. "But now, he's not. He's gone."

They all wasted a moment craning their necks to try to locate Galen, but he was nowhere to be seen. All there was to mark where he'd been was a patch of dirt where everything else was tangles of grass.

Kylara wondered if Cassandra had left a similar mark in the dirt when she had vanished. She had no more time to think about it, though, as Amy and her team approached from the woods.

"Am I glad to see all of you!" she shouted by way of hello.

The young dragon mage was stunned when, instead of the old hero-worship she'd felt for the powerful mage, what rose in her chest upon seeing her was fury and rage.

"The feeling is not mutual," she snapped.

"I'm sorry?" Amy stopped in her tracks, taken aback.

"This mess is on you." Kylara gestured vehemently at the vegetation and pieces of bone that protruded from the ground. "First, you hollered at Galen in front of the class and chased him away. That was unprofessional but you were worried about all of us, so it was understandable."

"I—" The mage started to speak but she cut her off before she could.

"But then you used your magic when Amythist tried to keep that horde of dragons from running rampant. You made Galen lose control. If anyone had died here today, their blood would be on your hands."

The young woman looked ready to make an angry retort of her own and she was prepared to respond with considerably more vitriol if she did. Fortunately, before the two could escalate the confrontation, Amythist joined them.

"The young lady has a point, Amy," the headmaster announced. "A little restraint might help you in the future."

Amy lowered her head like she'd been punched. "Yes, ma'am."

That was the moment when Kylara truly saw her hero as she was for the first time. She was only a few years older than she was. In the short time since she'd discovered her powers, the young mage had killed dragons, fled, been recruited into a war, and acquitted herself famously during the worst battles.

But she wasn't that different than her. Both of them tended to go off half-cocked, and either of them would lay their lives down for the people they protected. They were far more alike than different.

The realization hit hard and pushed through her anger. She broke into a smile instead. "It's okay, Amy. No one's perfect."

The mage walked closer to her and held a hand up. "Friends, then?"

Kylara shook her hand, then pulled her into a hug. "Definitely."

Amythist smiled at them and placed a hand on each of their

shoulders. "Excellent! Since you two are such good friends, I'm sure you won't mind directing the cleanup of our campus?"

They groaned at the same time, then shared wry smiles.

"I thought we would be in trouble," Sam said.

"No," the headmaster said. "You've all done splendidly. If anything, you've demonstrated exactly why a place like the Lumos School is so important to us. Look at you. It took everyone working together to save the day—mages, dragons, and even a pixie power in there if I'm not mistaken. I thought we were done for before those trees up and swallowed the dragons we were fighting. Well done, Tanya."

"Thanks, but that wasn't me. That was Kylara," the young dragon admitted.

Amy nodded, impressed. "Chalk that down as a point for the mages, yeah?"

"Definitely!" Jasmine interjected, which forced nervous laughter from those who could manage it.

"I don't know what your teachers will say, but seriously, I'm glad you were here for the fight. Plus, it's not like this will be the last one, huh?" Amy said.

"What makes you say that?" Sam asked.

"I don't see the bone lord or the queen of the elements around. That means they got away. Which means, most of the time anyway, that it's only a matter of time before more trouble finds us."

"At least we know we can beat them together, though, right?" Tanya said.

Amythist nodded with a broad smile. "A small group of dedicated individuals can save the world. You're lucky to have already met some people as special as these, Kylara."

She knew she was. After everything that had happened these last few months, she understood better than ever what was important in her life. It was simple and even obvious. People were important.

Losing her home had hurt, but it was the thought of her mom being gone that had wrecked her emotionally. Going to the pixie realm was strange, but it was much harder to think she'd have to live her life without her friends. She'd face a thousand pig monsters or glowing balls with jolt powers as long as she could keep her friends.

She looked at them now—Sam and his too handsome smile and Tanya and her shredded dress. Even Karl had stood with her, sarcasm and all. And then there was Jasmine, who didn't seem all that keen to talk to them now that the fight was over, but she had been there in the thick of things when it mattered most.

Kylara couldn't believe how lucky she was. She had all these amazing people in her life although months before when her mom had been taken from her, she'd had no one.

She was almost ready for danger to come knocking, simply because she knew that when it did, she'd have her mom and her friends to face it beside her.

## CHAPTER THIRTY-NINE

Galen opened his eyes but couldn't understand what he saw.

It looked like his eyes had somehow sunk into his head and he was looking out through his broken skull. Everything above him was dark except for a gash of white light that ran from the bottom of his vision up to the zenith overhead, then split into two more, both of which ended within his viewpoint from the back of his skull.

"You're awake, thank goodness."

He turned to the voice and immediately disproved his hypothesis that his face had been crushed and he was somehow still alive. The blackness above wasn't the inside of his head but rather of some huge, man-made dome and the lines of light weren't the cracks of a head injury, but fissures in the massive structure.

It took a moment to realize that he lay in a shaft of light, which made it hard to see anything outside of the narrow strip he was in but blackness. He recognized the voice but it remained disembodied.

"Are your healing powers working on your head? I think you got a concussion."

"Where am I?" he asked.

"You're in a safe place. A place where no one else can hurt you."

The young dragon shook his head. "It was me who hurt everyone else. God, what if someone had died? That would mean I...that is, my powers—"

"You didn't kill anyone. My spirits watched the entire encounter. Your revenants were under control and behaving beautifully, in fact, until Amy Williams tried to overpower you."

"I thought she only made a shield." The events after that were fuzzy for him. He had begun to feel overwhelmed by the dragons as if all of them demanded more power from him. It felt like they had all required a flood of energy to fight whereas before, they had only needed a trickle.

"She made a shield at first but then she used her magic to capture you. She denied you the very air you breathe and struck you at your weakest moment to knock you unconscious. That's when you suffered a concussion."

Galen could vaguely remember the whirlwind of energy, but he didn't remember being hit by anything "What happened when I was unconscious?"

"Your revenants—denied the calming presence of their master —lost control. But the mage Kylara Diamantine saved the day."

He tried to process the information that he had lost control and a fellow student had been forced to protect the entire campus from his power run amok. "They must all hate me."

"Many people hate what they cannot understand," the woman said, still hidden in shadow.

Cautiously, he moved from the shaft of light and into the safety of the darkness. He didn't feel so blinded there, or as over-whelmed. As his dragon sight adjusted quickly to the dark, he saw the woman who'd spoken. It was the mage who had tried to help him at school when everything had gone so wrong.

She wore well-worn leathers and was wrapped in a cloak of

white fur against the cold wind that blasted into the dome through the cracks. Her hair was dark and marked here and there with gray, and her face was lined, especially around the eyes, which looked like they too had seen things in the darkness and been driven from the light long before.

"I don't understand this power either," he confessed to Cassandra—he seemed to recall she had told him her name.

"I'm not sure anyone on this planet does," she said softly.

"Then I need to get rid of it!" he stated, suddenly sure that his power was the abomination Amy had made it out to be. "Maybe if I can get rid of it, they'll forgive me. I won't have to be a rogue dragon if I get rid of it, right? You said those dragon bodies didn't kill anyone. Maybe if I get rid of this power before they do, I won't have to live as an outcast."

"I'm so sorry, Galen, but that's not wise," the woman said gently, stood from her kneeling position, and walked slowly toward him. As she moved through the space, he studied his surroundings a little more closely. It wasn't only the dome over-head that was broken. This entire place—whatever and wherever it was—could only be described as a wreck.

Rubble lay in disarray, and twisted pieces of metal were strewn about as well as if a giant had made a tossed salad of broken concrete and steel. In the distance behind Cassandra, he could barely make out what appeared to be the shape of a giant lighting set-up. Every bulb had been shattered and he could understand the feeling.

"But you were trying to help me turn it off, weren't you?" Galen asked. "In the field—I remember you being there. You tried to help me stop them."

"I tried to help because I didn't want you to get hurt, but I would never try to take your power away, Galen. Do you truly think the dragons would respect if you became simply another vanilla dragon again? Do you think your family would respect you if you returned powerless instead of more powerful?"

He bit the inside of his cheek at the thought of his family discovering he had given up an ability so powerful that it had overwhelmed Amy Williams and her mage guards. They would never forgive him for something they would see as a pointless sacrifice. "But you said no one on earth can help."

"No one can, yes. Not anymore, anyway."

"What do you mean by not anymore?" he asked.

"Perhaps this power the pixies granted you could be understood if you had the proper tutor—a dragon who gained powers in the same way, for example. It's funny, I would never have thought of him but with your power, it seems obvious. He would have been the perfect tutor. Maybe, with your help, he can still be."

"I don't understand what you're talking about. Are you saying there was a dragon who could have taught me but that he's…he's dead?"

Cassandra nodded. "Indeed. But he is gone. I thought that by coming to his final resting place I might have been able to sense something of his spirit, but I was wrong. He's too far gone and has been dead for too long."

"How long is too long?" Galen asked. "I raised those dragons from that graveyard and they must have been hundreds of years old."

"That is a good point." Her tone had become almost a purr. "He hasn't been dead nearly that long. Maybe this could work."

"No, wait, it can't," he said and the tiny confidence he had managed to build in himself was immediately snuffed out. "When I bring them back, it's only their bodies. They're still mindless and they feel soulless. There's no way one of them could teach me."

"You're so perceptive, Galen. I don't know how someone so young can have a power so formidable and still be able to recognize his weaknesses."

"I guess I'm used to failing," he said, although it didn't feel like failure when he talked to Cassandra. It was nice to discuss it with someone who finally treated him with respect. For once, he could enjoy being able to earn praise instead of more not-good-enough responses like the teachers at the Lumos school always piled on.

"Failure is how we learn," she agreed. "I failed many times in trying to contact this spirit. But now I see that perhaps I wasn't thinking broadly enough. I can summon spirits, but without a body to anchor them, they cannot remain here for any amount of time. If only there was some way to—"

"What if I raise the body and you bring its spirit back?" he suggested eagerly. "It could work! Okay, there's no guarantee, right? But if it did work, I would have the tutor I need, wouldn't I?"

"Well, yes, I suppose that is possible." Cassandra wore a bemused expression on her face. "I don't know if it would work, though. Tell me, have you practiced with only one skeleton? Would you be able to protect me from it?"

"One dragon won't be a problem for us," he said and gained new confidence now. "If I lose control, I can fight it while you use the earth spirit to bury it."

"Yes, yes, that's a good plan." She took a few steps toward a pile of rubble. "Shall we try?"

"You mean now?" he asked.

"Yes, we are already at his resting place, after all." The mage gestured for him to follow her.

He complied and moved through the light and deeper into the darkness. "Why did you bring me here?"

"I didn't know if the Steel Dragon would be hunting you." She stopped in front of the pile of rubble and he could already feel the bones buried beneath it. They were jagged, the bones of a dragon with a special ability that changed their very structure. Galen could only think of one dragon who had been such a special one and the Steel Dragon herself had killed him. "I know she would never come here. Even in death, she fears him."

"Is it smart to bring him back, then?" he asked, suddenly unsure.

"He is one of three dragons who obtained powers from the pixies—not including the students, of course. Now that the Steel Dragon and Amythist are treating you as a pariah, he's your only choice if you want to use your power. There is no one else who would be both willing and able to teach you. Without him, are you sure you'll be able to control your abilities?"

"Maybe it would make more sense if I simply never use them," Galen said. His hands shook and he couldn't believe he stood near the grave of the infamous dragon.

"That's hardly realistic," Cassandra snapped.

"Excuse me?"

"What if you're attacked? What if someone comes to kill you? Are you telling me you won't defend yourself? What if someone tries to kill your brother or your parents? Will you sit idly by and waste your potential because you're too afraid to use it?"

After a long moment, he shook his head. "No. You're right. We have to do this."

"Precisely. Now, raise his bones into one of your revenants. As you do so, I will usher his spirit into its former home. With luck, we will soon have a mentor fit enough to teach you and hone your formidable powers."

Galen nodded, closed his eyes, and reached out for the bones. He could feel them under the pile of rubble—every jagged edge and wicked point. Carefully, he began to pour his inner magic into them and tried to fill them with magic so they could animate themselves. They drank greedily as if they were thirstier than any of the other skeletons he had raised, even the hulk dragon.

It didn't feel like raising the body of a recently deceased creature. It felt like these bones had last lived—last *truly* lived—thousands of years before and that unearthing them from their resting place was a supremely unnatural thing to do.

There was more to the skeleton than only age, though. It felt like a thousand other lives held onto this one—as if every dragon or human who had ever died at the cruel, bony claws of this corpse now struggled to stop him from being successful.

"Ignore the lesser souls!" Cassandra shouted. She sounded strained as if she also had to expend more energy than she had anticipated. "They do not understand what we hope to accomplish. The dead are bitter. They always are. Ignore them and focus on the sweet taste of success, of power, and of mastery!"

Galen heard her encouragement and thrust more of his magic into the cruelly shaped, twisted bones. His strength left him and his healing power failed. Soon after, his ability to change into a dragon started to fade. It was a slow process but soon, it too would be gone.

He cried out, desperate not to lose his ability to become a dragon, but when he was about to lose everything, it was over.

Gradually, his strength began to return. He was still a dragon, thank goodness, and still had his powers. And he had done his part of the magic. He had raised the body of the dead dragon.

Cassandra still labored at her part of their agreement. Her arms were outstretched as wind whipped past her. Her eyes were as black as shadow, and a low, ragged, uncomfortable growl issued from her throat.

Her nose began to bleed, then an ear. She screamed and her chest shuddered as what appeared to be a living shadow seeped from the earth beneath the feet of the now standing dragon skeleton.

It extended slowly and found the claws of the dragon body where it stood placidly. Inch by inch, it crawled up and around the bones, wound through them, and when it reached the neck vertebrae, some spread down its spine, legs, and tail. It sent other tendrils of itself that looked like spilled ink through the great skull with its jagged bony points.

The dark soul of the dead dragon flowed into the skull and something about the skeleton changed. It no longer stood so robotically and so stiffly. There was something to its posture now —something intelligent and even organic.

The beast turned its head, still bone-white but lined with veins of blackness that crept around the skull and beyond to the entire skeleton. It was like the soul attempted to completely wrap around the bones but there wasn't enough of it to complete the job. So, instead of a pure white skeleton, it was a dracolich made of bones that were wound with veins of black that addressed Cassandra and Galen.

"Who dares to disturb Lord Boneclaw's rest?"

As I write this, Michael and I are kicking off work on the sixth and (probably) final book in the Dragon's Daughter series. It's going to be called *The Sum of All Magic*, and won't be out until Spring, but it's shaping up to be a truly epic conclusion to this fun storyline!

Which begs the question: what would you like to read next??

Michael and I have enjoyed working together this past year and a half. During that time we've managed to create fifteen *Steel Dragon* novels (bundled into five volumes) and we'll soon have six *Dragon's Daughter* novels as well. We're almost certainly doing something else fun after this series is complete, but…what?

This is your chance to have a little something to say about that. I'd like to invite any readers dedicated enough that they're taking the time to read our author notes to send me an email. You can reach me at author@kevinomclaughlin.com — I do try to reply to everyone who writes me.

Would you like to see more Kristen Hall? More Kylara Diamantine? A new story featuring entirely different characters, but still set in the same world? (I have visions of a pixie-focused series that could be fun!) Or perhaps it's time for us to move on from this world and try something entirely different. Send us your thoughts! (I'll share them with Michael.) We'd love to hear what you're interested in reading next!

This year has been a momentous one for me. I'm not *quite* to my million word goal yet, but I'm definitely on track to hit it by the end of December, 2020. This is the first time I'll have cracked that barrier. A million new words in a calendar year is pretty cool stuff. Oh, I know a lot of writers who are miles faster than that, but for *me*, it's pretty awesome!

Of course, that means I'll need to up my game yet another notch for 2021. This will be an especially fun year for me, since August 2021 will mark ten years since the publication of my first solo book. I'd had short stories published and a co-credit on a nonfiction book back in the '90s, but 2011 was my first solo, professional publishing credit.

Wow, it's been ten years already? That's wild!

Not quite sure yet how I'll 'celebrate' this particular birthday, but I figure I need to come up with something especially cool and writing-related to make this year stand out.

As always, folks, thanks *so* much for reading!

Kevin McLaughlin

## MICHAEL'S AUTHOR NOTES
### DECEMBER 14, 2020

Thank you for not only reading our story but reading our Author Notes here in the back!

I am staring out my office window at my backyard, preparing these Author Notes as the first COVID immunization shot was administered this morning.

While we still have a crest of the pandemic to go, it is a major milestone going into the future.

I have about seventeen days until the end of the year. For about seven of them, I hope to be mostly off. Now, off doesn't mean not working. It just means fewer meetings and a very unstructured day.

**My New Year's Resolution**

I need to lose weight but making that my resolution this year would probably doom it, so I think I will refrain. I will work to lower my weight, but abstaining from Coca-Cola might be a goal too far.

I like to think I am smart enough to hack my future, if only for a little bit. So, I have decided to hack my way to creating a solid story that feels a little faster and a bit better. My experience creating the Kris Kringle story (*Christmas Kringle: Silent Night*) was fun and sincerely a group effort.

If you have not heard, LMBPN Publishing is giving away the…umm…intense Christmas story for free, or you can buy it on Amazon for $0.99 (no Kindle Unlimited – sorry! To give it away, we can't put it into the program too.) Do look on our Facebook group or join our email list. I'm sure we are placing the link in multiple places.

Now, we plan on testing a lot of ways to reach out and find new fans for our stories in 2021. I'm sure Pinterest advertising is on the list, as well as social influencers, extending to multiple languages.

You know what is not on the list?

Slowing down. Well, not exactly.

**Slowing Down**

Right now, LMBPN is in the process of breaking apart our mega-book releases (including *Witch of the Federation, Rogue, Steel Dragon,* and a couple of others), where the books were actually three books in one. Think of our test as the opposite of releasing three books, then creating the boxed set. For mega-books, we created the three stories but released them as one mega-book first. Now, we are breaking them back apart, giving them new covers, and making them available for those who do not like reading six-hundred-page stories.

While this means we have over a hundred titles to release this year, it doesn't mean we aren't creating new stories and storylines, which brings me back to *Dragon's Daughter* and Kevin's comments in his Author Notes.

It's time to mention that you should reach out to Kevin and let him know what you did and did not enjoy with our stories. What do you think is missing nowadays? For example, during the spring, I was feeling that the old sword & sorcery genre was missing new blood.

So I created Skharr DeathEater the Barbarian. We have just

released the third book in that series and have plans to go to at least seven, maybe more if I can find enough readers to go along with me for the ride. (Just a warning, that series has adult language and adult situations, all closed-door.)

If you reach out to Kevin, let him know a bit about your reading history. What genres do you think are missing now? Have authors (us included) stopped writing new stories in genres you enjoy?

While I hope not, let us know. Maybe one of your favorites is also one of ours.

I hope your holidays are or were fantastic, and that 2021 is the year we got past the Pandemic.

Ad Aeternitatem,

Michael Anderle

Book 11 - Brave New Worlds (2019)

Book 12 - Warrior's Marque (2020)

## The Ragnarok Saga (Military SF)

Accord of Fire - Free prequel short story, available only to email list fans!

Book 1 - Accord of Honor

Book 2 - Accord of Mars

Book 3 - Accord of Valor

Book 4 - Ghost Wing

Book 5 - Ghost Squadron

Book 6 - Ghost Fleet (2019)

## Valhalla Online Series (A Ragnarok Saga Story)

Book 1 - Valhalla Online

Book 2 - Raiding Jotunheim

Book 3 - Vengeance Over Vanaheim

Book 4 - Hel Hath No Fury

## Blackwell Magic Series (Urban Fantasy)

Book 1 - By Darkness Revealed

Book 2 - Ashes Ascendant

Book 3 - Dead In Winter

Book 4 - Claws That Catch

Book 5 - Darkness Awakes

Book 6 - Spellbinding Entanglements

By A Whisker (short story)

The Raven and the Rose - Free novelette for email list fans!

## Dead Brittania Series:

Dead Brittania (short prequel story)

Book 1 - King of the Dead

Book 2 - Queen of Demons

Raven's Heart Series (Urban Fantasy)

Book 1 - Stolen Light

Book 2 - Webs in the Dark

Book 3 - Shades of Moonlight

## **Other Titles:**

Over the Moon (SF romance)

Midnight Visitors (Steampunk Cat short story)

Demon Ex Machina (Steampunk Cat short story)

The Coffee Break Novelist (help for writers!)

You Must Write (Heinlein's rules for writers)